# Break Out

## A Vancouver Knights Novel
### Book 1

Kylie Kent

ISBN 13: 978-1-922816-91-7(ebook)
978-1-923137-05-9 (paperback)

Editing by - Kat Pagan

# Club Omerta

**Are you a part of the Club?**

Don't want to wait for the next book to be released to the public?
Come and Club Omerta for an all access pass!

This includes:
• daily chapter reveals,
• first to see - everything, covers, teasers, blurbs
• Advanced reader copies of every book
• Bonus scenes from the characters you love!
• and so much more

**Click the link to be inducted to the club!!!**
CLUB OMERTA

*To Aaliyah,*

*The extremely sweet and bubbly and very fashionable reader I met at a signing event in London. Thank you for giving me the inspiration for Aliyah Monroe as well as for all of your support throughout my authoring journey.*

*Xx*
*Kylie*

# Chapter One

"He's a liability this team doesn't need, Jacob," Uncle Lou yells at my father, hitting the large oval conference table with his fist. My uncle's face is red, the little vein in his forehead pulsing rapidly.

I look to my father, who's the complete opposite.

Calm, relaxed, and leaning back in his chair like he doesn't have a care in the world. If I could give anyone a piece of advice, it would be to never play poker with my dad. His face is unmovable in any situation. I honestly can't remember the last time I've seen him smile *or* laugh. Probably when my mother was still here. Fifteen years ago. That's a long time to go without smiling.

If it were anyone else yelling at Dad, and not his own brother, I'd be looking to make a hasty escape from this room. Alexander McQueen dresses and blood splatters don't tend to mix too well. And I'm fond of this outfit.

"Last I checked, this was my team, Lou," Dad retorts with a single raised brow.

"Pops, Uncle Lou might be right. King is a lawsuit waiting to happen. The man brings bad press and everything else you don't want in a league looking to score the Cup this year." This comes from my older brother, Grayson, AKA the Vancouver Knights' enforcer.

"He's the best sniper the league has seen since Hull, except this kid has a better slapshot. I want 'em. We're signing 'em," Dad says with a finality that means no one is going to argue with him.

"What about that?" Uncle Lou points to the tv

screen mounted on the wall at the end of the conference room.

Liam King's smirking, cocky-ass face is front and center. He's sprawled out on a black leather sofa with three half-naked puck bunnies climbing all over him. But it's not his questionable choice in bedmates that's set the media into a frenzy this time. No, it's the white powder and rolled-up hundred-dollar bill sitting on the table in front of him that's caused quite the stir.

I've spent years wondering what went on behind the closed doors of this conference room. To say I'm disappointed by how mundane and boring this meeting has been would be an understatement. I don't know what I was expecting, but when my father called and told me I was needed, I jumped at the chance to be part of the *team*. As the only girl in the family, it was never my place to be one of the boys. I wasn't supposed to know the inner workings of my father's businesses. Not that it takes a genius to figure out just how my family's amassed its wealth.

We don't choose the families we're born into. We just have to learn to live with them, right? Do I agree with everything my father and brothers do? No, but they're the only family I have and I love them regardless of the blood that may stain their hands. Unlike my mother, my father stuck around. He'd never leave me alone or feed me to the wolves.

"That's what we have Aliyah for. She's going to babysit King and make sure he doesn't gain any negative attention from the press," Dad says.

"Wait... what?" I ask. I take it back. It seems my father would feed me to the wolves—these bastards just happened to be disguised as a bunch of brutish hockey players.

"Absolutely not. Are we not looking at the same fucking pictures, Dad? That asshole is not going within an inch of my sister. He's a womanizer, who's seen more bunny ass than Bugs Bunny himself." Gray pushes to his feet, his chair falling backwards in the process.

"Sit your ass down." Dad's voice rises. One thing about Jacob Monroe? The man does not tolerate temper tantrums. From anyone. Especially my brothers. My moods and outbursts, he's way more lenient on. But theirs? Not so much.

My lips tip up at the sides. It's a sibling thing. Also, I'm glad someone finally told Gray to shut up when it comes to the whole overbearing big brother act.

"Do you really think I'd put my daughter at risk, Grayson? You're going to be on the ice with King.

4

You're his teammate and I trust that you'll put the fear of the devil in him—let the bastard know exactly what will happen if he so much as thinks about touching your sister," Dad says.

Guess that whole *sticking it to Gray* thing didn't last long. I should have known it was too good to be true.

"You know I'm right here," I say.

"Your point?" Dad asks.

"I have a mind and will of my own. Last I checked, we live in the twenty-first century. If I want to give the whole damn team free rein of my body, I can and I will," I tell him.

My dad blinks. Twice. His knuckles turn white around the pen he's holding. I'm surprised it hasn't snapped under the pressure yet. Throwing the pen onto the table, he stands and walks over to the large floor-to-ceiling window behind his desk.

"Come here, Aliyah," he says, staring out the glass.

I push to my feet and straighten my shoulders. I'm not backing down. These men need to learn that I'm not a little girl anymore. I'm twenty-four years old. I should be able to make my own decisions. I approach my father, as his gaze focuses on the rink below.

"You see that ice out there?" he asks.

"Yes," I answer.

"What color is it?" He doesn't look at me. His eyes are glued to the rink.

"White," I tell him.

"White," he repeats. "If you let any of my players touch you, that ice will be painted red with their blood, and it'll be your job to come up with a creative way to explain how a whole team of NHL players went missing," he says before turning his icy glare on me.

I swallow. It's not the first time my father has threatened to kill any guy I've ever shown an interest in. I've gotten really good at hiding the fact that I date. I figure it's not worth the headache until I'm sure the guy is worth going toe-to-toe with my family over.

"I wouldn't do that, Dad. You know that," I tell him. I may talk a big game, but I'm a three-date minimum kind of girl. I don't just jump into bed with anyone with a nice smile.

That thought makes me turn and peek at Liam King's picture. He does have a pretty face *and* a nice smile. I'm sure those perfectly white teeth are fake though. He's a hockey player after all. However, that knowledge doesn't stop the flutter that starts up in my stomach when I look at him. I'm usually immune to hockey players. I've been around them my whole life. But there's something about Liam King that seems to seep into my skin and send a need I'm not going to acknowledge right to my core.

"Surely there's someone more qualified for this job than me, Dad. Make someone else do it, please," I practically beg him.

"There are few people I trust in this world, Aliyah, and you just so happen to be one of them. I need you to do this for the team. For me. All you have to do is make sure he stays away from parties, clubs—anything he deems fun, really," Dad says with a twitch of his lip. Not a smirk but the closest thing I'm going to get.

I groan. I can't say no to him. The last time I heard a man even try, well, I never saw that man again. So I'm not a hundred percent sure what happened to him but my imagination can come up with a few ideas.

"He'll be here tomorrow morning. I want you in his apartment when he arrives. Introduce yourself. Make sure you read him the riot act, Aliyah. Show him who's boss," Dad says, handing me a slip of paper.

"Fine, but I want a pay raise." I turn and walk back over to the desk.

"You're not even on the payroll." Grayson shakes his head.

"Well, guess I am now." I smile at him. "Who knows, Gray? I might even be good at this job. Then I'll be able to hang out with you and your little hockey friends more often."

"For the love of God, Lia, don't go near my friends." Gray scowls at me.

"Enough. Aliyah, I'm sure you've got plenty to do before tomorrow." Dad dismisses me.

"Yep, plenty. I'm going to need a new wardrobe, something a little more *puck bunny chic* maybe." I pick up my bag and walk out of the room, leaving Grayson's groans and grumbles behind me.

My hands are sweaty. *Why the hell am I so nervous?*

He's just an athlete, like any of the others you've met before. Sure, he's hotter than any human should be, but he's just a man.

I look in the gold-framed mirror that hangs in my new friend's foyer... No, not friend.

Assignment? Nope.

Target? Maybe.

Whatever he is, it's his apartment I'm waiting inside. I fiddle with the white headband that was already sitting perfectly in place atop my head. My long dark hair hanging in loose waves, parted straight down the middle of my face. I'm wearing an iconic black and white Chanel dress, paired with a set of black Louboutin Mary Jane pumps. I pull the nude lipstick out of my bag and reapply the shade for the fifth time in the last half hour.

He's late. *Why is he late?*

For all I know, the idiot got off the plane, found a party, and is already passed out drunk somewhere. That could be a good thing. If I fail before I even meet him, maybe my father will see that I'm really not suited for this job and assign someone else.

The door opens, and I turn on my heel and force a smile on my face. Liam King—who is so much larger in real life, mind you—stops just inside the foyer.

"Ah, shit, sorry, ma'am. I thought this was my apartment," he says, looking at the key in his hand.

"It is, and it's Aliyah, not ma'am." I smile,

holding out my hand to him while trying to remain professional. Professional is good. I can do professional politeness without trying to ride this man like he's the bucking-bull ride down at the local bar. "I'm your welcoming party, your new best friend, really."

"They gave me a fucking babysitter?" he grunts, briefly shaking my hand. Then he hefts the huge bag he's carrying onto his shoulder and walks right past me. "You can go now. I don't need a minder," he says.

"Actually, you do," I say, my heels clanking on the marble floor as I follow him through the apartment. He walks down a hall and opens a few doors before finally choosing one. I follow him and stop abruptly. This isn't just a room. No, it's his... bedroom.

*Shit! Abort, Aliyah, abort!* Do not look at that bed. Do not imagine him on top of you on that bed.

Liam turns. His gaze goes from me, to the bed, and then back to me. His lips tip up at one side of his mouth.

Shit, this is not good. I take a step backwards, realizing my mistake. Professional politeness doesn't include entering a man's bedroom.

# Chapter Two

A fucking babysitter. The team assigned me a representative from the cock-blocking fun police. I can't believe this shit.

Although, as my eyes rake up and down her body, taking in the way her dress perfectly clings to her curves, I realize it might not be all that bad.

"You're right. Perhaps I do need a babysitter. It was a long flight. I need a shower and I certainly could use help reaching my back."

Her eyes widen before she schools her features. "I don't think I properly introduced myself. I'm Aliyah Monroe."

"Okay, Aliyah Monroe, I'm Liam King but you already knew that. So how about that hand?" I nod towards a door that I'm assuming is the bathroom.

"Sure, you go on ahead. I'll join you," she says, and then spins around and turns back to the door.

My cock stirs at the thought of getting wet and soapy with my new *best friend.* Fuck, if you've got to have a babysitter, at least I got a hot one.

I make quick work of stripping down and turning the water on. I step under the stream as soon as it starts to warm up. The bathroom is fully stocked with soaps, shampoos, and shit already. I avoid the loofah and pump some shower gel into the palm of my hand.

"Ready whenever you are, babe," I call out, wrapping my fist around my dick. I give it a few pumps while eyeing the door.

I don't get a response. She's probably stripping off in the bedroom, and any minute now, she'll walk in here buck naked and hand that tight little body of hers over to me on a silver platter.

They all do. She won't be any different—can't say I've ever had the pleasure of sleeping with the babysitter before, though. Not that my previous team ever dared to do such bullshit. I'm not a fucking kid who needs monitoring 24/7.

Although the fuckers did throw me away for one little fucking mess up. Okay, maybe not one, but still. Fuck them. Their loss. They're not going to replace me with anyone better. That's for damn sure.

Then again, if I would have known fucking up would result in having that hot little babysitter as my welcoming gift, I would have knocked that fucker out years ago. My ex-coach, the guy I laid out cold on the ice right before the Stanley Cup game last year, deserved the broken jaw and missing teeth. There's only so much a man can take, finding your coach in bed with your married mother, and then having him look you in the eye the next morning and make comments about her. Yeah, that's not something even a saint would tolerate.

Of course, no one fucking knows what the asshole did and I'm made out to be the bad guy, the loose cannon who can't control his rage. I have plenty of fucking control. Though I'm beginning to lose it at the moment.

Fuck, this chick needs to hurry up and get her ass in here. I close my eyes and picture the curves she's hiding under that prim-and-proper dress of hers. I imagine ripping that headband off before grabbing a fistful of her hair, tugging on it just hard enough so she's at my mercy but not enough to actually cause damage.

Again, I'm not the monster the media is making me out to be right now.

I'd run my tongue, my teeth, up and down the delicious curve of her neck. Opening my eyes, I'm blinded by the bright white lighting reflecting off the too-white marble walls. I tighten my hand around my dick and increase my movements. Little Miss Monroe not joining me isn't going to stop me from getting off. Just thinking about her is enough to have my dick rock-hard and leaking precum. I picture throwing her down on the bed, tearing her dress right down the middle. I imagine burying my face between her legs. I bet she tastes sweet too. The good girl types always do. I increase the speed of my movements. I can feel it. I'm so fucking close. My balls tighten, tingles run up my spine, and—

"AHHH!!! FUCK."

That scream has me dropping my cock and sprinting from the bathroom. Ever tried running on smooth marble tiles when you're soaking wet? Yeah, it ain't fucking fun. It's a good thing I'm used to skating around on ice.

"What happened?" I ask, skidding to a stop in the living room.

Aliyah is standing on the coffee table, her mouth and eyes both open wide and staring right back at me.

"What the fuck?" I ask again, my gaze flicking around the room.

"Where are your clothes?" she asks, staring at my still-erect cock.

"Back in the bathroom, where I was showering before you screamed bloody murder out here." Clearly, the girl's fine, not injured. "If you wanted to see me naked, sweetheart, you had an open invitation to join me." I smirk.

"There's a spider," she says in way of explanation.

My blood goes cold. There isn't a lot that scares me in this world, but spiders? Yeah, I don't fuck with those creepy bastards. In my opinion, anything with eight legs is from outer space or some shit.

I jump up next to her on the coffee table so

quickly that she stumbles back and loses her balance. My arm snakes out, catching her around the waist and pulling her flat against my chest. Against my naked, wet chest.

My hands are shaking. The fact that there's a spider in here has me ready to find a match and burn the building down. Do the Ghostbusters actually exist? Maybe they can come and exterminate the little fucker.

"Where..." I gulp. "Where is it?" I force out, my eyes glued to the ground.

"I don't know. Oh my god! Get off me." Her palms land against my chest and she pushes.

I take a tiny step back, creating as much space between us as possible on this small surface. I'm scanning the area for the creature that has likely come to take me out—no doubt employed by my former coach—but I can't see it.

"You cannot be scared of spiders. You need to kill it," Aliyah says.

"Me?" I point to my chest. "No fucking way am I going near it. Wherever it is."

"It went under the sofa," she tells me. "And I'm not killing it, so you have to."

I open my mouth to respond when I hear the crack, and then we're both stumbling as our makeshift platform collapses underfoot. Again, I reach a hand out and catch her so she doesn't fall to her ass. Without thinking, I pick her up and run to the kitchen counter, jumping on it with my babysitter still in my arms. Aliyah shrieks, and I swear the sound nearly deafens me.

Great, now I won't even be able to hear the spider coming for me. *Do spiders make sounds?*

"Get off me. Let me go," Aliyah hisses, and I drop my hands from her waist. "You need some clothes. Stop touching me when you're naked."

"That's usually when women want me to touch them, sweetheart. It's even more fun if you're naked too." I wink at her.

"Ew, and never going to happen," she says. "You need to find and kill that spider. We can't stay up here all day."

"I'm not going anywhere near that thing."

"Fine. I'll call one of my brothers." She smiles with an added twinkle in her eye. "It'll be like killing two birds with one stone, because when they come over and see you up here with me, *naked,* they will shoot first and ask questions later. Then they'll handle the spider, and I can go on with my life like this whole day never happened."

I don't even know how to unpack all that. "I'm

not afraid of your brothers," I tell her. I'm a professional hockey player. Fighting is part of the deal.

"You'd be the first." She laughs. "I don't think I introduced myself to you properly." She holds out a hand. "I'm Aliyah. Aliyah Monroe," she repeats, and that's when it hits me. The name. I finally recognize it.

Fuck me. Aliyah Monroe, the daughter of my new boss, Jacob *Monroe*. The man who owns me. Owns my new team anyway. But that's not all he is. Word on the street is that he's the leader of Canada's criminal underground. And those brothers she mentioned, one of them happens to be my new teammate. Yeah, this is not how I planned to start my life here in Vancouver.

"Fine, I'll kill it. But not because I'm scared of your brothers," I grunt.

"Whatever you say," she sing-songs, appearing a little too happy with herself.

"I'm killing it because I'm not about to have my new boss hate me on day one. *This*..." I point between us. "...never happened."

# Chapter Three

I'm sitting on the kitchen counter watching Liam walk very tentatively down the hall, his naked back on full display. What a back it is, though. Rippling with muscles and still dripping water. I can't believe I just got a front-row seat to all that is Liam King.

And I mean *all*. Every last inch of his nakedness is now burned into my memory. He returns to the living room with a hockey stick.

*A hockey stick.*

"You couldn't have put on some clothes while you were in there?" I ask him, unable to take my eyes off his cock. I mean, it's a freaking work of art. It deserves to be appreciated, right?

"You want this spider dead or what?" he fires back.

"Yes. But a hockey stick? How on earth are you planning to kill it with that?"

"The only thing I can work better than a hockey stick is the dick you can't seem to stop staring at."

When I look up at his face, he winks at me. "I hope that spider jumps up and bites it *and* that the venom makes it swell and fall off," I tell him.

"That is literally the meanest thing anyone has ever said to me," he huffs, sounding wounded. He looks at the floor. "It can't actually jump up and bite my dick, right?"

I shrug. "God works in mysterious ways."

"You're evil. Cute as fuck, but evil nonetheless."

I sit and watch as he kicks the sofa out of the way. The spider is still there, just staring up at me. Okay, well, probably not at me.

Liam lifts the stick and smashes it down on top of the eight-legged creature. Once he's certain it's dead, he drops the stick to the ground, walks over to the other sofa, and falls onto the seat.

"Are you okay?" I ask him.

"Not in the slightest," he tells me.

I notice his hands are shaking. I could feel them trembling when he was holding me, but now, it looks like he's really struggling. His chest rises and falls in rapid succession.

I jump off the counter and open the fridge. I made sure it was fully stocked for his arrival. I grab a bottle of water and take it over to him. "Drink this."

He takes the water and gulps the whole bottle down in one go before peering up at me again. "You know, if you really want to make me feel better, you could come and join me in that shower I never got to finish." He smirks.

I look down at his half-hard dick. "Mmm, tempting, but I think I'll pass. I'm really not in the mood for catching herpes this week. Maybe next time." I turn around, swipe the empty bottle from his hands, and throw it into the trash. Pivoting to face him with my hands resting on my hips, I add, "You're expected to be on the ice at five a.m. My advice? If you don't want to piss on what has to be your last Hail Mary, don't be late."

With that, I storm over to the foyer, heavier footed than I would usually walk while loving the sound of my heels clicking on the marble floor. Then I pick up my purse from the entrance table, stab at the elevator button, and wait.

Argh, I hate apartments with elevator entrances. They really ruin the whole *storm out of the house* thing I was trying to do. As I wait for the doors to open, the hairs on the back of my neck rise on end, and I know he's staring right at me. No matter how much I want to turn around and get another glimpse of him, I don't. When the doors finally decide to put me out of my misery, I step onto the platform, spin on my heel, and press the G button for the garage.

I smile at him as he stares back at me with a look of shock on his face. Guess he's not used to women with self-control. "This is what self-respect looks like," I tell him right as the doors close.

It's not until I'm in my car, pulling out of his building, that my shoulders finally sink. I sigh and silently curse my father for putting me in this position. Never in my life have I wanted to say *fuck it* and do something completely reckless.

That something being Liam King.

I really hope the guy learns to put clothes on. If not, it's going to be a long season and, honestly, I'm not sure my vibrator is up for the task.

It's only midmorning, but I need something to calm my rattled nerves. I hit the button on my car. "Call Charlie," I say into the speakers.

Charlie is my best friend, has been since kindergarten. She's really more like a sister to me than anything else. Like me, Charlie comes from a family who makes their money on the other side of that right-and-wrong line. Her father is in business with mine, and thankfully neither has given the other a reason to *terminate* that partnership—otherwise, it would really put a damper on our friendship.

"Hey, babes, how's it going?" Charlie answers the call.

"It's an emergency brunch kind of day. Get the girls and meet me at the Four Seasons?"

"On it," she replies, then asks, "Wait... What's the emergency?"

"The job my father gave me yesterday, it's going to suck a lot more than I originally thought," I groan.

"Back the truck up. You mean to tell me you met the Liam Fucking-Sex-On-Legs King already?" Her voice raises in both volume and pitch.

I wince. "I'll tell you all about it when I see you."

I press the button, disconnecting the call. I'm so not getting into the details of just how much of him I saw. Not over the phone. I need a bucketload of mimosas and some pastries first.

An hour and three mimosas later, my closest friends are looking at me with their mouths gaping.

I met Amanda in fifth grade when her family moved here from England. She's from old money, the royal kind—we like to call her *princess*. In reality, she's only a duchess. Although she refuses to use the title and insists on paving her own way in the world. Which she's doing a mighty fine job at. Amanda started an online retail store, where people sell high-end secondhand goods. She basically gets her money from others selling their shit, and she makes a lot of it.

Nicole, I met through Charlie, who says she found her lost at a frat party. What really went down was that Nicole was drugged and being taken advantage of by some college douchebag. Charlie stumbled into the room and clocked the bastard over the head with a lamp. She then called her brothers and, well, we don't actually know what happened to the guy after that because no one's ever heard from him again.

Phoebe, we met recently at a charity event. She's an oil heiress and is in training to take over her family's business. We immediately hit it off when she looked at my brother Jonah with nothing but disgust and outrage on her face. Any chick who doesn't instantly drop her panties for my brothers is golden in my book.

Me? I'm the youngest of four children. I have three over-the-top protective brothers, who I love to hate on a daily basis. First, there's Grayson, the Vancouver Knights' enforcer. Then there's Jonah. He's currently in grad school, studying business. Followed by Vinny. He's... well, he's learning the ropes from my father. Vinny was always landing himself knee-deep in academic shit at school, so Dad ended up making him drop out of college and start working for him. Which I know is probably not the smartest thing for everyone, but for Vinny, it's been the best decision. He doesn't stay out partying all night while finding more trouble than one person ever should anymore. Probably because most of the "work" he does is conducted at night.

"Wait, you mean to say you've seen Liam King's dick? Like in real life?" Nicole asks a little too loudly.

"Shhh, why not put out a press release? Jesus, Nic. I don't think the old couple over in the far corner heard you." I scowl at her.

"Sorry, but really. How was it?" She leans in with an overeager grin.

"How was what?" I ask, playing dumb.

"His dick. What are we talking? You don't have to specify. Just say stop when it matches." Phoebe starts with her palms pressed together and slowly separates them.

I frown at her and shake my head. "It was a dick, not the Mona Lisa. And he's an ass. If I never have to see him again, it'll be too soon," I tell them.

"She's protesting waaaaay too much for someone who wasn't impressed," Charlie interjects.

"I *wasn't* impressed. Like I said, it took the guy 0.5 seconds to ask me to fuck him. He's an ass," I repeat.

"What I'm not understanding here is why in the ever-loving heck did you not fuck him?" Charlie asks.

"Because I don't want a shopping list of STDs," I deadpan.

"That's what condoms are for," Nicole adds, not helping my case.

"Nope, I think it's your whole three-date rule thing. So if we count this morning as number one, you only have to see him two more times before you can take him up on his offer," Phoebe tries to reason with me.

"Ew, and no. Hell will freeze over before I go anywhere near that man's dick," I say, leaving out the fact that I've already had it pressed up against me.

"Oh, look, here's your shot at number two. He just walked in," Charlie says, smiling wide. "Introduce us."

"No, and bullshit. He's not here," I tell her.

"You sure? Because that guy right there looks just like him. I mean, he'd look better without the leggy blonde hanging off his arm. But, eh, you work with what you got, right?" Charlie points behind me.

I turn my head and my eyes bug out of their sockets. "OH MY FREAKING GOD. I'm going to fucking kill him," I say, already pushing to my feet. It's not until I'm halfway through the lobby that a plan on how to get rid of this bimbo comes to mind.

# Chapter Four

I breathe a sigh of relief when I enter the doors of the Four Seasons. As soon as the babysitter left, I called an exterminator to come and clean out the apartment. No fucking way am I sleeping there when there's a chance of that spider's family members coming after me, looking to take out their eight-legged revenge.

The hot blonde on my arm doesn't hurt to ease my rattled nerves after that near-death experience. The thought of bending her like a pretzel and fucking her until we both can't walk anymore is exactly the distraction I need to unwind from the shitshow that is my life.

Lindsey? Or is it Lauren? Who the fuck knows? She presses her tits against my side. They're hard, fake. I prefer real ones, soft pillows I can sink my fingers into. But real tits are hard to come by these days—well, with the kind of chicks I know anyway.

"Babe, I'm going to suck you off so good you'll be begging for seconds," she purrs.

I smile down at her, my cock hardening in my pants as we make our way through the foyer. *Seconds* is not something I'll ever be begging for, especially from Lindsey... or Lauren?

"I like your confidence, but don't count on it, sugarcakes," I tell her.

"Oh my god, Liam, babe. Thank god you're still here. I thought you might have checked out already. I was worried I wouldn't see you again and, well..."

I look up and my eyes connect with hers. The babysitter. She's here.

"...I thought I'd give you *this*. I'm sorry. I should have told you last night before we, well, you know. But you're just so hot and I couldn't say no, even though I knew I wasn't supposed to. Anyhoo, this doctor will help clear you right up. But don't worry, every time I've had crabs in the past, they clear up within a week. So you should be good to go in no time."

I watch in horror as Aliyah digs through her purse, retrieving a business card, and then proceeds to hold it out for me to take. I'm so shocked at the moment all I can do is stare at her.

"Uh, look, Liam, maybe give me a call in a couple of months. I gotta go," Lindsey or Lauren stammers out while prying her fake-as-fuck body out from under my arm.

"Wait, Lindsey, this isn't..."

"It's Laura, asshole," she says right before storming back towards the entrance of the hotel.

I turn around to a very satisfied-looking babysitter. "Are you fucking kidding me? I'm pretty sure cock-blocking isn't in your job description."

"Actually, it kind of is. You've been in town all of five minutes and you couldn't keep yourself out of a possible scandal," Aliyah says, dropping the card back into her purse with a little more flair than necessary.

"There was no scandal," I growl in response. "And if I want to get laid, that's my business, not yours, and certainly not the team's."

"Actually, that nine million dollar contract you signed makes everything you do the team's business. Why the hell my father chose to invest in you, I have no idea. But he did, so here we are. Why are you *here* anyway?"

"Because I beat the shit out of my former coach and got kicked off the team. I needed a job." I shrug.

"No, here, in this hotel," she clarifies.

"I'm having the apartment fumigated. I can't sleep there."

"Well, you can't sleep here either," she tells me.

"Why the fuck not?" I wait as she pulls out her phone and taps on the screen before she turns it around to show me a picture of myself. It's not one of my finer moments. After I got dropped by Montreal, I went on a bender. Girls, booze, and more girls. Although this picture would have you believe I was using coke, I've never touched the shit and never will. I'm an athlete, not a fucking idiot. "That isn't what it looks like," I say, shaking my head.

"It's a photo. It's exactly what it looks like. You

whoring around with a bunch of puck bunnies is one thing. But don't pretend like it's anything more than what it is. They don't like you. They like your sperm, so they have a meal ticket for the rest of their lives. Don't believe for one second that they're with you for any other reason. No self-respecting woman would be caught in a position like this."

I'm starting to think this Little Miss Goody Two-shoes attitude needs to be rumpled a bit, and I know just how to do it. "You sound jealous. We could fix that, you know. Come up to the room with me and I'll show you exactly what those girls were there for." I rub a hand along my jawline. "By the way, in case you're wondering." I lean in so that my mouth is a breath away from hers. "It was for the earth-shattering orgasms I can give them, not my babymakers."

"Yeah, you're not staying here. Follow me. I'm taking you home," she says, pulling back before maneuvering around me.

"Well, when you ask so politely, how can I refuse?" I grin while stepping up next to her. Without thinking, I rest my palm on the lower curve of her back. Which she instantly shakes off, then moves to the side to create more space between us.

"It's my job to make sure you don't get yourself into trouble and create bad press for the team. I happen to take my job seriously. We can't all skate by on pure luck."

Okay, that stings. I pride myself on how hard I've fucking worked to get to where I am. Ask any pro athlete—luck has nothing to do with it. It takes hours of training, early mornings, constantly aching muscles. I could respond, let her know just how hard I've worked to get here, but what's the point? This chick has some preconceived notion about who I am. It ain't my job to prove her wrong.

Instead, I follow her to the front of the hotel. She hands the valet a ticket stub and looks everywhere but at me as she waits for her car to be brought around. A few minutes later, the valet pulls up in a bright-yellow Lamborghini Urus. He hands the key fob over to Aliyah, and she finally turns and looks my way.

"Get in," she says right before she hops into the driver's seat and closes her door.

I look behind me. I could just walk back inside the hotel. It's a free world after all. And then the flashing of cameras starts. My name being screamed as people practically run towards me has me climbing in her car and slamming the door shut. Blocking out the noise of the paparazzi.

"How the fuck did they know I was here?" I grunt.

"Probably Laura." Aliyah smirks. "Girls like that would pay anything to be seen with someone like you."

"Who?" I ask, my brows drawn down in confusion. Aliyah rolls her eyes as she puts her foot down and peels out of the hotel's porte cochère. I scramble to get my seat belt buckled. "Nice car. I didn't know babysitters were so well paid," I comment while admiring the vehicle's interior.

"It was a gift," she says, gripping the steering wheel tighter.

"From your hockey player boyfriend?"

Am I probing to find out if she's single? *Yes.*

Am I trying to get under her skin while I do it? *Also yes.*

"From a hockey player, yes. Boyfriend, no," she responds cryptically.

"You just have hockey players buying you luxury vehicles? You must be a good babysitter."

"Actually, you're my first assignment. And, trust me, it's not something I willingly signed up for. Honestly, if today is any indication of how this season is going to go, then I may just get one of my brothers to kill you," she says.

"They could try," I reply. To which, she just shakes her head and laughs.

Twenty minutes later, we're pulling into a gated estate, the long driveway leading up to a massive mansion. "This is where you live?" I ask Aliyah.

"Uh-huh. Sure," she says before pulling the car to a stop, cutting the engine, and turning to me with a frown. "Word of advice? If you want to keep your tongue in your mouth, refrain from making any inappropriate sexual comments. And if you want to keep your fingers attached to your hands, also refrain from touching me." With that said, she gets out of the car.

I'd like to think she's kidding, but I've heard the rumors about her family, which is the real reason a babysitter can afford to live in a house like that and drive a car like this. I slide out of the passenger's side and quickly fall into step with Aliyah. I throw one last glance over my shoulder at the Lambo. I am curious, though, as to which player bought her that thing. And why.

The sound of my phone startles me. Pulling it out of my pocket, I stare at the name "Mom" flashing on the screen.

"You need to get that?" Aliyah asks.

"Nope." I turn off the phone, rejecting the call. This can be added to the other hundreds of calls I've refused to answer over the years. I follow Aliyah into the house. "You live here alone?" I ask. But then I hear the sound of male voices the farther we go.

"Nope," she parrots while popping the P.

We end up in a living room that looks like it's straight out of *Bachelor's Paradise Magazine*, if that were an actual thing. The room is decked out with a black leather sectional, a pinball machine stands in the corner, and a billiard table takes up half of the floor space. A flat screen television larger than a jumbotron hangs on the wall.

Everyone in the room stops what they're doing, some putting down game controllers, others holding cue sticks in their hands. All now unapologetically glaring at me.

# Chapter Five

Aliyah

I t's not until every occupant in my brother's living room is sending silent death threats in Liam's direction that I think maybe this wasn't the best idea. But no way in hell was I taking him to my actual place. At least if he's here, I can put him up in one of my brother's guest rooms... and leave.

Honestly, I think I need to talk to my father, tell him that I really am not the right person for this job. How on earth am I meant to spend a whole season shadowing this man when every time I look at him, I get that funny feeling in my stomach—not to mention how often I've had to clench my thighs together to ward off the need deep within my core. I can't even look at the guy and not see him naked. Dripping with water. Not remember the feel of that hard, naked body pressed up against mine as he caught me, stopping me from falling flat on my ass when the coffee table broke.

I know without a doubt if I told my dad I had the hots for Liam King, he'd find a replacement babysitter in a heartbeat. He'd also ban me from entering or going anywhere near The Castle, AKA the home of the Vancouver Knights. In fact, I wouldn't put it past him to find a chastity belt and lock me in a tower.

"Lia, you good?" my brother asks, using the shortened name he gave me when I was a baby. *Lie-ah.*

"Just dandy. Gray, this is Liam King, the Vancouver Knights' latest recruit." I wave a hand up and down, motioning to Liam's body.

"I know who he is, Lia, but what I don't know is why he's standing in my house?" Grayson raises an eyebrow in question.

I force my eyes not to roll into the back of my head. My brother is the team's enforcer, but he's also a different type of *enforcer* for my father. Something not many actually know. I would never willingly bring a guy to his house, not one I liked anyway.

Not that I *like* Liam King. If anything, I despise the bastard. I like his body, a whole freaking lot. But the actual man? Not so much. If only personality transplants were a thing...

"He needs a place to crash. His apartment is being fumigated," I tell Grayson.

"And this is my problem, how, exactly?" My brother raises a questioning brow.

I look around the room. There are two other Vancouver Knights players here watching this whole interaction, and I know that they're going to follow Grayson's lead, how ever he decides to handle this. Meaning if he makes a statement to not like the new guy, the whole team will follow suit. If you assumed professional sports players grew out of that high school jock phase, you're wrong. They didn't, probably never will. People think middle-aged housewives like to gossip. Yeah, I'd put money on it that these guys talk shit more than any bored housewife or mom at school pickup.

There are also a few of my brother's other friends, AKA soldiers, loitering about. They look casual, playing pool and drinking beer, but I know without a doubt they're strapped up and ready to fight at a moment's notice.

"You know what? You're right. It's not your problem. It's mine." I make a point of turning and touching Liam on his forearm. His very toned and tanned forearm. "You can just come and stay at my place, Liam. I only have a one-bedroom apartment but I'm sure we can make it work." I bat my eyelashes up at him.

Within two seconds, Grayson is marching over. Four seconds, and he's practically ripping my hand off Liam and holding out a palm. "I'm Gray, your enforcer. Welcome to the team. Follow me. I'll show you where you can crash for the night, then I'll bring you back and you can get acquainted with these morons." Grayson gestures a thumb over his shoulder to the rest of the room.

I smile, because I knew that would get my brother to change his tune real quick, and the over-protective brute played right into my hand. "Okay, well, now that you guys are developing a deep and meaningful bromance, I'm out of here. I have other things to do with my life," I tell them.

Liam smirks at me while Grayson grunts, "This is my sister. Just in case you missed the memo, she's very fucking off-limits to you."

"Sister, got it." Liam holds up his hands in surrender.

"Good, you'd be best to not forget it either. Men have taken a blade to the face for less," Grayson huffs. He then proceeds to clap Liam on the shoulder. "Come on, if I don't hurry up and get back in there, they'll drink all the good stuff."

"All right, catch you later. Don't forget: you need to be out on the ice first thing tomorrow morning," I tell Liam before walking away. I turn as I reach the foyer. "Oh and, Gray, no girls," I remind him.

"What?" My brother's head practically pivots off his neck.

"He cannot be seen with any girls. Don't invite any over," I warn.

"You can't be serious, Lia. That's a stupid rule no man should have to endure," Grayson argues with his arms crossed over his chest like a properly scolded child.

"I agree," Liam pipes in with a grin and a nod.

"I don't care. My player, my rules," I throw over my shoulder before walking out through the large foyer.

Once I'm in my car, I exhale the breath I didn't know I was holding. Is the *no girls* rule purely because of the press issues? Or is it because when I saw that bimbo attached to Liam's arm in the lobby, an uneasy feeling overtook me?

I shake my head and press the start button. I don't have the time nor the want to analyze that right now. What I need is to go home, do some laundry, read a book, and soak in a hot bath. I don't think that's too much to ask for. A quiet afternoon before the craziness of the season starts tomorrow.

Ominous clouds cover the sky and drizzly raindrops fall onto my head and shoulders as I make my way into The Castle. I look up and let the water hit my face. It's still dark but the lights from the building put out enough illumination to not make it creepy. I doubt anyone is going to jump out of the shadows here.

It's odd. This is one place I feel both the most afraid and the safest at the same time. Afraid because, well... I can't skate, don't skate, and won't skate. The whole sliding around on razor-thin blades terrifies me. I tried it when I was little, but every time I fell, I would get this overwhelming fear that someone was going to skate right by and slice my fingers off. That never happened, obviously, but it *could*.

Then there's the safety I feel being near or in this building. The knowledge that it's owned by my family and the fact that no one in their right mind wants to cross Jacob Monroe. There's a reason people fear my father, cross the street whenever they see any of my brothers. The Monroe name has been at the top of the underground food chain, so to speak, for generations.

I push through the heavy steel doors that put me right into the hallway that leads to the locker room. I'm early. I wanted to make sure Liam actually showed up—and I was hoping to try to talk to my father. First things first, though. I need to lay eyes on the man in question.

I walk straight into the locker room. The guys who were in the process of changing are quick to grab towels and cover themselves. Every single one of them except Liam King, who stands there with a white towel wrapped around his neck and nothing else.

What is it with this guy and his unashamed nakedness?

This is the second day I've seen him and the *second* time I've been offered a full frontal in return. My eyes have a mind of their own as they make their way down to his cock before snapping back up to his face when I see him twitch and harden.

"Aliyah, what the fuck are you doing here?" My brother's voice growls from the opposite side of the room.

I turn my head in his direction and smirk. "I needed material for my spank bank." I then look over at every player in the room—every player except Liam. "Thanks, boys." With that, I turn on my heel and walk back out, listening as my brother threatens violence against his teammates as the door closes behind me.

I make my way up to my father's office, stopping in the kitchen to make him a cup of coffee and fill a plate with pastries. His door is open when I get there. Walking in, I place the cup on his desk, followed by the plate.

"Morning, sweetheart. What do I owe the pleasure?" he asks, already knowing I want something.

"Can't you just accept a visit from your only daughter without thinking I have a motive? I just wanted to see you—that's all." I smile and sit in one of the chairs in front of his desk.

From where I'm seated, you can see directly out onto the rink. Chills run through me just thinking about the ice. I've never really been one to love the cold. Although I'm Canadian, born and bred, I think I lived my previous life on a tropical island somewhere.

"Okay, how are you?" His voice is hesitant. Untrusting.

"I'm glad you asked, because I'm tired, Daddy." I pout while putting extra emphasis on the endearment, knowing I'm my father's one weakness. Don't get me wrong, my dad loves all of his children, but it's obvious I get a little extra-special treatment. "I was thinking... maybe Europe or Australia for a few months."

"Were you now?" my father asks, sipping at his coffee while his eyes never leave mine.

"Uh-huh, I think it'll do me some good. You know, put me in a better headspace for the rest of the year." I nod, hoping it'll get him to do the same—in business, it's called mirroring, a subtle manipulation to get someone to agree to your terms.

"Tell me, Aliyah, how exactly will you perform your job if you're on the other side of the world?"

"Well, I was thinking you could get someone else to babysit Liam King." I shrug.

"No." My father's voice is stern. I can't hide the shock on my face. "I know it's not a word you're accustomed to hearing, especially from me. But this... I need you to do *this* for me," he adds as if reading my mind.

I shrink into the chair, still a little unsure how to deal with the fact that my father told me no. *I know...* I sound like a spoiled brat, but it's not my fault I've grown up getting everything I've ever asked for. And I've never tried to abuse my father's good will.

"I have done everything in my power to make sure you've never wanted for a single thing, Aliyah. I've never asked anything of you. This is the first, and I really don't believe I'm asking you for much," he says, placing the coffee cup down on the table.

Well, now I feel like shit. Talk about laying the guilt on thick.

"I'm sorry. Like I said, I'm just tired. I'll figure it out, and I won't let you down," I say.

"Good, now tell me how yesterday went?"

Images of a naked Liam King killing a spider with a hockey stick fill my head. Yeah, probably not a good thing to report back on. The naked part, that is. I can't help the grin that curls my lips at the memory.

# Chapter Six

My new coach hates me—scratch that. My new *team* hates me. It's clear I'm not wanted here, but I'm not here to win them over. I'm here to win them games, plain and simple. And that's something I happen to be good at.

A point I'm proving to all of these haters right now as I continue to run the endless drills the coach yells in my direction. Hitting the net with my puck each and every time. Even when the fucker put two goalies up against me, I still managed to make that red light shine.

I'm determined to make this work. I'm not an idiot. I know that this team is my last shot at any kind of pro career. If I don't, I doubt I'll even get a job coaching a youth league.

My thighs burn as I skate up and down the ice as fast as I can, trying to be quicker and better than everyone else. I get body-checked into the boards by Monroe, fucking Grayson Monroe. AKA the owner's son and my babysitter's older brother. Also the guy whose house I slept at last night for fear of said babysitter finding out I didn't stay.

Right as I hit the wall, I look up into the stands, not expecting to see her staring right back at me. A small smile on her too-pretty face.

*Fuck, King, get your head on straight.* I internally curse myself. I can't be thinking of her, or that she's fucking pretty. Or that I want to know what her naked body feels like pressed beneath me. I bet I could make her come alight with pleasure, make her scream my name so loud the whole city hears it.

I shake my head and skate after Monroe—no fucking way is he getting that puck away from me. I manage to catch up to him just as he's swinging for a goal. Swooping in, I get a hold of the puck and I'm off towards the other end of the ice. I can feel him on my heels as I dodge the rest of the useless fuckers trying to stop me. Skating around them like they're nothing more than an orange cone on the ice. I don't see the obstacles when I skate. I see the clear paths around them and I take those.

The puck hits the back of the net and I spin around to a fuming Grayson Monroe. He's not happy I just showed him up, but I don't give a fuck. Like I said, I'm not here to make him fucking happy. Although I must admit there is one Monroe whose face I'd like to put a happy, contented, orgasmic smile on...

I look back up to the stands, but she's no longer standing there. *Did she see me score?*

Why the hell do I want her to see me score? I don't work to impress chicks. I don't need to. I know. I sound like an ass, but the truth is the truth. Why this particular girl is taking over my thoughts, I have no idea. It's probably because I need to get laid. If she didn't ruin my plans last night, I wouldn't be so wound up today. Not getting laid and sleeping in a house where I clearly wasn't wanted—yeah, let's just say that tonight I'll be staying at my own apartment, no matter how many fucking spiders are inside it.

"Hit the showers. Same time tomorrow. Don't be late," Coach yells out to the team. Just as I turn to skate off the ice, I hear him call my name. "King, hold back," he grunts.

It takes everything in me not to roll my eyes. Instead, I grit my teeth, biting down on my mouth guard. And face him. I know what's coming. It's not the first time I've had a coach who hates me on day one. They're all fucking pissed that I'm good at what I do. I make their job easy. I get wins. Any normal person would think that would make them fucking love me. But, no, they fucking hate it for reasons unbeknownst to me.

He takes his time. I could close the gap, but I'm not moving an inch. He wants to talk to me? He can fucking walk his ass over here. He stops two feet in front of me and has to crane his neck slightly to look up at my face.

"You think you're God's gift to hockey, don't you?" he asks.

"No, Coach," I answer. Do I think I'm great at

what I do? *Yes.* But a gift? *Hell no.* I've fucking worked my ass off to be this good.

"Your time here is limited. You know it and I know it. Don't get too comfortable, son. This is temporary. This team doesn't need a player like you," he spits out.

"A player like me?" I point to my chest. "Oh, you mean a player who scores? A player who wins championships?" It's no secret that this team makes the playoffs and then fails, every single year.

"A player who will only bring bad press and the bad vibes that come with it. Word of advice? The owner of this team isn't going to put up with your kind of bullshit. And I'm not the type of coach who will take your shit laying down, not like your last one," he says right before he shoulder-barges past me.

Well, at least now I get why he hates me so damn much. I wonder if they knew the reason I beat the fuck out of my coach if they'd still be so offended. He fucking deserved it. You don't fuck with family. I don't care who you are.

I'm the last one in the locker room. Everyone else has cleared out. Pulling my bag down, I quickly get dressed. I'm sore and tired but also really fucking bored. There has to be something to do in this godforsaken town. Something to keep me entertained. I pick up my phone and make the mistake of looking at the screen. Ten missed calls from my mother. Five text messages that I have no plans of reading anytime soon.

I might not let anyone else fuck with my family, but that doesn't mean I'm not allowed to be pissed at them. I'm honestly not sure how I'll ever be able to look at my mother and not see fucking red after what she did.

Shoving my phone into the pocket of my jeans, I swing my bag over my shoulder and walk out of the locker room. Only to stop at the sight that greets me the moment I step out.

Aliyah Monroe, sitting crossed-legged on the floor, leaning against the wall opposite the door. She has a large coffee cup next to her alongside her oversized Dior bag. Is she planning a camping trip? Because I swear she could fit a tent and a sleep sack in there.

I tilt my head and observe her. She either hasn't

noticed me yet or is doing a great job of pretending she hasn't, with her face glued to the screen of her phone as she scrolls through some social media account.

I clear my throat, causing her to sigh, roll her eyes, and then slowly raise them to meet mine. "I was hoping you drowned in there, or slipped on the soap and broke your neck," she says in a very monotone voice that has me questioning if she's joking, or if this woman seriously wishes me bodily harm.

"I'm not usually in the business of disappointing women, but in this case, I'm not sorry," I say. "What are you doing sitting out here?" I ask, looking up and down the very empty corridor.

"Waiting for you. What else would I be doing?" she fires back.

"Why?"

"Because my dad seems to think you're the best thing since electricity was invented. And he's made it my job to ensure you don't get into any trouble."

"Best thing since sliced bread," I correct her.

"Huh?"

"The saying, it's *the best thing since sliced bread*, not electricity," I explain.

"Yeah, but that's stupid. It's easy to slice bread.

Do you know how hard it is to live in today's world without electricity? I don't imagine it'd be fun," she says.

What I don't tell her is that I *do* know how hard it is to live without electricity—it's fucking cold is what it is. Growing up, my mom would pretend it was a game. My brother and I knew better, but we always went along with her "blackout" rounds whenever the power was cut off. I very much doubt Little Miss Princess here has ever had to go a day in her life without all the modern comforts she has at her disposal.

"I'm hungry. Where's a good place to eat around here?" I ask, looking to change the subject.

"You're in luck. Eating just happens to be one of my favorite pastimes." Aliyah smiles as she pushes to her feet, then turns and bends over to pick up her bag and coffee cup.

When she straightens and spins back around, I do nothing to hide the fact I was checking out her ass. Her delicious, heart-shaped ass that would fit perfectly in the palms of my hands. If she's going to put it in my face, I'm going to look.

"Ready whenever you are," I say with a smirk.

"Let's go. I'm driving," she says, walking ahead of

me. "And stop staring at my ass," she adds, while putting an extra sway to her hips.

"That ass was made to be appreciated, sweetheart," I mumble low enough that she doesn't hear me.

## Chapter Seven

"Hey, Ms. Monroe, usual spot?" Cal asks as I walk into his restaurant, appropriately named Cal's Diner.

"That'd be great. Thanks, Cal," I reply and lead Liam, who is currently getting the death glare from

Cal, over to the booth in the far back—it's where I always sit when I come here.

The place is very 1950s. An American-style diner with a retro feel, complete with the jukebox that still plays vinyls. The booths are red and white, the floors a black-and-white checkered pattern, with an odd mixture of neon signs and random pinup girl posters scattered all over the walls. I've been coming here since I discovered the diner's existence when I was fifteen, when it became a kind of sanctuary, a place I could go and be alone and not be bothered by anyone. It's on the outskirts of town.

As Liam's huge-ass body fills the seat opposite me, I'm wondering what the hell I was thinking. This is my spot. I don't even bring Charlie here. But when Liam asked if I knew of any good places to eat, Cal's immediately came to mind. The food is to die for.

Liam turns his head as he eyes the interior. I wish I knew what he was thinking. No, scrap that. I don't care what he's thinking because *he* doesn't matter. He's a job. That's it. I don't need to get to know him or learn his inner thoughts. I don't need to know what his lips would taste like pressed against mine... how his hands would feel...

"Not really a place I was expecting a princess to

frequent," Liam says, turning his body back around and landing those dark blue eyes of his on me.

"I'm not the princess. That's Amanda. And I'll have you know this place has better food than any Michelin-star restaurant I've ever dined at," I tell him.

"Who's Amanda?" he asks.

"My friend."

"What makes her a princess?"

"The fact that she's literal royalty. She's a duchess, not a princess, but that's a lot closer to being a princess than I'll ever be."

"Sure, if you say so," he says, then mutters under his breath. "*Princess.*"

I grab my knife from the table. "Call me that one more time. I dare you," I bluff. I wouldn't be able to stab him. I can't stand the sight of blood, haven't been able to since I was eight years old, but that's a story for another time. I don't need those kinds of thoughts in my head right now.

"So, what's good?" Liam hums, picking up the menu, seemingly unfazed by my threat of violence. I don't know what I was expecting. He's a goddamn hockey player. Violence is in his blood. Me wielding a butter knife isn't the least bit intimidating. He was more scared of that spider yesterday.

"Everything's good here. But if you want to experience the ultimate *foodgasm*, get the double beef and bacon burger paired with a strawberry shake." I almost moan at the thought of sinking my teeth into that burger.

"A foodgasm? What the hell is a foodgasm?" Liam sets his menu back on the table and looks up at me with a grin.

"It's like an orgasm, but better. You get it when you have the best tasting food ever."

"Nothing is better than an orgasm, sweetheart—and if you think food can beat it, then, well, I'm sorry but you clearly haven't experienced a real orgasm."

My mouth drops open. "I've had plenty of orgasms, not that it's any of your business," I tell him.

"No, you haven't," he says, sounding so sure of himself. *Cocky.* "I can help you out with that though."

*Why does his voice go deeper whenever he suggests I jump into bed with him?*

"Pass." I smile while also squeezing my thighs together, trying to ebb off the need this man is creating in me.

"It's an open offer?" He shrugs, like offering sex is nothing more than offering something as simple as a cup of coffee.

The waitress comes up to the table. Her eyes take their time checking out Liam, and I mean she takes in *every single inch* of him. Maybe I could get over my fear of blood and stab her in those eyes?

I clear my throat. It's not because I'm jealous. That'd be ludicrous. No, I want her attention because I'm hungry and would like to place my order sometime this century, not when she's done eye-fucking the man sitting across from me. The same man who either doesn't notice the attention he's getting or is choosing not to as he studies the menu.

"What will it be?" the waitress asks in a snappy tone, her annoyance obvious.

*Well, too bad, love.* I'm hungry. You can eye-fuck the asshole as much as you want, after I get my food.

"I'll have the double beef and bacon burger, side of fries and onion rings, and a strawberry shake," I tell her.

She writes my order down on her pad before turning to face Liam. "And for you?" she sings in a much more pleasant tone.

"I'll have the same, thanks," he says, handing the woman his menu along with a full-dimpled smile.

"It'll be r-right out," she stutters and grabs the menus before sauntering off.

"Can you not?" I ask, rolling my eyes.

"What'd I do?"

"The charm, making her think she has a chance with you. It's cruel," I tell him.

"How do you know she doesn't have a chance? And I can't help it if I'm naturally charming."

"I'm sorry... I guess I didn't know horny, middle-aged women were your type. But, by all means, don't let me stop you." I wave a hand in the direction of where the waitress walked off.

"Meh, I prefer horny, petite brunettes," he says. I'm going to need to see an optometrist with how much eye-rolling I'm doing around this guy. It's becoming a problem. "Also, I thought it was your job to cock-block me."

"My job is to make sure you don't get yourself into any more trouble and to keep you out of the press as much as I can."

"So, cock-blocking wasn't in the job description then?"

"No, I took initiative and added that task all on my own." I smirk.

"You're a real go-getter, going above and beyond for the cause, right?" he asks.

"Exactly." I slide out of the booth and stand. "I'll be back." I make a dash for the bathroom. I don't want to sit here and continue to share small talk with him.

What the hell was I thinking? I should have asked my father to clarify what this assignment actually entailed. Am I really meant to be his shadow? Just follow him around all day and night?

The moment I enter the bathroom, I turn on the faucet and wet my hands. I splash the cold water on my neck and my elbows. I read somewhere that water helps you relax. I think it's bullshit, because right now I'm not relaxed. I'm at my comfort spot, about to eat my favorite food. I should be as relaxed as they come. But, no, I'm on pins and needles because I've turned into a damn hussy and all I can think about is jumping the bones—or boner—of the guy sitting across from me.

Liam fucking King. Argh... why? What did I do in a previous life to have to endure this kind of torture?

I reach into my pocket, looking for my phone, but it's not there. I must have left it on the table. Great, now I can't even hide out in here and scroll on social media to pass the time until my food is cooked.

Staring at my reflection in the mirror, I straighten my shoulders, tuck back the flyaway hairs, and smooth out my clothes. "You are Aliyah Monroe.

You can handle this. This man does not affect you in the slightest," I say to myself before walking out of the bathroom.

I will not let him ruin my happy place. I wonder if I can find one of those little devices they used in that alien movie, the ones that can erase your memory. Then I could make it so he doesn't remember this diner exists.

I slip back into the booth and stare at my phone, which is still sitting face-down where I left it.

"It's been blowing up. You might want to check it," Liam says.

I swipe up my cell at the same time it dings with an incoming text. I open the messaging app and see my group chat with the girls has ten unread messages. I open the thread and regret it immediately.

CHARLIE:

@AliyahMonroe Are you on date #3? Is that why we haven't heard from you?

AMANDA:

@AliyahMonroe I want all the details. Was he good?

CHARLIE:

@DuchessAmanda Was he good? Like that man could possibly be anything but good. Have you seen him on the ice?

AMANDA:

@CharlieBear I don't think someone's skating ability has a single thing to do with their fucking ability.

That one does make me chuckle. I've never dated a hockey player, so I can neither confirm nor deny that their agility on the ice helps with their movements off it.

"Something funny?" Liam asks.

I look up. I almost forgot he was sitting there. Almost. "My friends want to know if being able to skate well has any correlation with your skills in the bedroom," I tell him.

"Well, tell your friends I'm happy to give them a personal demonstration, both on and off the ice." He winks.

"You don't even know what they look like. Are you really that much of a whore you'd stick your dick into anything?"

"It's hot girl logic." He shrugs.

"What the hell is *hot girl logic*?" I ask, switching

my phone to silent and putting it back down on the table. I'll answer the girls later.

"It's just the way things are. Hot girls group together in bunches. You're hot, which means your friends will be hot too. I mean, usually there's one in the group who's a standing five instead of a ten. But don't worry, you're not it."

He can't be serious. Do men actually think like this? It's ridiculous.

But then I consider my friends. They're all hot in their own way. Charlie could have gone into modeling if she wanted to. She's tall, thin, with long sandy-blonde hair that's worthy of being in a shampoo commercial. Amanda is everything you'd expect a princess to be, always perfectly put together and elegant. She has fair skin and dark hair, with amazing bright-blue eyes. And then Nicole is the typical girl next door, or rather that head cheerleader you hated in high school. Blonde as blonde can be. She's tall with curves in all the right places and huge D-cup breasts that she's not afraid to flaunt. Finally, there's Phoebe. Olive skin tone, dark hair, and dark eyes that I swear you're likely to get lost in if you stare for too long. She has a way of drawing you into her orbit.

I'd hate to break it to Mr. King here, but if he saw

me amongst those girls, I'd probably be *the five* he mentioned. "Remind me to never bring you around my friends," I tell him.

"Why?"

"Because I don't want the hassle of taking them to the health clinic to get scanned for STDs," I say.

Liam picks up his phone, taps on it a few times, and then hands the device over to me. "Just so we're clear, this was done the day before I arrived. I'm as clean as a whistle, sweetheart."

I stare at the report on his screen. Who the hell carries around their labwork like this? Manwhores, that's who. I hand the phone back to Liam just as the waitress approaches and places our food down in front of us.

# Chapter Eight

I've never really cared too much what people think of me. They either love or hate me. I don't try to change their minds. As far as I'm concerned, it's on them to determine what they think, not me.

But for some reason, here I am, sitting across

from the owner's daughter, trying to change her opinion. It fucking irritates the shit out of me that all she sees is an NHL superstar, a player with only one thing on his mind. Okay, *superstar* might not be the exact word she would use—that may have been reaching.

Why the fuck do I even care? That's the question I can't figure out the answer to. I don't even know this chick. I don't need her approval or any shit like that. However, knowing I don't need it does nothing to change the fact that I want it. I want her to see me for me, not the Liam King the media portrays me to be. Just boring, old me.

The kid who spent all his free time perfecting his game. When I wasn't looking out for my little brother, making sure he had at least one meal a day, I was the kid skating or sliding around a puck. I was the kid who kept to himself, out of fear that everyone at school would find out that he was poor. The kid who had to steal food sometimes just to be able to feed his mother and brother. I'm the kid my father never wanted. The kid who had so many fucking insecurities growing up.

Insecurities that I thought I didn't possess anymore. Turns out, I was wrong. Because sitting across from this perfect little ice princess, I feel less-than. I hate her for making me feel like this again, like I'm not good enough.

I watch as she picks up her burger and takes as big of a bite out of it as her mouth can fit. She doesn't care that the sauce and grease drip down her chin as she closes her eyes and tips her head back... *moaning*.

Fucking foodgasms. This is what she was talking about. Now my dick is rock-hard as I think about all the ways I could force those sounds out of her myself. When she swallows, I get a clear image of her swallowing me.

Aliyah opens her eyes and looks my way. "What?" she asks, picking up a napkin and swiping it across her face.

I shake my head. "Nothing," I grunt and reach for my own burger. I don't usually eat shit like this during the season. I have a strict diet plan that I stick to. I'll just have to find a way to burn off the excess calories later. I wrap my mouth around the bun, and the second I bite into the meat, a taste explosion hits my tongue. Holy shit, she wasn't wrong. This has to be one of the best burgers I've ever eaten.

"Well?" Aliyah prompts.

I lift one shoulder. "It's okay," I tell her.

"Oh, come on, it's better than okay. Admit it," she says.

"Admit that you like me first," I dare her to say the words.

"The problem with that is... I'm not a liar. So, sorry, not gonna happen."

Well, shit, that stings. "You lied to me yesterday," I point out.

"When?"

"When you took me to your brother's house under the guise that you lived there."

"I didn't lie. I said I didn't live alone, and I *do* have a bedroom at Gray's, so *technically* I kinda do live there," she says and then proceeds to sink her teeth into her burger again.

I close my eyes as the sounds of her moans go right through me. "If you keep moaning like that, we're going to have a problem," I tell her.

"What? Like what? I'm not moaning," she insists as her cheeks turn a new shade of pink.

"My cock says otherwise. It happens to like the sounds of your moans, a fucking lot. Which is a problem for both of us."

"That seems like it's definitely a *you* problem, and not a *me* problem." Aliyah pops a fry into her mouth.

"No, it's an *us* problem, because if you keep turning me on, I'm going to do everything in my power to wear you down until you let me fuck you. Which won't take long, especially if I pull out everything in my arsenal." I lift an eyebrow before adding, "And we both know it'll be an *us* problem if I fuck you. Because, one, I work for your father and, two, *I work for your father.*"

"Your ego knows no bounds, you know that? You don't need to worry, because there is absolutely nothing you can do that will ever make me want to fuck you."

"You see, now, that's just a challenge, which only turns me on more. It's been a while since I've been challenged."

Aliyah rolls her eyes. "Shut up and eat your burger before it gets cold."

For some fucked-up reason, I follow her instructions and do just that. After inhaling the burger, barely remembering to chew, I wipe my face with a napkin. "What are your plans for the rest of the day?" I ask her, trying to make polite conversation.

"Whatever your plans are. My job is to follow you around and stop you from making mistakes."

"I don't make mistakes," I tell her.

"Beating up your coach wasn't a mistake?" she throws back, her jaw slightly dropped in shock.

"Nope."

"Allowing yourself to be photographed with puck bunnies and a shit-ton of cocaine on the table wasn't a mistake?"

"Okay, that wasn't my finest moment, but that picture was staged. I don't touch drugs. Never have, never will." I shrug. It's the truth. I have no reason to lie about that.

"Well, it doesn't matter. We're going to find a way to clean up your image, turn you into *Canada's prince* again."

"So, you follow me in the media, huh?" I smile. Her use of the name the tabloids gave me early in my career tells me she's read up on me. Even if most of it is a bunch of fucking lies, made-up stories that should get a New York Times bestseller sticker for fiction because that's really all they print.

"I did my research. It's what any good employee would do. I needed to know what I was getting myself into when my dad gave me you to babysit."

I make a point to look over my shoulder and around at the otherwise empty diner. "You know it's okay. You can admit you like me. No one will ever know. There's no one here but us," I tell her.

"Why does it matter to you if I like you or not?" She folds her arms over her chest and leans back in the booth to eye me from across the table.

"It doesn't." I shrug, annoyed that she can see right through me.

"Right, sure it doesn't." She nods to my empty plate. "You done?"

"Seems that way," I say, standing from the booth while adjusting my still half-hard cock in my pants. Aliyah pulls her wallet out of her oversized purse. Before she can grab any cash from inside, I throw two hundred-dollar bills on the table. "I've got it," I tell her.

She takes out a hundred and tosses it on top of mine. "I don't need or want you to pay for my meal." She purses her lips together in defiance.

I don't say anything. I wait for her to slide out of the booth. When she walks past, I swipe her bill off the table and slide it into the opening of her bag before following her out of the diner.

"Where to?" Aliyah asks as soon as I shut the passenger-side door of her car. I look over to her and smirk.

*Is she my new personal driver too?*

"Home," I tell her. I haven't had a chance to check out the building I'm going to be living in for how ever long the Knights decide to keep me. There's supposed to be a state-of-the-art gym as well as a heated lap pool. It's one of the reasons I chose the place.

Right now, I have a lot of energy to burn off. You'd think that training this morning would have worn me out, but I have a ton of pent-up energy coursing through my body. I'm telling myself it has nothing to do with the tempting little vixen sitting next to me. The completely *off-limits* tempting little vixen. I mean, I don't think you could get any more off-limits than Aliyah Monroe.

Knowing *that* doesn't stop me from wanting her, though. If anything, it only makes me want her more. Without a word, Aliyah pulls out of the parking lot. I rack my brain, trying to find something to say, a way to break this silence that's fallen over us. It's off-putting, because it's not completely uncomfortable.

*How can you be so comfortable around a stranger?*

Aliyah turns into the underground garage, entering the code into the panel—a code that I never gave her. Then she maneuvers into the spot designated for my apartment. "Where would you have parked if I had a car?"

"I'm sure I would have figured something out." She grins in a way that tells me I won't like whatever it is she's thinking.

"Thanks for the ride," I say, climbing out of the car. I reach in, grab my bag from the back seat, and pause when I see her doing the same. "What are you doing?" I ask aloud.

"Following you, obviously. It's kind of my job."

"You're going to be bored out of your mind," I warn her.

"I have no doubt. But that's why I have this." She hefts her oversized bag onto one shoulder.

"What's in that thing anyway?" I ask. I'd offer to carry it for her if I weren't so afraid of having my head chewed off. *Literally.* I wouldn't put it past her to sink those pearly white teeth right into the side of my neck and start munching.

"Everything and nothing at all." She smiles.

That fucking smile is going to get me in trouble, and then it's going to get her in trouble too. Because if I fall on that sword, there won't be any fucking stopping. Something tells me one taste of this woman will never be enough.

Yeah, I need to find that gym ASAP. I need to

distract both my mind and my cock from all thoughts of Aliyah Monroe. "Just try to stay out of my way. I don't do well when my space's cramped," I grunt out and head to the bank of elevators.

Maybe I can piss her off so she leaves. It can't be that hard, right? I've pissed off plenty of women before. Usually, it's because I won't go back for seconds with them, or I turn down their advances or some shit. I glance over my shoulder. I wonder what it'll take to make this walking, talking temptation on two legs blow a fuse.

Fuck, thinking about her pissed off and fuming, yelling at me, should not be such a turn-on. Maybe I need a shrink. These thoughts are not normal.

Aliyah follows me into the elevator and beats me to the punch, pressing the button to take us up to my apartment. "Just so you know, I have three older brothers. I'm very adept at speaking grump. But don't expect me to sit around and be all rainbows and sunshine if you're going to resort to grunting at me."

"Noted," I say, keeping my voice as neutral as possible.

# Chapter Nine

This was a mistake, a mistake of epic proportions. And I mean EPIC. I should have stayed in the apartment, or sat in the hall and waited for him. What I should never have done was blindly and stupidly follow Liam-freaking-King into the gym.

What on earth was I thinking? I wasn't, obviously. I've sat in the gym with my brothers countless times before. I've even worked out with them. But Liam King is not my brother and the way my body is responding to seeing this man lift weights is not okay. No matter how much I try to tell myself he doesn't affect me, I can't deny the attraction. My brain is on board with living in denial but my body—particularly those traitorous lady parts downstairs—seems to have a mind of its own.

I'm surprised I don't have a pool of drool at my feet right now. I feel like I should be on one of those documentaries about animals in heat on the Discovery Channel. I can imagine the commentary now.

*"Here, we have the not-so-elusive horny female. And it's hockey season, folks, which means that mating season is also in session, and this particular female is looking to start hers out with a bang!"*

Argh, I hate him for making me feel this needy. I'm trying not to look. It was easier when I knew he could see me, but right now, Liam has his back to me, his shirtless muscles rippling under the overhead lights and dripping with sweat as he performs a ridiculous number of pull-ups. Surely his arms are going to tire soon. How many times can one guy lift himself like this? My head tilts to the side, appreciating the view he's giving me more than I'll ever admit out loud. And then, like I'm snapped out of my trance, I dart my eyes away as his feet hit the mat and he turns around.

I dig through my bag and find my phone. If my brain cells hadn't taken a vacation over the last ten minutes, I would have snapped a picture of that scene. I probably could have sold it to the tabloids, or auctioned it off to my friends.

Speaking of, I open up the text message thread. There are twenty new messages in our group chat. I don't read through them; instead, I type out my own message.

ME:

@All How much would you pay for a shirtless picture of Liam King working out in the gym???

Within seconds, I see the little bubbles pop up on the bottom of the screen—the ones that let me know someone is replying.

AMANDA:

@AliyahMonroe Don't you dare tease me like that. I'd give you a kidney.

CHARLIE:

@AliyahMonroe A real best friend would have already sent the picture.

NICOLE:

@AliyahMonroe How does five hundred thousand sound?

PHOEBE:

@AliyahMonroe I've just used "Find My Friend" to track you. I'll be out front in ten. Let me in!!!

My eyes bug out of my head. They absolutely cannot turn up here. Shit, shit, shit! I wouldn't put it past any of them to actually track me down and pop up unannounced.

ME:

@All DO NOT and I mean DO NOT turn up here. You'll get me fired.

NICOLE:

@AliyahMonroe Don't be so dramatic. Your dad is not going to fire you.

CHARLIE:

@AliyahMonroe He might when he finds out you're screwing his latest investment.

My phone vibrates excessively, the notification

with an incoming video chat from Phoebe flashing across the screen. I hit decline and drop my phone. Nope, no way am I answering that right now.

"Lia, don't hold out on me. I swear, if you're screwing the Liam fucking King, I want deets," I hear her scream through the receiver. I peer up as I scramble to grab my phone and silence the video call.

In my haste to *not* answer it, I must have hit *accept* instead of *decline.* Any hopes that Liam didn't hear my friend screeching through the speakerphone are halted when he stops moving and looks directly at me with a smirk.

"Oh my god, shut up. Phoebe, stop talking right now!" I yell, finally managing to pick up my phone.

"I want to know too. How big is it? Because the only reason you wouldn't have already told us would be if it was tiny, like pinprick tiny, and you feel bad for the guy. Lia, don't feel bad," Charlie says, followed by a barrage of laughter coming out of my phone's speaker.

I hold the camera up to my face. "It's so small you'd have trouble identifying it if it were next to a bobby pin," I deadpan. "I didn't even come," I add, right before the phone is snatched out of my hands.

"*Clearly* she's lying. She doesn't want to let on to how extremely well-endowed I am. And just so you know, she was too busy screaming my name before she passed out after the fifth orgasm I gave her to take precise measurements," Liam says, looking directly into my phone.

I'm on my feet and reaching for my phone in seconds, which only makes him lift it higher. "He's lying. I have not and *would not* go anywhere near that disease-infested package of his," I yell out, jumping up in a lame attempt to swipe the device from his hands.

"I have no problem getting up close and personal. I mean, they have all kinds of medications for clearing up that sort of thing these days." *This* comes from Amanda.

"Right? I agree. Why let a little STD get in the way of a good time?" Charlie adds with a laugh.

"Oh. My. God. Stop. This isn't funny," I growl.

"It kind of is," Nicole counters.

I flop back to the ground. "You know what? You all want the infamous Liam King? Then have at 'em. I don't even care," I huff.

Liam looks down at me. Without a word, he disconnects the call and crouches in front of me while holding out my phone. "Your friends seem fun," he says.

"Yeah, they are," I tell him, taking the device and tossing it back into my bag.

"Between you and me, I'd pick you. Every fucking time." He winks, stands to his full height, and then walks over to the bench press. Leaving me sitting here with my mouth hanging open in shock.

*He'd pick me?* What does that even mean? I don't know how much time passes, but when Liam stops in front of me again, my butt is numb from sitting on the floor.

"Come on, we're done in here." He holds out a hand for me to take.

I look at his open palm like it's the snake offering Eve that damned poisoned apple in the Garden of Eden. I know I want to take it, but I also know I shouldn't. In the end, my manners win out and I place my hand in his large, warm palm. Liam tugs his arm back and I'm on my feet within seconds. He releases his hold when he bends down to pick up my bag. Then, without another word, he takes my hand again and leads me over to the elevator.

Why is he holding my hand? Or the better question is why don't I want him to let go?

As soon as we're inside the elevator, Liam glances down at our joined palms. His brows draw together, and he quickly releases his grip on me before tucking his now-free hand into his pocket.

*Is he just as confused by that whole gesture as I was?*

"I'm going to hit the shower and then order some dinner. Unless you want to join me and I can start with dessert?" He wags his brows up and down suggestively as his eyes roam the length of my body. The elevator doors open into his foyer.

"Tempting, but I'll pass. I'll sit out here. We actually have some PR stuff to go over before I head home."

"PR stuff?"

"Yeah, like what charity events you're going to attend, things you can do to make the people fall in love with you again," I tell him as I make a mental list.

"I have one question," he says.

"Go on."

"How do I stop you from falling in love with me in the process? If I'm going to turn into the Canadian poster child for hockey again and all, that is? I mean, you've put up a good fight so far, but that'll all change when you come to learn just how much of a nice guy I actually am."

"I think I can refrain from developing feelings for you, Mr. King," I tell him.

"And I think you're going to fall so hard in love with me that you'll be begging me to break the rules with you."

"I don't beg. Ever."

"See? That just seems like another challenge, princess," he says with a wink.

"Ew, and it's not a challenge. Go take that shower. You stink."

His laughter follows him down the hall, and I can't help but wonder if he's right... *Could I actually develop feelings for him?*

I shake my head. That is highly unlikely. My body might be attracted to the guy, but that's just a physical, chemical reaction. There's no way on God's green earth that I could fall in love with Liam King.

# Chapter Ten

Aliyah just left. How she managed to talk me into agreeing to all of those events she wants me to attend and donate to, I have no idea. She seemed so passionate when she talked about the causes. It was like I was seeing a completely different side of her and I liked it. A lot. I was captivated by her. It's probably why I'm now staring at a printed-out list of dates, which all involve me wearing a tux.

I put the list on the refrigerator, pinning it under a Vancouver Knights magnet. It's going to take me a while to get used to the fact that the Knights are now my team.

I sit on the sofa and turn on the television. I promised Aliyah I'd be staying in for the night, assuring her that she didn't need to stay and babysit. She looked tired. Fuck, I'm tired myself. Probably too tired to go out even if I wanted to.

I flick through the channels until I land on sports news. I know I should keep scrolling, but like a moth to the flame, I'm drawn in. Especially when I hear my name mentioned by the commentator. They're talking shit. They always do. Which is why I change the channel, deciding I don't want to hear it. I used to spend my downtime obsessing over the highlights. Back when my name was only ever mentioned with praise. Now everyone is waiting for me to fall even farther from the pedestal they all had me on.

I'm not going to, though. This is going to work. No matter what I have to do, I will make this work. I'll take the Vancouver Knights to the Stanley Cup and win. It's not like it's gonna be hard. They're already a good team without me. They've come pretty fucking close to making it for the past few years. But this will be the year they go all the way. I'll prove to everyone who doubted me, betted against me, that I'm still the fucking best at my job. Even better than that, I'll beat *him*. My old fucking coach. The one who made the mistake of sleeping with my mother.

I settle for some horror flick I've seen before. It's really just background noise at this point. I close my eyes, feeling the exhaustion of the day. I need to get up to skate before the sun rises. It's nothing I'm not used to, but after the extra workout I did today— mostly as a distraction and to keep my hands busy so I wasn't tempted to touch the forbidden fruit, so to speak—I'm struggling.

The worst part is, it didn't work. I still wanted to touch her. Especially when I saw her checking me out. She thought I didn't know she was watching. I had my back to her, but I could see her reflection in the mirror on the wall beside me. She was enjoying the show. Which made me do a million more pull-ups than I normally would. I liked knowing she was watching. Even as I think it, I know this woman has reduced me to a stupid teenage boy trying to show off for the pretty girl. A girl I shouldn't be trying to impress at all.

*What the fuck happened to my plan to just piss her off enough to get her to leave?*

Oh, that's right. My hard dick seemed to take over and erase that plan from my mind. It can start tomorrow... if I even see her. I'm sure I'm not going to see her every day.

Fuck, it's going to be a long-ass season if I do. I run a hand down my face. I sink farther into the sofa and let my body start to relax.

"What the fuck?" I groan, waking up from what feels like a five-minute nap.

It's dark outside, so I pick up my phone and check the time. It's eleven thirty at night. Then I hear a buzzing noise. I look around, wondering what the fuck is making that god-awful sound before pushing to my feet and following the noise into the foyer. The buzz rings out through the apartment again, and that's when I spot the culprit. The intercom on the wall. I don't know a single soul in this town, apart from Aliyah, so why the hell is my door buzzing in the middle of the night?

Pressing the button, I grunt into the speaker, "What?"

"Open up, big bro. I'm freezing my balls off out here." My little brother's voice grates through the intercom *and* my patience. What the fuck is he doing here?

"Matty? What the hell?" I say into the speaker at the same time I press the button that allows him access to the building.

I pace up and down the foyer, waiting for the elevator to ding and indicate his arrival into the apartment. Don't get me wrong, I love my baby brother. He's the most important person in my life. I'd do anything for the little shit. Which he knows and takes full advantage of at times. For as long as I can remember, it's been me and him against the world. We've always had to look out for each other. My mom tried. She did her best. I know that. Her best just wasn't good enough. It didn't keep us fed, warm, clothed. I also know I sound like an ungrateful shit, but when you watch your mother suffer from depression every other month because of a broken heart, courtesy of her latest great love, you tend to develop some resentment. She did that to herself.

She chose to chase a love story, instead of taking care of her children. And unfortunately for all of us, they never came with a happy ending.

That was until she met Glen, her current husband. I actually thought she'd got it right this time, that she found a guy worthy of her attention. I even took the time to get to know him. Now I wish I never did, because it turns out my mom isn't capable of reaching the end of her love story. I don't know if she self-sabotages on purpose, or if she's just fucking hopeless. I can't even talk to her after I found out she cheated on Glen with my fucking coach.

The elevator buzzes and Matty walks in. But he's not alone. He has four extremely scantily clad women in tow.

"Matty, what the fuck? Do you know what time it is?" I yell while pulling him into a hug. I know... mixed-as-fuck messages going on right here. But he's my brother and I haven't seen him in two months.

"Nice to see you too, bro. And I do know what time it is. It's P.A.R.T.Y time," he says, spelling out the word for emphasis.

"No, it's not. I have morning skate. I'm going to bed," I tell him.

"Come on. I haven't seen you in months. Just come and have one drink with me. Please, Liam, one drink and then we can come back here. I'll even tuck you into bed myself," he says.

Fuck, I know I'm going to regret this. "One drink. And I mean it, Matty. I have practice, and the new coach already hates me."

"Until you start winning him games. Don't worry so much. You're Liam fucking King. Or have you already forgotten that?" Matty slaps a hand across my cheek.

"No, but it appears you have," I say, wrapping an arm around his neck. I twist and have him in a head-lock in minutes. His guests gasp and step out of the way as Matty kicks his feet out in a lame attempt to trip me up.

"Okay, I give," he wheezes.

I let him go. "Wait here. I need to get my wallet and phone," I tell him, walking towards the bedroom.

What the fuck am I doing? I shouldn't be going out. I promised Aliyah I would stay in. Shit. Why the fuck do I even care? I pull up her contact and dial her number.

It almost rings out before she answers. "Hello?"

I can tell by the sound of her voice that she was sleeping. "Quick question," I ask her.

"Liam?"

"On a scale of one to ten, how pissed are you

going to be in the morning when you find out I went out and had one drink? Not two, not three. One." Though I'm not sure that specifying the number really matters.

I hear a muffled scream and some ruffling of what sounds like sheets. "Liam King, I swear to God if you go out right now, I will find you and I will drag you back home. But not before I stop at the closest pet store, buy every fucking tarantula they have in stock, and empty them onto your bed. You won't even see them until they're crawling all over you."

Fuck, that's actually not a vision I need. "Anyone ever tell you you're mean?"

"Plenty of people," she deadpans. "I mean it, Liam. Do not go out."

"I can't *not* go out. My brother just showed up. I have to go and have one drink with him, or I'll never get rid of the kid."

"You can say no. That's what grown-ups do, Liam."

"Guess you better start hunting me down, princess," I say before hanging up.

My phone immediately starts ringing. I silence it and shove it into my pocket with a smile on my face. For some reason, having Aliyah hunt me down isn't all that unappealing. I just fucking hope like hell that no pet stores are open this late.

I walk out of the bedroom and find Matty sprawled out on my sofa, two of the girls squished up next to him. The other two are on the opposite sofa, making out.

"Let's go. And they are not coming back with us," I tell him, pointing to the harem of women he brought.

"What? Who are you and what have you done with my brother?" he asks.

"Hurry up before I change my mind, Matty."

We settle into a booth at the back of a bar called ICE. If the name didn't already give it away, it's heavily hockey focused. I probably should have chosen somewhere else, but this was close. I remembered walking past it yesterday.

I paid the bartender to fill my glass with just soda when I ordered a vodka soda. I have no plans of drinking before a morning skate. I'm not a fucking rookie. I've made that mistake more than once before and it's never a good time.

"So, how's Vancouver treating ya?" Matty asks.

"I've only been here two days," I say.

"Another one then." He slams his cup down on the table.

"No, I said one. Let's go."

"Come on, you don't have to join me. I just want one more." He pouts.

"Fine, one more. But then I'm leaving, with or without you," I warn him. Matty smiles wide. He knows my threat is empty. I'd never leave my little brother alone in a city he doesn't know. "How'd you get here? Why aren't you at school?" I ask him.

"I took the weekend off to see you. Mom says you won't answer her calls." He shrugs.

"And I'll stop answering yours too if you bring her up again."

"Come on, Liam, just tell me what happened. How am I supposed to play peacekeeper if you don't tell me what she did to piss you off this time?" he huffs.

I stare at him, keeping my face neutral. I am not telling him what she did. It's bad enough I know. He has no idea how much I wish like fuck I didn't.

"Liam fucking King, I hope you know a good

doctor because you're going to need one when I'm through with you," Aliyah's voice screams out from across the bar. Aliyah's very pissed-off voice. I look up, and sure enough, the hot little brunette is stomping her way towards our booth.

*How the fuck did she find me so quickly? And what the hell is she wearing?*

# Chapter Eleven

*Aliyah*

Sometimes being Aliyah Monroe comes in handy. Like right now. The fact that it took me less than ten minutes to track down my prodigal hockey player is great. For me. Not so much for him, because I am going to ruin his damn night and give him hell for making me drag my ass out of bed.

I stop in front of him. One drink with my brother, my ass. He's sitting in a booth with a guy who *could* pass for his brother. They have the same stupidly handsome face. But they're not alone. They have four girls sitting with them.

I fold my arms over my chest. "Get up. We're leaving," I tell him.

Liam ever so slowly runs his eyes up my body, from head to toe. It's only now, as he's undressing me with those eyes, that I take note of what I'm wearing. I didn't bother to get dressed. I was so pissed I jumped out of bed, slid my feet into some slippers, and grabbed my keys. I was already driving when I started reaching out to all the bars around his apartment complex.

"What the fuck, Aliyah?" he finally asks, pushing to his feet.

"I could ask you the same thing. You promised you'd stay in," I remind him, trying to hide how hurt I am that he broke his first promise to me already.

Liam shrugs out of his jacket. "Put this on. You're cold."

"No, what I am is tired and freaking pissed off

that I had to chase your ass down in the middle of the night," I tell him, stepping back.

"Aliyah, put the fucking coat on," he grits out between his teeth. "You're wearing underwear in the middle of a fucking bar."

"Actually, it's sleepwear. Not *underwear*. And I wouldn't be in the middle of a fucking bar if it weren't for you." I look down and notice my nipples are poking out of the thin cotton of my singlet. Goosebumps rise all over my exposed skin. I meant what I said. I'm wearing sleep shorts, not underwear, but they really aren't that much better. Liam steps closer, and this time, I let him wrap the coat around my shoulders.

"Two days, huh, bro?" the kid sitting at his table asks.

"Shut up," Liam tells him, without taking his eyes off me.

"Let's go," I say.

"Aliyah, this is my brother, Matty. Matty, Aliyah, the babysitter the team assigned to me." Liam waves a hand between the two of us.

"You got yourself a babysitter? What the fuck for?" Matty asks.

"Because he's incapable of making responsible decisions like a grown-ass adult, and we're not about to piss away a multi-million dollar contract on bad press," I answer for him.

"Man, when you're done babysitting him, can you come babysit me? I could use a lesson or two." The kid grins, and I definitely see the resemblance now.

Liam turns around. "Shut the fuck up. Don't talk to her like that. Don't even think about her like that. Get up. We're leaving," he says, swiping his phone up from the table.

"Okay, jeez. You could have just told me you were hot for the babysitter," Matty replies.

I pivot on my heel, hoping like hell they can't see the blush creeping up my face under the darkness of the diminished bar lighting. A hand lands on the small of my back. A very large hand. One that I know belongs to Liam just from the reaction my body has to the touch.

*Traitorous freaking body.* I want a damn refund.

"Ignore him. Our mother dropped him on his head a lot as an infant," Liam whispers into my ear.

"It's fine. Let's go." I take one step forward when Liam reaches out and wraps his palm around mine.

*Why is he holding my hand? What the hell is happening to me right now?*

Shit. I need to shake this guy loose before I get

myself into the sort of trouble my dad won't want to bail me out of. Instead, Jacob Monroe will enjoy following through on his promise to paint the ice red.

Even with that image in mind, I don't let go of Liam's hand until we reach the curb where my car is still waiting. I told the valet to keep it there, that I wouldn't be long.

"Shit, nice car, A," Matty says, reaching for the passenger side door.

Liam slaps him over the head and shoves him towards the back. "Get in, and for once in your life, just be quiet."

I walk around to the driver's side. By the time I get into the car, both Liam and his brother are buckled in. "How much did you drink?" I ask Liam. "You do know you have to be up and ready for morning skate in four hours, right?"

"I'm aware and capable of meeting my responsibilities, Aliyah. This isn't my first job," Liam says, his lips tilting up at the sides like he's trying not to smile.

Two minutes later, I'm pulling into his garage. "Get out, and don't make me come back in the middle of the night, Liam," I tell him.

"Nice meeting you, A. I'm sure I'll be seeing more of you," Matty says, closing the door as he exits the car. Leaving just me and Liam inside.

I don't know what he's waiting for. Then I remember I'm still wearing his jacket. I take it off and hand it to him. "Sorry. Forgot I was wearing it."

"It's past midnight, Aliyah. You shouldn't be out on these roads. It's not safe," he says.

"I'm a big girl, Liam. I'm also the daughter of Jacob Monroe. Do you really think anything is going to happen to me?"

"Not even your father can stop the ice from freezing over," he counters. "I have a guest room. Stay here until it's at least daylight."

"Is this your way of trying to get me in your bed, Liam? 'Cause it's not going to work," I tell him.

"No, it's my way of making sure you don't die because I was an idiot and let my brother talk me into going to that bar. I can't live with that on my conscience," he says.

"Fine, I'll crash in your guest room. But I'm locking the door," I huff.

"Thank you. And you should. A man only has so much restraint when it comes to your kind of temptation." He looks down at the jacket in my outstretched arm. His eyes focus on the long scar that runs up the inside of my wrist. I drop the jacket and climb out of the car. I usually wear huge bracelets or cuffs to cover the mark. It's the one reminder of who I really am that I can't escape.

I'm the daughter a mother couldn't love. The daughter a mother would do the most unthinkable and heinous things to when no one else was watching. It wasn't until the slicing of my wrist in the bathtub, the same day I got this scar, that someone noticed. It was also the day she finally decided to leave, after her failed attempt to get rid of me for good. I never saw her again after that. I remember my father being sad. He'd look at me with tears in his eyes. And I knew it was my fault he lost his wife. Not that he'd ever say it.

I walk up to where Matty is waiting. I really don't want Liam to ask me about what he thinks he saw. I know what it looks like, but the truth is so much worse. Because I didn't get that scar from not loving myself. I got it from being *unlovable*.

I mean, if your own mother can't love you, then how can anyone else?

Liam stands between me and his brother in the elevator at an odd angle that fully prevents Matty from being able to see me. It's weird, and the small chuckle that comes out of Matty's mouth tells me that I'm not the only one who thinks so.

"Matty, you've got the sofa," Liam says, taking

my hand in his again and pulling me down the hall. He opens the door to his guest room. It's decorated in light blues and whites. The king-size bed has a million pillows on it, the large pile just calling my name, while the floor-length dark-navy velvet drapes are already closed. "You can sleep here. The door locks. Wake me up if you need anything. You remember where my bedroom is, right?" Liam says, his tone serious until that last comment, when it resumes its playful lilt.

"What could I possibly need?" I ask him, confused.

"A cuddle? An orgasm? The list is endless, really," he says with a smirk.

"I think I'll be fine." I walk over to the bed and pull the covers back. Just before he closes the door, I call out to him. He stops and turns around to look at me. "Thank you for not asking about it," I tell him, wrapping my right hand over my left wrist.

Liam glances from my wrist to my eyes. "Everyone has a past, Aliyah. It's usually never what people think or expect it to be, because nothing is ever as it seems in life. Goodnight." He doesn't say anything more before he shuts the door behind him.

I think I prefer it when he's being flirtatious. I can pretend not to like that Liam. It's so much harder when he's nice and sensitive and makes sense. I have been judging him based on his past, even though I wasn't there and have no way of knowing what really happened. I don't know why he beat up his coach, or why he went on that bender and found himself in numerous precarious situations that ended up plastered all over the tabloids.

I climb into the bed. The sheets are cool and soft on my skin as I sink into the mattress. Pulling the blankets up over my chest, I look back to the door. I really should get up and lock it, but I don't feel unsafe. I don't think Liam or his brother will come in here when I'm sleeping. So, instead of locking the door, I close my eyes and let sleep take over.

# Chapter Twelve

"**T**hanks." I hand the cab driver a fifty and make a mental note to contact the company that should have had my car delivered to me by now. I hate not having my own way to get around.

I pull my gym bag over my shoulder and walk

into my building. Training was just as shitty today as it was yesterday. It seems the whole *let's hate on the new guy* routine isn't going to end anytime soon. I can't blame the guys for being salty towards me though. I have beat their asses out on that ice during every game I ever played against them over the last few years.

Then, all of a sudden, they're expected to play *with* me, which is not always an easy adjustment. It just sucks to be on the receiving end of their dislike. I honestly thought I'd play for Montreal until I retired. I wanted to be a one-team kind of player. Now, all I want to do is play my old team and annihilate them. People I considered friends, family even, all turned their backs on me the minute I got traded. Not a single fucking one of my former teammates has reached out since I left.

Does it sting? *Not gonna lie. You bet your sweet ass it does.*

I was always there for any one of them. Whenever they needed shit, I was the one to help them out. Not that I need them, because I learned from a young age not to need anyone. The only person in life you can rely on is yourself. Though I have to admit I've let myself down a lot lately too.

I walk into my apartment, tossing my bag on the

floor in the foyer. I'll deal with that later. I look towards the hallway, where I left Aliyah asleep in the guest room. I stuck my head in before leaving this morning, and she was out of it. I didn't want to wake her, so I closed the door and left. I'm certain she won't still be there though. It's eleven a.m. There's no way she's still asleep.

I find Matty in the living room eating a bowl of my cereal and watching some shitty reality television show.

"Why the fuck do you watch that BS?" I ask, plopping myself down beside him.

"Because they're all MILFs," he says.

My gaze shifts back to the hallway. I don't know why I'm obsessing over checking that room. Do I want her to be here? *No, I don't.*

*But, also, I kind of do.*

"She hasn't surfaced yet, if that's what you're wondering," Matty says.

"Why would I be wondering?"

"Because you've got that look on your face and you can't stop glancing down the hall."

"I'm not wondering. I couldn't care less." I get up off the sofa. "I'm hitting the shower."

"Your hair is still wet from the shower you clearly just took." The little fucker smirks.

I flip him the bird as I walk in the direction of the room I really shouldn't be walking towards. Then again, it's my fucking guest room. If I need to go in there, I can. Indecision fills my head as I stare at the door handle. I shouldn't open it. I should just leave her. This could be my opportunity to go out and spread my wings. She's asleep and won't be able to cock-block me.

My hand reaches out just as the door swings open, and a distressed Aliyah walks right into me. My arm wraps around her back to keep her from falling.

"We really need to stop meeting like this, princess," I tell her.

"Ew. And cut it out with the whole *princess* thing. Why didn't you wake me up?" Her hands push against my chest. I don't want to let her go, so I don't.

"Because I told you no one would go into that room while you were in there." I shrug.

"Please tell me you went to morning skate?" she asks, shoving harder to get out of my hold.

This time, I let her go. I'm not supposed to like how good she feels pressed up against me anyway. And, honestly, if it weren't for her shoving at my chest, I wouldn't have dropped my arms. I would have pushed her back into that bedroom, down onto that bed I can see behind her, and covered her body with mine. Preferably naked-style.

"I went. So don't you worry that pretty little head of yours. I *am* capable of doing my job." I roll my eyes. I've never missed a fucking practice session in my whole career. Even when I was injured and unable to skate, I'd still show up. I'd watch from the bench or work out in the gym with the trainers.

"I don't doubt that. No one gets to the NHL without dedication and commitment. *But* you've made some questionable decisions lately, and it's my job to ensure that you don't fuck up again."

"Or fuck at all, apparently," I mutter under my breath. Then I take her hand. "Come on, I'll lend you some clothes."

"What for?"

"Because you're not wearing any and I'm not about to let you walk out of my apartment without clothes on," I tell her, tugging her towards my bedroom.

"I have clothes on," she fires back.

"Barely." I look at her, letting my eyes take in all of that creamy skin on full display. My gaze lands on her breasts, her nipples pebbled under the skin-tight cotton of her sleep top. Fuck me, I'm going to hell. Or, at the very least, I'm going to have my kneecaps blown out, because I already know there is no way I'm going to be able to withstand temptation. I need a taste of this woman. I let out a groan and force myself to turn back around. But not before I catch the blush creeping up Aliyah's neck.

"I don't need your clothes, Liam. I'm going home to change."

"It's freezing out there, Aliyah, and it's my fault you're running around town practically naked." I walk into the closet and pull out one of the Vancouver Knights sweaters that was sent to me when I first signed. It has my number and name on it. "Put this on, then you can go home."

"I'm not wearing your clothes, and I'm not going home alone. You're coming with me," she says, crossing her arms over her chest.

I make a point to look behind me, at my bed, where the sheets are still rumpled from when I got out of it this morning. I need to hire a cleaner— another thing to add to my ever-growing to-do list. "I have a perfectly good bed here, babe. We don't need to go back to your place," I tell her with a grin.

Aliyah looks at where I'm pointing and bites down on her bottom lip. I watch as she walks around me and towards the bed. Holy shit, is she actually going to...

Nope, she's not. Fuck me. My cock just went from hard to fucking *harder* at the thought of her climbing onto my bed and spreading those thighs for me. Instead, she's... fixing the sheets.

"What are you doing?" I ask, dumbfounded. Any other time I've invited a chick to my bed, I barely get the words out before they're on it, offering up their bodies, their pleasure to me.

"Making your bed. You can't leave the house without making your bed. It's sloppy," she says.

"I haven't had time to get a cleaner yet. You don't need to do that," I tell her.

"It's fine. You can't leave the house without making your bed," she repeats. I stand there and stare at her, not knowing what to say or do as she continues to smooth out the top sheet. When she's done, she turns around. "You're going to need your skates today."

"What for?"

"It's day one of the new and improved Liam King," she tells me. "Let's go."

I reach out and stop her as she tries to walk past me. Lifting the sweater in my hand, I pull it down over her head. "Wear it," I tell her.

"Fine, but only because it's cold and not because you want me to." She threads her arms through the sleeves.

Shit, I should have thought about this a bit more. I thought seeing her practically naked was hot, but this... Seeing her in my sweater, with my number on her. Fuck, it's sinful. I blink. The hemline falls halfway down her thighs. It's huge on her, but I don't think I've ever seen anything more stunning.

"You should keep it," I say. My voice comes out hoarse as I swallow the lump in my throat.

"I'm not keeping your sweater. As soon as I get home, you're getting it back." She glances at the bed and furrows her brows before looking my way again. "Grab your skates. Let's go," she reminds me.

I should ask her where we're going. Instead, I follow her out of the room and pick up the bag I dumped in the foyer. "Matty, I'm heading out. Don't eat my cereal," I yell in his direction.

"Whoa, hold up," my brother replies, jumping over the back of the sofa and heading towards us. "Holy shitballs," he says, eyeing Aliyah up and down. "A, babe, what do I have to do to get you to babysit me? Like for real."

I reach out and slap him upside the head. It's becoming a habit, I guess. "Shut the fuck up and don't talk to her like that," I remind him. "Also, stop undressing her with your eyes before I rip them out of their sockets."

Both Aliyah and Matty stare at me. I'm not sure if it's the words or the growl that just escaped my throat that has them gaping.

"I don't need you to defend me, Liam," Aliyah says. Then she turns to Matty. "If you want me to babysit you, all you have to do is put at least sixteen hours a day out on the ice, live and breathe hockey. Make it to the NHL, draft twenty-third. Become one of the best in the league, and then go and fuck it all up to the point that your own team doesn't want you anymore and lets my dad buy you. It's not that hard really. Your brother managed it. I'm sure you can too." She smiles.

Matty just blinks at her. He's at a loss for words for once in his life.

"You know my stats?" I ask her, shocked.

"Don't let that ego of yours get to you. I only know them because there was a mandatory meeting before your arrival, and your stats were mentioned. Although the main focus was on how everyone but my father didn't want you on the team."

"Yeah, the welcoming party's been warm," I tell

115

her sarcastically. I press the button on the wall and the doors to the elevator open.

"It was nice to meet you, Matty," Aliyah says as she steps inside.

"Yeah, you too," he replies as he looks from me to Aliyah, and then back to me again. "Drinks tonight. I'll arrange the entertainment," he adds.

"No," both Aliyah and I tell him at the same time the elevator doors close.

# Chapter Thirteen

The whole way down to the garage, I can't stop thinking about the fact that I made his bed. What was I thinking? I wasn't. I was on autopilot. It's one of those childhood coping mechanisms I haven't been able to shake.

Even as I heard my mother's voice in my head,

I couldn't stop myself. *Never leave without making your bed. It's sloppy. Why are you such a sloppy bitch, Aliyah?* I know I shouldn't let her words affect me after all these years, but some things are just ingrained. I can't leave without making the bed.

Trust me, I've tried, only to get five minutes down the road and have to turn around and go back. What if I crashed and someone had to go into my room and saw the bed unmade?

I unlock my car and climb into the driver's seat, waiting for Liam as he puts his bag in the back and then hops in next to me. I maneuver us out of his garage. "What happened this morning?" I ask him.

"What do you mean?"

"At morning skate. What happened?"

"We *skated*, discussed plays, nothing out of the ordinary," he says, looking out the windshield.

"Are the guys treating you okay? I can talk to Gray..."

"Do not do that. I'm fine, Aliyah. The last thing I need is for you to talk your brother into being nice to me. Honestly, it's just teething issues. Nothing I didn't expect and certainly nothing I can't handle."

"Okay, but I can tell him to be nicer. Just saying."

Liam groans and shakes his head. "You are really

118

taking this whole babysitting gig to the next level. I'm not an actual child, babe."

"I'm aware," I mumble to myself. This man is just that, all man. Trust me, I know. I've had his *man*hood pressed up against me. His long, thick, hard manhood. My thighs squeeze together at the thought of feeling that piece of meat in other places. Places like my vagina.

Shit... I can't let him get to me. I do not need complications like Liam King in my life. Also, I don't date hockey players. Although sleeping with him isn't really dating. I wonder if that can be my loophole?

Then there's the whole *my father painting the ice with Liam's blood* thing screaming in my head. I'd like to think it was all bark, but I know better. His bite is even worse. I've heard the stories.

"What are we actually doing today, anyway?" Liam asks.

"It was on your schedule. If you wanted to know, you should have read it," I tell him.

"What schedule?"

"The one I emailed you last night. You might have seen it if you didn't break your promise and go out with your brother."

"I called you. And between you and me, I didn't

actually want to go out."

"Yeah, it looked like you were having the worst time of your life with that bunny tucked up on your lap," I say.

Liam smiles at me. "She wasn't on my lap. Are you jealous? Because if you are, I can make space for you *on my lap*."

"Not even a little bit."

"You sound jealous," he says.

I wasn't jealous. I was pissed off that I had to get out of bed to drag his ass home. I *was not* jealous. I'm not a jealous person.

"I'm tempted to tell my dad how much you keep offering to fuck me. That'd be my ticket off babysitting duty for sure." I shrug.

"Why haven't you told him then?"

"Because he just spent millions of dollars on you. He thinks you're the answer to us winning the Cup this year. And if I tell him you want to get in my panties, then he's going to kill you *and* our dream of bringing home that Cup."

"So you do care? You don't want me to get hurt. Aw, I'm touched." His hand falls to his chest.

"I don't care if you're hurt. I care if the Knights win the Cup. They're my inheritance, after all, and nobody wants to inherit a losing team, Liam," I say.

It's not true. I actually love hockey, whether or not it's part of the family business. I love the game and I love the high of winning. That feeling you get when everyone skates onto the ice. The crowd, the fans— it's all intoxicating, really.

"The Knights will win the Cup," he tells me.

"How can you be so sure?"

"Because it was already a great team without me. But with me, it's the greatest in the league."

"Riiight," I draw out while giving him the side-eye.

"So this is where you live?" Liam asks, bending his head to look up at the building I'm driving up to.

"Yep."

"Alone?"

"Nope, I have a roommate, of the male variety," I say, leaving out the fact that he's also a cat.

"You have a boyfriend? You never mentioned it..."

"You never asked," I remind him.

"Who is he?"

"Why?"

"I like to size up my competition. If I'm going to win you over, then I need to know what I'm up against." Liam smirks.

"You won't win against Casper. He's perfect,

loves cuddling up to me, listens to me talk all the time, and never complains. Oh, and he's always there when I need him."

"Sounds like a douche," Liam pouts.

I gasp. "Take that back. Casper is not a douche."

"Nope, he's most definitely a douche. I have a sixth sense about these things."

I park the car and switch the engine off. "Come on, I won't be long. I'm just going to shower and change."

Liam follows me into the elevator, his hand resting on the lower part of my back. I step aside to get out of his reach. Not that it works. The guy is so huge it's hard to create distance in such a small space. And when he takes a step closer to me, again resting his hand on my lower back, I look up and glare at him. "Stop it," I warn.

"Stop what?" he asks me.

"You know what. Stop touching me," I say right as the door opens.

"You like it when I touch you." He grins.

I'm still glaring up at him, trying to deny his claim, even though my body very much agrees with it, when I hear the familiar click of a safety being taken off a gun. My head turns to see my brother Vinny pointing a pistol directly at Liam's head.

I jump in front of him. "Vinny, put that away, damn it. What the hell are you doing here?" As I'm asking this, Liam effortlessly picks me up and shoves me behind him, while wrapping an arm around his back to hold me in place.

"You have two seconds to let my sister go before I shoot you," Vinny says in that eerily calm voice that he's mastered. He almost sounds bored. But I know better. He is out of his damn mind right now. Raging on the inside.

"Yeah, I'm not letting her go until you put that down," Liam says.

*What the hell is he thinking?* My brother isn't going to hurt me. I lower my mouth onto Liam's back and bite down.

"Ow, did you just bite me?" he asks, turning his head to look at me, while keeping his eye on Vinny and that damn gun.

"Yes, let me go. He's not going to shoot me, idiot. But you, he most certainly will."

"Aliyah, I'm not letting you stand in front of a loaded gun. Are you insane?" he asks me.

"Lia, who the fuck is this fuckwit?" Vinny says at the same time.

I push at Liam and manage to get out of his hold. Stepping to the side, I take the gun from my brother, who I know only lets me because he has several others strapped to his body. "This fuckwit is Liam King, the Knights' latest asset. You can't shoot him. Dad paid millions to get him here, Vinny."

"I don't think Dad will care when I mention how I found this guy with his hands all over you." Vinny hasn't stopped staring at Liam. "And what the hell are you wearing? Where've you been all night?"

"I stayed at a friend's. And I borrowed a sweater. Shesh, are you the fashion police now too?"

"You look like you just rolled out of bed. A man's bed," Vinny grunts.

"I wish I did. Unfortunately, I didn't. So don't fret. You can go on about your day, pretending I'm an innocent little virgin who'll never get laid," I say, walking past him and into my apartment.

"I'm not pretending, Lia. You are a virgin," Vinny says from behind me.

I roll my eyes. Not that he can see me. "Whatever, Vinny. I don't have time for this today. I have shit to do. And that shit doesn't include dealing with your overbearing ways."

"Why are you here? And why the fuck do you think you can touch my sister?" I hear Vinny ask Liam.

"He's here because Dad wants me to fix him.

And he wasn't touching me."

"I heard what you said, Lia. You told him to stop touching you."

"I was being dramatic. Do you really think I'd bring anyone up to my apartment who was touching me in a way I didn't want?" I ask Vinny.

"I'm going to assign some guys to your door, Lia. No man should be stepping foot in this apartment."

"Oh my god, kill me now." I pull my phone out of my pocket and call my dad.

"Aliyah, everything okay?" he answers.

"It would be better if your son wasn't in my apartment threatening to kill your favorite player, Daddy."

"Why is Liam King in your apartment, Aliyah?" my dad asks. Not denying that the man in question is *in fact* his favorite player. Anyone else would assume it's Grayson, but my dad doesn't work like that.

"He's here because I picked him up on my way, and I needed to stop by home before I took him to the rink, where he's going to be teaching the local youth league how not to be a disappointment."

"Okay, put Vinny on the phone."

I smirk as I hold my cell out to my brother. "Dad wants to talk to you."

Vinny scowls at me, snatching the phone out of

my hand. "Dad?... Uh-huh... Sure..."

I don't know what Dad says to him, but my brother disconnects the call and then hands my phone back before he goes into my kitchen and starts pulling out food. "What are you doing?" I ask him.

"Dad told me I can't leave until *he's* out of your apartment, and I'm hungry." Vinny shrugs.

"Oh my god, I'm changing my locks. You people are unbelievable. You know what? I'm gonna go to Vegas, get married, and get myself knocked up just to spite you all." Liam's eyes go wide before his lips start to twitch. "Don't say it," I warn him.

"Lia, if you did that, I'd slaughter the fucker and then help you raise the kid." Vinny cuts into a tomato. He's making himself a sandwich... and a mess of my kitchen.

"Be sure to clean up after yourself. I'm jumping in the shower. Do not kill him." I point at Liam while addressing Vinny.

"Yeah, you were right. Dad wants him alive," Vinny says, then adds, "For now."

I walk down the hall to my bedroom and slam the door shut. Casper looks up from his spot on my bed before he lowers his head again and ignores me.

"Great chat, Casper." I give him a little pat as I make my way into the bathroom.

# Chapter Fourteen

I can't say teaching youth hockey has ever been on the list of things I wanted to do. I wouldn't have signed up for this shit if it weren't for Aliyah forcing my hand. Although I do have to say I'd much rather be stuck in a rink with a bunch of six-year-olds who can barely stay upright on their skates than be back in her apartment with her psychotic brother.

When Aliyah went to have a shower, he made sure to explain, step by step, how he'd kill me and enjoy it if I ever so much as thought of touching his sister. It was graphic, and very *Godfather*-like. It probably should have been enough to stop me from thinking about her. It wasn't. Because even as he was explaining how he'd slowly slice into me, piece by piece while demonstrating his handiwork with a tomato and a paring knife, my mind was filled with thoughts of his sister in the shower, naked, wet, soapy. And how much fun we'd have if I were in there with her.

Shit, maybe Aliyah was right. I *am* on the path to self-destruction. Even knowing what will happen to me for touching her, I want to do it. I want to touch every fucking inch of her.

I look over to where she's seated at the side of the rink. She's dressed in a pair of jeans and a white sweater. Light-pink gloves cover her hands and a matching scarf is wrapped around her neck. She's completely covered from head to toe and still utterly alluring.

The youth league coach blows his whistle. "Huddle around," he calls out, and the kids slowly make their way over to where we're standing. Thankfully, my role here is purely to serve as inspiration. *Practice your skills and you could be me.* Not sure why anyone would want their kids to turn out like me, though. I'm fucked up. "What do you say to Mr. King for spending the day with us?" the coach asks.

"Thank you, Mr. King," they all call out in chorus.

"You're welcome." I nod, unsure of what else to say. I showed them some plays, and they watched in awe as I skated up and down the ice before hitting the puck into the net.

"Okay, off you go. And remember: practice, practice, practice," the coach reminds them.

The kids all skate off towards the exit, all except one little girl who stays behind. She comes up to me and cranes her neck. "Mr. King, do you think girls can make it to the NHL too?" she asks me.

I blink down at the kid before crouching to meet her at eye level, so she doesn't have to crane her neck so much. "I think girls can do anything they want to do, sweetheart. And between you and me, you're the best player on this team." I wink at her, and a big, huge, gap-toothed smile covers her face.

"I know. I've tried to tell them that, but all the boys say I'm a girl and I shouldn't play hockey."

"Well, boys are dumb," I assure her. It's not a lie. We're all really fucking dumb most of the time, especially when it comes to girls.

"They are... and gross too." She laughs. "Thank you, Mr. King," she calls out before skating off towards a woman who is waiting for her on the sidelines. It must be the kid's mom—she also happens to be the only woman who hasn't been giving me that *come hither* look all session.

I follow the kid off the ice, reaching down to grab the puck we've been using. "Aliyah, you got a marker?" I ask her. Aliyah reaches into her bag and pulls out a gold Sharpie. I swear this woman is always prepared for everything. I take the marker, sign the puck, and walk up to where that little girl is standing with her mother. "What's your name?"

"Graycee." The kid smiles.

"Well, Graycee, this is for you." I hand her the puck and look up to her mom. "She's really good on those skates," I tell the woman.

"I know. We spend most of our free time here. She doesn't want to do anything else but skate and play hockey," her mom says.

"It was nice meeting you, Graycee. And don't forget: boys suck and girls can do anything they want," I say, then nod at her mom before walking back to where Aliyah is sitting with a confused look on her face. "What's wrong?" I ask her.

"Nothing. I just think I know that woman, but I can't for the life of me remember why or from where." Aliyah shrugs. "That was really nice... what you did."

"Kid said the boys told her she shouldn't be playing hockey. It pissed me off. If I had a daughter, I wouldn't want some fucker telling her she couldn't do something just because she's a girl," I say.

"My whole life I've been told I don't need to know things. My brothers and my dad treat me like I'm this fragile little thing. A prized possession they have to protect at all costs."

"Well, that's not a bad thing either, you know. That you have a family who loves you enough to protect you. And considering who that family is, they're probably right. You shouldn't get yourself involved in their shit. You're better than that," I tell her.

"You don't know that."

"I do. And if you ever want anyone to treat you like you won't break, I'll do it." I lean into her. "I'd fuck you so hard and rough you'd be feeling me between your legs for weeks afterwards," I whisper.

Aliyah's eyes widen; her mouth hangs open. "I

can't believe you just said that to me. Did that gun pointed at your head this morning not teach you anything?"

"It taught me that your brother is a psychopath." I shrug. "Somehow, I think fucking you would be worth facing off with him again."

"Okay, you really need to stop. The only reason you think you want me is because I'm probably the first girl to say no to you. Get over it. I'm not sleeping with you, Liam." Aliyah picks up her bag. "Come on, I'm dropping you off at your place and I really hope you actually stay home tonight," she says.

I follow her out to her car, my eyes glued to the sway of her ass. An ass I want to fill my hands with, preferably with her legs wrapped around my waist as I fuck her up against a wall. Though part of me has to wonder if she's right. Do I only want to fuck her because she's not jumping in my bed? I don't think so. But I can't say the chase isn't thrilling. I haven't even looked at another chick these past couple of days. Even the ones my brother brought around. Nope, my cock didn't so much as stir at the sight of them. One look at Aliyah, though, and I'm rock-hard. I don't think it's because she's denying this attraction between us. I think it's because she has to be hands-down the hottest chick I've ever met.

"I didn't say anything about sleeping. There wouldn't be any sleeping, Aliyah. I don't know who you've been having sex with, but apparently you've been doing it all wrong," I tell her, shutting the door to her car.

She rolls her eyes at me, something I find she does a lot when we're together. "Liam King, I'm not fucking you. Get over it."

"I didn't notice any guy stuff in your apartment. This Casper dude doesn't exist, does he?" I ask her.

"He exists. Though I didn't say anything about Casper being a dude. I just said he was my roommate. My white, furry, male roommate, who happens to meow a lot."

"Casper's a cat? I'm competing with *a cat* to get into your bed?" I laugh.

"There's no competition. You're not getting into my bed."

"Fine, we'll use mine," I suggest.

Aliyah shakes her head and starts the car. She doesn't continue the conversation. I think I'm wearing her down though. I hope I am. Or maybe I just need to go out and get laid, erase her from my mind. When she stops in front of my building, she gives me a stern look. "Please don't make me hunt you down again. I have plans tonight. Plans I don't want interrupted."

"What are you doing?" I ask. Does she have a date? Because if that's the case, I'm definitely interrupting those plans.

"Girls' night." She smiles.

"With your friends? You know I can hang at girls' night."

"You're not a girl," she says.

"That's sexist and not very inclusive of you, Miss Monroe."

"Sue me. Get out of my car first, though." She grins.

"Have fun, but not too much. I'll be right here if you change your mind and decide to have the real kind of fun. With me. In my bed," I tell her before jumping out of the car. She drives off so fast that it's not until I get up to my apartment that I realize I left my bag on her back seat. I send her a message.

ME:

> My skates are in the back of your car. You can drop them off later, when you finally decide to take me up on my offer.

I can see the *read* message, but she doesn't respond. I tuck my phone into my pocket and head up to my apartment. "What are you smiling about?" Matty asks as soon as I step through the door.

"Nothing. Why are you still here?" I ask him.

"I've been waiting for you. We need to talk. About mom," he says.

"No, we don't." I walk to the fridge and pull out a beer.

"Yes, we do. Why aren't you talking to her? What'd she do?" he presses. "She won't stop blowing up my phone asking about you."

"It's nothing, Matty. Drop it."

"It's something, or you'd answer her calls," he counters.

"She knows damn well what she did, and the fact she's involving you is shitty. Ignore her. It's not that hard," I tell him.

"Does it have anything to do with the reason you beat the shit out of your coach?" he says, and my back stiffens. "It does. I fucking knew it," he spits out.

"You know nothing."

"She fucked him, didn't she?" he says. "It's not hard to work out. She's our mother. She can't stop herself from being a damn train wreck." He shakes his head. "Shit, does Glen know?"

Glen, my mother's nice, caring, blue-collared

husband. "I have no idea. It's not my job to tell him his wife is a cheating..." I leave off the rest. As pissed as I am, I can't call her the word that was in my head. She *is* still my mom.

"I can't believe she'd do this to you," Matty says. "I'm sorry, Liam. I didn't know."

"I didn't want you to know. This is between me and her. It has nothing to do with you."

"Bullshit. We're a team. It's always you and me. I will always have your back, bro."

As messed up as my little brother can be, there is no one else on this earth I trust more than him. He's the one person I know without a doubt would never betray me. "When are you heading back to school? You're cramping my style," I say, changing the subject.

"Why? So you can hit up your babysitter? You know that's a stupid idea, right? She's the daughter of your boss, Liam. Red flag! Huge fucking red flag." He waves his hands around to emphasize his point.

"Red happens to be my new favorite color." I smirk, bringing the beer bottle to my lips.

My phone vibrates in my pocket and I pull it out, hoping it's a message from Aliyah. It's not. It's from a different Monroe.

GRAY:

LK, drinks @MelvinsBar tonight.
Seven p.m.

ME:

Your sister told me I can't go out.

GRAY:

It's a team thing. And don't worry...
her bark is far worse than her bite.

ME:

I find that hard to believe. But, fine,
I'll be there.

I mean, how can I say no? I'm supposed to be making friends with my new teammates. I can't do that if I don't go and hang out with them. Grayson doesn't message back.

"I gotta go out and meet the team tonight. You wanna come?" I ask Matty.

"Nah, I'm gonna head back to school. If you need me, call me. And I'll keep Mom at bay, tell her to leave you alone for a bit."

"Thanks." I nod my head. "I'm real glad you visited." I didn't realize how much I missed him.

# Chapter Fifteen

"This is too sweet," I say, holding up my glass of sugary white wine.

"I like it." Nicole shrugs.

"You like any wine," Charlie reminds her.

"This is true." Nicole nods her head.

"Okay, so have you banged him yet?" Charlie

asks, quickly changing the subject to what the rest of them are thinking. I knew the question was coming. We've been sitting in this bar for a whole ten minutes. I'm surprised she's held out this long, honestly.

"No, and I don't plan to," I assure them.

"You stayed at his house. How did you not screw that man's brains out?"

"He'd have to have brains first." I smirk. I don't think Liam is stupid. In fact, I know he's not. But I cannot give my friends even the slightest inclination that I *might* have a small crush on the guy. They are relentless in their pursuit of getting me laid.

So what if I might be having a dry spell? It's only been six months. Which is not that long in the grand scheme of things. Besides, my vibrator does a much better job at giving me orgasms than any guy ever has.

"It's a crime to all womankind, Aliyah. You have an all-access pass to Liam fucking King and you're not going to use it?" Amanda says.

"He's not an object, you know. He's an actual person. And, no, I'm not sleeping with him." No matter how much he keeps giving me the option.

"I'm sure he wouldn't object to being used by you. No man in their right mind would. Shit, I've even considered switching teams for you." Charlie laughs. She's not lying. During our first year at college, she suggested we just date each other. I quickly shut down that idea by reminding her how much she liked penises and that I didn't and still don't have one of those.

"Next topic, please." I gulp down the wine that is way too sugary to be classed as anything but a confectionary. How do people drink this stuff? And whose idea was it to meet at a wine bar anyway?

"Nope, you still haven't given us all the hot goss. How big is it?" Amanda asks.

"I wouldn't know," I lie.

"You're lying. You're a terrible liar, by the way. You have so many tells." Nicole points at my face.

"I do not have tells. And I'm not lying."

"You do and you are," Phoebe says.

"Argh, I hate you all right now." I throw my hands up in the air.

"You love us. So, just tell us how big, and we'll leave it at that. Won't mention he who shall not be named for the rest of the night," Charlie says.

"Fine, it's big, huge, like I've never seen anything like it before." I hold up my hands, separating them in an effort to show my friends an estimated size.

Four sets of eyes bug out in response. "You need

a shrink, because there is something not right in that brain of yours if you haven't jumped on that yet," Nicole says while gesturing to my hands.

I roll my eyes at her and shake my head as I drop my palms to the table.

"You don't need a shrink," Charlie says. She's the only one of our friends who knows my real history. She also knows just how many hours I've spent in a shrink's office talking about the things my mom did to me over the years. "But you do need to jump on that D. ASAP."

"Sure, I'll get right on that," I say, knowing full well that I have no intention of *jumping on Liam's D*. Not now or ever. That doesn't mean I can't think about it, though, right? I mean, I'm already anticipating going home and getting out my buzzing toy, closing my eyes, and thinking about just how good Liam would feel on top of me. In me.

I look at the empty cup sitting on the table. What the hell kind of potion was in that thing? I will not be thinking about Liam King while I masturbate. Well, I probably won't.

Argh, maybe I need to find someone else to date. I don't know when exactly I'll find the time, but surely someone in this city can stand me long enough to get to my third-date rule. The only reason I've been having a dry spell is because I've met two guys who've made it to date number two in the last six months. All the others dropped out of the running before date number one was halfway through.

I might be a tad picky—okay, I'm a lot picky. But I don't want to date a dud. I want someone who will treat me right. I just want to feel that all-encompassing passion that drives you wild and has you throwing caution to the wind. The kind of ride-or-die love between Harley Quinn and the Joker, just with a little less crazy.

I don't think that kind of love is actually in the cards for me though. I'm just not all that lovable. I know my father loves me, my brothers too. But that's different. There's something wrong with a child whose own mother couldn't love her, right? There has to be. Why else would she have done the things she did to me? She never treated my brothers with such animosity.

"Let's get out of here." Charlie squeezes my hand and gives me the look. She knows where my thoughts have gone, that dark place that I try really hard to never go back to.

"Sounds like a good plan." I smile, silently thanking her for the distraction.

This is why I love her. She might be pushy when

it comes to certain things, like getting me to bang Liam King. But she's patient, she's kind, *and* she's understanding about the important stuff. Always has been. I remember when I was in the hospital after the last time I saw my mother. Charlie demanded that her father bring her to see me, and when she finally got to my room, she climbed onto my bed and curled up next to me. She didn't say anything, just clung to me as we both cried silent tears. Our fathers watched us from a distance. I don't think either of them knew what to do.

"Let's hit up Jay's," Nicole, who is already staggering on two feet, says as we exit the wine bar.

"Jay's? I don't know, guys. It's late," I say. I really don't feel up to doing a nightclub.

"Come on, Lia, we haven't been out dancing in ages. I need you to come, because these three will just go and find themselves men for the night and leave me behind," Phoebe says.

"You could find yourself a man too," Charlie tells her.

"I don't need a man. Or want one." Phoebe doesn't date a lot. She's more like me and prefers to stay in rather than go out and socialize.

"Fine, but I'm not staying late," I tell her.

"Deal." She grins.

"Woohoo! Let's pretend we're twenty-one again, get white-girl wasted, and make really bad decisions," Charlie hollers while throwing an arm in the air.

"Remind me again why we're friends with her?" I ask Amanda.

"Because we couldn't get rid of her if we tried, so we might as well accept it." She laughs.

We all pile into the back of the car provided by Charlie's family. It's the only way her brothers let her leave the house. If she doesn't take one of their drivers, AKA soldiers, along with her, then they'll lock her in. I've seen them do it too. Don't get me wrong, I think my brothers would try that themselves... if they didn't think it'd break me down mentally.

Being locked in any room freaks me out. Gotta love childhood trauma, right?

It doesn't take long before we're walking into Jay's. Charlie's driver leading the way, his bulky shoulders creating a clear path for us to follow behind him. We all grab a drink from the bar and then head straight to the dance floor. I throw back the vodka soda I ordered way faster than I usually would. But I need to let loose. If I'm stuck in here with a crowd of people I don't know, I need to relax, and alcohol will help with that. The buzz starts to run through my body and I feel good, really good. I'm dancing with Phoebe when I look behind me to see all three of our other friends grinding on some poor, helpless man.

"How do they just do that?" I ask Phoebe. I can't imagine letting go and grinding on someone I don't know. It seems so easy for them. Although I could imagine grinding on a certain hockey player I shouldn't be thinking about at all. "Never mind. I need another drink," I yell into Phoebe's ear before walking in the direction of the bar.

I lean over the sticky counter and raise my voice to order my drink from the bartender. Just as I turn around to head back to Phoebe, a guy approaches me. His eyes rake up and down my body. He's good looking, and I can tell by the pull of his lips that he knows it. Clean shaven, a sculpted jaw, cheekbones people pay a great deal of money to have. And piercing green eyes.

"I need your help," he says.

"With what?" I ask, my gaze flicking around the room.

"I need you to dance with me. Otherwise, I might be forced to live out the rest of my life with nothing but regret and a bunch of *what ifs*." He smiles.

"I doubt that," I say, though I can't help but smile back at him.

"Please, one dance. Just one. If I have to walk back over there to my buddies, alone, they're going to know you blew me off, and they'll never let me live it down," he says.

"Well, I'd sure hate that for you." I laugh. "One dance, but you should know I have no intention of going home with you or hooking up in a dark corner of this club."

"Noted." He nods, then holds out a palm. "One dance."

Taking his proffered hand, I let him lead me onto the dance floor as I quickly down what's left of my liquid courage and discard the cup. "What's your name?" I lean into his ear to ask the question.

"Oliver. What's yours?"

"Aliyah."

"Well, Aliyah, I do believe this dance is mine," he says, wrapping an arm around my waist and pulling me tight up against his chest. He has a nice enough body. I can feel the hardness of his muscles beneath his shirt. Though it's nothing compared to when I was pressed up against Liam.

*Damn it, Aliyah. We are not thinking about him.*

I turn around and start dancing in a way I wouldn't usually. I need to take my mind off a certain hockey player. I can't touch him. But I can touch Oliver, and more than that, I can let him touch me.

Oliver's hands grip my hips as I move my ass against his groin. "Shit, Aliyah, I think I might die out on this dance floor. Are you sure I can't change your mind on the whole coming home with me thing?" he asks, bending down to brush his lips against my ear.

"I'm sure. Sorry, I'm not that kind of girl," I say. "But I will dance with you."

"I'll take it." He grins.

I feel Oliver step back from me. I spin around to see what he's doing, only to find Liam fucking King fisting my dance partner's shirt while growling something in the guy's face. Oliver looks at me, then back to Liam. As soon as Liam lets him go, Oliver practically runs in the other direction.

# Chapter Sixteen

*H*ow did I let myself end up in this situation? And what the fuck just came over me?

The evening started out simple enough. Me, just hanging out with my new teammates. I was standing up on the VIP level of Jay's, a nightclub I let the boys drag me to after a stint at the bar, despite my better judgment. McIntosh, one of the team's wingers, was standing next to me when he pointed down at the dance floor and cursed.

"There's going to be a bloodbath in here when Gray sees that," he said.

I looked to where he was pointing to see Aliyah grinding her hot little ass on some random dude. And then the only thing I *saw* after that was fucking red.

I have no idea what came over me. I'm not a jealous person. Why would I be? But seeing another guy with their hands on her had me fuming.

I stormed down to the dance floor and pried him off her; then I told him if I ever caught him with his hands on her again, I'd tear them from his body. The little prick ran away practically pissing himself. And that, ladies and gentlemen, leads me to right now, where I'm presently standing in the middle of the dance floor in front of a less-than-pleased babysitter.

"What the fuck, Liam?" she screams.

I nod my head to the balcony where the whole fucking team seems to have gathered to watch my demise. How the hell am I going to explain what I've just done?

"It was either me or your brother. I figured that guy had a better chance of surviving with me," I lie.

149

I didn't even give Gray a second thought when I was pushing my way through the crowd to get to Aliyah.

She glances up at the balcony and shakes her head. "He can go to hell, along with you. I'm a grown-ass woman, which means I can dance with whomever the fuck I want whenever the fuck I want," she says.

A group of girls comes and stands next to her. Her friends. I remember their faces from the video call I interrupted.

"Sure, go on and tell your brother that." I cross my arms over my chest.

"Oh, I plan to. Don't worry," she growls.

I hold out an arm, gesturing for her to go first. "After you, princess."

Aliyah barges past me. My hand lands on the small of her back as I follow her. I don't know why I keep touching her like this. It's almost like it's instinctual.

"I should have let Vinny shoot you." Aliyah turns her head just enough to yell at me over her shoulder.

I step up closer to her and lower my mouth to her ear. "Probably, but then you'd never know."

"Know what?" Her brows furrow. Then she stumbles on the step and bumps into me.

"How good my cock feels filling your sweet little cunt." I smirk.

"Argh, get off me." She shoves at my chest and stumbles again. I grab her by the elbows to keep her from falling.

"How much have you had to drink?" I ask her.

"How ever much I wanted to," she throws back.

*Oh, she's even nastier when she's drunk.* Which doesn't make her any less hot, mind you. In fact, I think I'm into it. I could definitely think of a way to correct that mouth of hers. Fuck, now my cock is harder than ever.

I follow Aliyah as she makes her way over to her brother. I do remove my hand from her back but remain within arm's reach in case I need to catch her again.

"Gray, seriously, what the hell? Now you're sending your goons to cock-block me?" she hisses.

"I didn't send him, Aliyah. He did that all on his own." Gray grins while holding out a fist to me.

I lift my hand and bump knuckles, ignoring the icy glare I get from Aliyah. "Anytime, bro," I say.

"You can't stop me from having sex, Gray."

"Wanna bet?" He lifts a challenging brow in her direction.

"Yeah, actually, I do. Please, for the love of God,

don't tell me you still think I'm a virgin?" Aliyah huffs out.

"You are," Gray says, so sure of himself.

I can't help but laugh and thank fuck I have a brother and not a sister. Because as much as I feel for Gray right now, he's wrong. There's no way that girl is a virgin. She's too fucking hot to not have been snatched up already. Although the thought of her being with other men doesn't bode well with me either. Fuck, can't she just be a virgin? I'd gladly help her lose that V-card.

"No. I'm not," Aliyah says.

Gray covers his ears. "I'm not listening to this. Nope, I can't hear you," he says, shaking his head.

Aliyah's friends, who all appeared to have followed us up here, are laughing. So is the rest of the team. I'm the only one who doesn't find this conversation amusing. Aliyah and sex shouldn't be in my head.

Who am I kidding? It's the only thing I've been thinking about since I first saw her standing in my apartment that day.

Virgin or not, it doesn't make any difference to me. Once I've fucked her, she won't remember anyone who came before me anyway.

"I'm going. You're being ridiculous," Aliyah says,

spinning around on her heel—I'm assuming to leave. She stumbles again and I reach out an arm to stop her from falling, also again.

"We really need to stop meeting like this, princess," I tell her.

"I'm going to fill your apartment with spiders," she fires back.

"You're a mean drunk, you know that?" I tell her.

"She is," one of her friends agrees with me. "Come on, Lia, let's go. There are plenty of other clubs in this town filled to the brim with plenty of other available men, all just waiting to take us home."

"She's not going to another club," I answer for her.

"Oh, yeah? And who's going to stop her? You?" the friend challenges me.

"Yep," I say, then turn to Gray. "I'm taking her home. She's too drunk to make responsible decisions right now."

Grayson has been drinking just as much as his sister has. The whole team has been. I'm the only one who's been sipping on water all night. "Thanks, man, 'preciate it," he says, and then steps up to Aliyah and whispers something in her ear.

A mischievous smirk curls her lips as she looks at me. "I don't know, Gray. He's really hot, and his cock *is* impressive. If what they say in the tabloids is true, I bet he really knows how to use it too."

"Lia, if you make me kill him, I'll make sure Dad takes the contract fee out of your trust," Gray is quick to reply.

"Nine mil? I think I can afford it." She laughs.

"No, you can't," I tell her. "Come on, let's go." I take hold of her arm, then look back at the guys. "I'll catch up with you in the morning." As I escort Aliyah outside of the club, her friends tag along behind us. Please tell me they have their own way home? I am not dealing with five drunk females right now. One is more than enough.

"Liam, you're bossy, you know that? And full of yourself," Aliyah says, as we push through the front doors.

"Thanks, princess. And here I was, thinking the falling part had started already." I laugh before spinning towards her friends. "Have you got a way home?"

"Yep. Take real good care of her. She could use it," one of the girls says, winking at me.

My brows furrow. I'm not sure about these friends of hers, who seem more than willing to let a strange man take Aliyah home while she's so wasted. They say their goodbyes, whispering something into her ear, before they all climb into the back of a big black SUV.

Great. I guess Aliyah doesn't have her car here. I fish my phone out of my pocket and order us an Uber. It's only two minutes away, thank god. As soon as our driver pulls up to the curb, I help Aliyah into the back and squeeze in beside her. I don't know her address off the top of my head, so I have to plug in mine. She can use the spare bed again.

"Why are we going to your place?" she asks, glancing out the window.

"Because you need to sleep it off," I tell her.

"No, I was having fun, Liam. Do you even know what that is? *Fun?*"

"I do." I nod.

"Well, then why can't anyone just let me have fun? I hate my brothers. They always cock-block me." She pouts.

"Apparently not always," I mumble under my breath. According to her declaration in the club, she's not as innocent and virginal as her family would like to believe. The car pulls up in front of my building, and I practically have to lift Aliyah up to help her get out. "Are you going to be able to walk?" I ask her.

"Yes," she says and stalks off towards the main

entrance. She's still swaying a little but it's not nearly as bad as before.

When we get up to my apartment, I grab a bottle of water and hand it to her. "Drink this. You can use the guest room."

"Why am I here, Liam?" she asks me.

"Because I don't remember your address, and I wasn't going to leave you drunk in a nightclub."

"Why?"

"Friends don't leave friends to make poor decisions," I say.

"We are not friends," she declares to an audience of two.

"Well, ouch, babe. If we're not friends, then what are we?"

"We are... I don't know what we are. But friends don't look at me the way you do," she tells me.

"And how do I look at you?"

"Like you want to devour me whole."

"That's because I do. I want to ravish every inch of that body of yours, princess," I admit while my cock twitches his agreement.

"You see, that's a problem, Liam. Because if I let you do that, we'll both be in trouble."

"Sometimes, trouble is *fun*," I repeat the word she's been so fond of using tonight.

"Not with my family, it isn't. People who get into trouble with my family don't fare too well."

"I'll survive, or I won't. Either way, you'd be worth it."

"No, I'm not." She shakes her head, all the amusement suddenly drained from her voice. "Thanks for the water, and the room," she says, but she doesn't lift her eyes to look at me.

I watch as she walks past me and down the hall. I pause for a few seconds, only to find myself following her into the guest room, where she's already climbing into bed.

"Why would you say that?" I ask before I can stop myself.

"Say what?"

"Say that you're not worth it?"

"Because I'm not loveable, Liam King, and putting your job and life on the line for someone who's not loveable isn't worth it," she says so simply that I know she really believes that.

I walk over to where she's curled up on the bed. How the fuck can she possibly think she's not loveable? I grab her chin, forcing her face to tilt upwards towards mine. I don't think. I just act as I slam my lips down onto hers. I push my tongue past the seam of her mouth, savoring her taste as I try to show her in this kiss just how worth it she is. Then I pull away again, still a little shocked that she kissed me back, to be honest. But I can't let this go any further, not while she's still intoxicated.

"You are *very* loveable, Aliyah Monroe," I say before standing to my full height and walking out of the room.

I don't know why I wanted to tell her that, why I needed her to realize just how worth it she is. Another thing I can't seem to understand is the sudden desire I have to find the asshole who put that thought into her head in the first place. I want to find him, them, whomever and show 'em exactly what it's like to feel less-than. Before I put them in the ground.

*Not loveable?* I shake my head as I step into the shower.

One of two things is going to happen in the morning. Either Aliyah's going to wake up and hope-fully not remember what happened between us, or remember it and want me to do it again.

It goes without saying that I'm hoping for option number two.

# Chapter Seventeen

"**N**o, please, Mommy. I didn't mean to. I'll do better. I will." I beg her not to hurt me as she drags me into the bathroom. I don't like it when she takes me in here.

She holds me under the water, and I can't breathe. "You little bitch! You did it on purpose. You just want *to make me mad. You want him all to yourself, don't you? Well, you can't have him. He's mine. He was mine first." She's screaming now, calling me horrible names at the top of her lungs.*

*I don't know who she's talking about. I don't know why she thinks I'm doing this. And I don't know how to stop her. "No, Mommy, please. I'll be good," I try again.*

*"You don't know how to be good. If I don't get rid of you, I'll always have to share him. You're a disgrace. Really pitiful. No wonder I don't love you, Aliyah. I can't. No one can. You're unlovable. You're not cute, though it's clear you think you are. You've bewitched him—that's it. You're a demon," she says, tapping a finger against her chin as she turns around and closes the door.*

*Now I'm alone in the bathroom with her. She says she has to wash the demons out of me. I don't know what a* demon *is, but it doesn't sound good, and I don't want her to hurt me again. "Please, Mommy, stop. Get Daddy. He can help us," I plead with her.*

*"No!" she hisses. "He's mine, not yours." Then she takes something shiny out of the cabinet, grabs my arm, and holds it out to one side. I don't know what she's planning to do, but then she presses the shiny thing against my wrist, into my skin, and drags it up*

*my arm. It hurts. It hurts so much and I feel dizzy. I scream as loud as I can.*

*There's a banging noise on the door and my mother lets go of me. I fall to the floor, clutch my arm to my chest, close my eyes, and scream louder.*

"Aliyah, wake up."

I hear my name being called but I can't open my eyes. I don't want her to see that it didn't work. I don't want her to try again...

"Aliyah, wake up," the voice repeats a little louder this time. "It was just a nightmare. You're okay, baby. Wake up."

I feel my body being moved, then a sudden warmth as strong arms wrap around me. I blink my eyes open as consciousness creeps in. I look around, trying to gain my bearings. I'm in Liam's guest bedroom. In his arms, as he rocks me back and forth.

"You're okay. I've got you," he whispers.

"I... I'm sorry," I tell him.

"It's okay." He pulls back and uses the pad of his thumb to wipe the tears from my cheek.

I'm mortified. I haven't had this nightmare in such a long time. What the hell? "I didn't mean to wake you," I whisper, though it sounds stupid when I say it out loud.

"It's okay. Can I get you anything?" he asks me.

I shake my head. "No, I'll be fine."

He's silent for a moment, before he pulls away again and stands. "I'm right next door... if you need anything."

I watch as he twists the knob, then quickly call out to him. He turns around. "Liam, can you... can you stay?"

"Of course," he says, dropping his arm and walking to the other side of the bed, where he proceeds to slide under the blanket with me. He reaches over and pulls me up next to him, my head now resting on his shoulder. "Go back to sleep. I'll be here," he tells me, gently kissing the top of my head.

I know I shouldn't, but I do it anyway. I let myself indulge in the safeness I feel when I'm wrapped in his arms.

*She can't hurt you. You're not a little girl anymore,* I remind myself. Then I close my eyes again and hope like hell my brain believes it.

There's a weight on me. A heavy, warm weight. When I open my eyes to have a look, I find a muscled, tattooed arm. An arm that belongs to one very off-limits, hot-as-sin hockey player. The very same hockey player I'm supposed to be keeping a professional distance from.

All the events from last night come crashing down on me. I was drunk but, unfortunately, not drunk enough to not remember everything. Dancing with some guy in the club. Liam pulling him off me, dragging me home, *kissing* me…

Me kissing Liam back.

The nightmare that followed, Liam comforting me, and then me asking him to stay. To say I'm embarrassed would be an understatement. I don't think there's a strong enough word for what I am right now.

*Shit, shit, shit.* This was not meant to happen.

As gently as I can, I slide out from under his arm and off the bed. I don't want to wake him. I pick up my phone from the nightstand and tug it free from the charging cable. He must have plugged it in for me last night. That's sweet. I bend down, grab my shoes, and tiptoe my way across the room. Just as my hand lands on the knob and I'm about to open the door, I jump ten feet in the air.

"You sneaking out on me, princess?" his voice calls out from the bed.

I turn around to find him sitting upright, his back propped against the headboard as he watches me. Shirtless, with the sheets rumpled around his waist. Damn does that man have a nice set of abs. I almost forgot how nice...

"I'm sorry, like really, really sorry for last night. I don't know what I was thinking. Please forgive me," I say, avoiding eye contact.

"What part? What part are you apologizing for, exactly?" he asks me.

"All of it?" I shrug.

Liam slides out of the bed, and even though I know I should start walking, get away while I can, I'm trapped. My legs won't work. He stops right in front of me, forcing me to tilt my head upwards to meet his gaze. "So you're sorry for grinding that hot little ass on some stranger's dick?"

"Nope, not that part." I smile.

Liam raises his eyebrows. "Are you sorry you got so drunk I had to bring you home?"

"A little." I nod.

"Are you sorry you kissed me?"

"You kissed me," I clarify.

"You kissed me *back*. Are you sorry about that?"

I blink. If I'm honest, truly honest, I'm not sorry, because that was one hell of a kiss. The once-in-a-lifetime kind of kiss. But I'm never going to admit that out loud. Especially not to him.

"Yes," I say instead.

Liam's lips tip up at the corner of his mouth, just one side. "You're lying. Are you sorry you asked me to stay?"

"Yes," I say again, because *that* I am sorry for. "I'm sorry you had to see me at my worst, and I'm sorry I woke you up."

"I'm not."

"What?" I ask, confused.

"I'm not sorry, for any of it," he says right before his lips slam down onto mine.

I'm telling myself just one more second and then I'll pull away. Just one. Maybe two. And then he has his tongue inside my mouth, devouring me, and I'm lost. Like I said, a once-in-a-lifetime kind of kiss.

*Or does this make it twice?*

It doesn't matter. All I know is that I could stand here and kiss him until my last breath. It's that good.

I don't want to stop, even though I know I should. I have to.

Liam's hand cups my cheek, holding my face exactly in the position he wants it, as he takes a step forward and I take a step back until my ass hits the wall. One more step and his body is pressed right up into mine. My hands roam over his naked chest, down his abs. *Damn it.* It's my only thought as my fingertips dig into his skin. I'm not supposed to like this as much as I do. I've never felt like this just because of a kiss before. I need more. More of him. I need him to touch me. Everywhere.

As that thought enters my head, Liam pulls away. "I don't believe you're sorry at all, princess." He smirks.

I push at his chest. I need space. I need to get out of here. "I'm going home, and you're getting your ass over to The Castle." I skirt around him and walk out to the foyer before repeatedly stabbing the button for the elevator.

"What's on the schedule for today?"

"Huh?" I spin around at Liam's question.

"The schedule you made me, what's on it?"

"You have your morning skate, then you're presenting a check to a local animal rescue center. Wear a suit," I tell him.

"A check?"

"Yeah, the team is making a donation, and you're repping the team."

"Why me?"

"Because you're the one who needs all the good PR opportunities."

"Okay." He nods, then asks, "Can I take you to dinner?"

I'm so stunned by his question that I don't even know what to say. *Can he take me to dinner?*

"I'm gonna assume your silence is a yes. *Wear a dress*," he says, mocking my tone. "I'll be taking you somewhere nice." Then he turns his back on me and disappears down the hallway.

*What in the ever-loving hell just happened?*

The doors to the elevator open and I step inside, leaning against the mirrored walls as the cab descends. My mind is whirling. I kissed Liam fucking King, not once but twice. And I freaking liked it.

# Chapter Eighteen

I'm trying to listen to the special teams coach. He's going on about some new power play he wants to try out. I should be paying attention, but that's really fucking hard to do when I can't stop thinking about her.

Especially when she's seated in the bench

section just off the ice, all bundled up again, like she's in Antarctica and not a hockey stadium. Cute as fuck.

*Whoa, where the fuck did that come from?*

I shake my head and try to clear my thoughts, but they all steer right back to her. Aliyah Monroe. I want to ask her about her nightmare. I've never in my life heard anyone scream like that, not even after breaking a bone on the ice. I thought someone had gotten into the house, was attacking her. But when I bolted into her room, she was tossing around on the bed, completely out of it. Screaming like she was experiencing the most intense pain. Alone.

I almost asked Gray about it this morning in the locker room but quickly decided that wasn't the best idea. I don't need him knowing I spent the night in bed with his sister. What I do need is to figure out what's happening between the two of us. This is new territory for me. I've only known her for a couple of days, and I can't get her out of my head. I want her around, which is fucking odd.

When I caught her trying to sneak out of the room this morning, I wanted to drag her ass back to my bed. That's never happened to me before. I've always been the one who wants the chick to leave, preferably sooner rather than later. There's just something different about this girl. I'm not sure what it is, but I'll figure it out.

"King, Monroe, and Jameson. You're up," the coach says, calling out our line.

We get into formation, me in the center, Gray on my left, and Luke Jameson on my right. The puck passes from Gray to Luke, and then to me as we make our way to the end zone. I pass it back to Luke and he sends it flying over the goalie's glove, hitting the back of the net.

"Again," the coach shouts from across the rink. "Faster, pass more aggressively."

We repeat the same play, over and over again until the moves become more muscle memory than anything else. A whistle blows, then the coach yells out for us to hit the showers.

"Nice footwork." Gray claps me on the top of my helmet, commenting on the way I skated around the opposition during the last play.

"Thanks." I nod at him, but my eyes are on his sister. Aliyah is staring down at her phone. As if she can feel my gaze, she looks up and locks those brown eyes of hers with mine. She then glances at her brother and returns her focus to the device in her hands.

"Thanks for taking her home last night," Gray says as we make our way off the ice.

"Don't mention it," I tell him.

"She likes to act like she's tough and independent, but she's not," he says.

"I don't know. She seems pretty fucking tough when she's chewing my ass out for whatever stupid shit I've done that day." I laugh.

"I don't doubt that." He chuckles, then looks back over at his sister and opens his mouth like he's going to say something else. He doesn't. Instead, he shakes his head and continues to walk down the corridor to the locker room.

I take my time stripping out of my gear and showering. I'm trying to figure out what to say to her, how to approach the subject of her nightmare. I need to know who the fuck hurt her so badly that it's left her traumatized and screaming in the middle of the night like that.

Then there's the little matter of her mouth. I want it again. I can't recall a time I've enjoyed kissing someone so fucking much.

I need to get my shit together. I dry off, cracking my neck from side to side to relieve some of the tension the hot water didn't seem to ease. The only one left in the locker room with me is Hunter Forbes, one of the team's defensemen.

"Hey, man, got any plans tonight? A bunch of us are heading over to Jasper's, a new club that's opened up around the corner," Hunter says.

"Not sure. I actually think I'm gonna crash early tonight," I say. How these fuckers continue to go out and then come and play the way they do, I have no idea. I know we've still got another week before the preseason games begin. But, fuck, these early morning skates aren't fucking easy.

"If you change your mind, hit us up," Hunter says.

I nod, knowing that's not gonna happen. What I'm really planning on doing is taking Aliyah out for dinner. I want to be able to talk to her, get to know her better. It might be the only way I'm ever going to figure out what this pull is I have towards her.

I'm exhausted, though, and ordering in is seeming like a much better idea. Between being out late, waking up to Aliyah, and then wondering who or what the fuck hurt her for the rest of the night, I didn't get much sleep.

I dress in a crisp clean suit, as per Aliyah's request, and shut my locker. I walk out to find her sitting crossed-legged on the floor again. She looks up at me. "Why are you always the last one out?" she asks.

"It takes time to look this good, princess," I say, spreading my arms to my sides to give her a better view of the merchandise.

"You don't look any different from when you rolled out of bed this morning, except you have more clothes on," she tells me.

"Would you prefer I didn't?" I raise my eyebrows at her.

"Nope. Clothes are good. You should wear them more often."

I hold out my hand to pull her up off the floor, and she looks at it like it's going to bite her head off. Instead of accepting my help, Aliyah unfolds her legs and stands. I drop my arm, trying not to let that little bit of rejection sting. It's a new feeling for me. Though something tells me I better get used to it if I am gonna be spending so much time around a certain ice queen. It seems Aliyah Monroe is the furthest thing from a "sure thing" bang. I never know where I stand with her. Although, when I was kissing her, owning that pouty little mouth of hers, she gave her whole self to me. Until she didn't. And she closed herself up tighter than she had been before.

"You were good out there this morning," Aliyah says.

And just like that, gone is that feeling of rejection. She watched me. She thought I was good. Not that I need her recognition. I *am* good on the ice. I know that, but hearing her say it makes me feel... something.

"Thanks. It's a good team," I say. Because it's true. The Knights have been so close to that big win. They just haven't been able to get to that final game. This is their year though. I'm certain of it.

It's only been a few days, but something has shifted with the team. They're accepting me. I'm sure it has a lot to do with Gray's change of opinion towards me, although that's not likely to last too long once he finds out what I've been doing with his sister. Or at least what I plan to do.

"Tell me about this animal rescue place," I say to fill the silence that fell over us as soon as we got into her car.

"They rehome cats. There's really not too much to tell."

"Cats? Just cats? What have they got against dogs?" I ask her.

"Nothing." She shrugs. "It's just a cat rescue place."

"Okay." I smile. "Cats. Got it. Guess it's a good thing I'm very fond of pussy."

Aliyah whips her head around so fast to glare at me I'm surprised it doesn't fall off her shoulders. "Gee, the dozens of tabloid pictures of you with all those puck bunnies on your dick would never have clued the world in on that one."

"My dick has never made it to the tabloids. Although it probably should have. It's fucking impressive."

"Your mother filled your head with too much self-importance. I've seen better."

"Lies. You have not."

Aliyah's lips twitch. She's trying not to smile. I really want to make her smile. "So... dinner tonight. I know I said I'd take you out but how do you feel about ordering in instead?"

"I never agreed to have dinner with you, Liam," she says, her tone dry.

"You didn't say *no* either."

"I'm not sleeping with you, and you can't kiss me again. It's not right."

"Kissing you might be the best thing I've ever done. You can't expect me to not want to do that again. Fuck, Aliyah, we'd be so good together," I tell her and mean it. Not sure why. But it's a gut feeling.

"Probably, but it doesn't make it right. We're adults. We can work together, refrain from getting involved personally."

"Sure, you keep telling yourself that, babe." I swear I'm going to get whiplash from the hot-and-cold vibes this woman is constantly putting out.

"I'm not trying to be difficult or play hard to get or whatever. I'm just trying to keep you alive and me from having to explain to my father why I failed the first job he's given me."

"Why is your father's approval so important to you?" I ask her.

"Because he's my father. Why wouldn't it be?"

"Because life should be about doing what you feel good doing. Don't look for approval from others. Look for it within yourself," I tell her.

"I owe it to my father to not fuck this up. He's done a lot for me."

"He's your father. He's supposed to do a lot for you." Even as I say this, I know that not all fathers, parents in general, fulfill their roles properly. Though I have a hard time believing Jacob Monroe doesn't dote on his only daughter. Fuck, I've seen firsthand how protective her brothers are of her.

"Maybe," Aliyah says and shuts the engine off.

# Chapter Nineteen

W omen always say that seeing a man holding a baby is a major turn-on, but they never mentioned anything about small, fuzzy animals. Cats in particular. Why wasn't I warned? I would have chosen a different charity.

My restraint is only so strong, more like paper thin at this point.

Watching Liam play and pet the homeless cats is giving me a whole new view of him. He seems genuinely interested when the manager of the rescue center talks to him about the costs and operations of keeping the place up and running.

Liam picks up a scrappy-looking ginger-and-white cat. "Hey, there, beautiful," he coos. "Mark, how does one go about adopting one of these little guys?"

"There's paperwork. We do a series of checks to make sure you're a suitable candidate. And then, once all the T's are crossed and I's are dotted, you get to take your new baby home."

"Okay, let's do that. I want her," Liam says.

"What?" I ask, shocked.

"I want her," Liam tells me with a shrug.

"You want a *cat*? This is a lifetime commitment, Liam. How are you going to look after a cat once the season is in full swing? You're on the road all the time," I remind him.

"How do you look after Casper when you're not home?" he fires back with a questioning brow.

"I'm usually home."

"You've spent the last two nights at my place," he whispers but I swear it feels like he's shouting.

I tug Liam aside, hoping Mark doesn't think I'm being rude. "I have friends who go over and check on him."

Liam looks to Mark. "She's right. I can't commit to full-time care. My schedule is hectic, but I want to give an additional twenty-thousand on top of whatever the team has agreed to donate. Keep it between us, please. They don't need to know," he says, gesturing a thumb over his shoulder to where the press is waiting on the other side of the glass wall.

Liam's custom-tailored suit is now covered in various shades of cat hair. And how do I know it's *custom-tailored*, you may ask? It fits him way too well not to be. He doesn't seem to care one bit though.

"Should we do this?" Liam asks, and it takes me a minute to realize what he's talking about.

"Ah, yeah." I follow him out of the indoor cat play area we've been holed up inside for thirty minutes, and we make our way to where the media outlets are set up and waiting for us. Liam and Mark stand on a makeshift stage as the former passes the latter a huge, oversized Vancouver Knights check for the sum of one hundred thousand dollars.

After a short speech, during which Liam surprises me again with his obvious passion for the animals' well-being, I'm left feeling a little guilty. I'm beginning to think that I don't know Liam King very well at all. And, maybe, I've rushed to conclusions where his character is concerned. Except for the whole jumping in bed with every puck bunny to come sniffing at his skates—that one's forgone. There's no question that the guy is a manwhore in every sense of the word. I know one when I see one. I've grown up with brothers who have a constant revolving door of women. I can't tell you how many times I've caught one of them sneaking a girl out of the house in the wee hours of the morning.

Once all the formalities are done, Liam and I head back to the car. "Well, that was fun. What's next?" he asks.

"I'm dropping you off at *your* home, and then I'm going to *mine*. I trust you can handle yourself for one afternoon."

"An afternoon, yes. Does that mean I'll be seeing you tonight? We have dinner plans, remember?" he says.

"No, we don't. And I really hope I don't have to come out and babysit you tonight. I just want one night of sleeping in my own bed. Being in my own apartment," I tell him.

"Okay, I'll stay in. I'm just sayin' it'd be way more fun if we *stayed in* together—clothing optional of course," he says with a too-big grin.

"You are relentless in your pursuits." I shake my head at him. "We're not spending the night together."

"Being relentless has gotten me to where I am today. It works well for me."

"Right, well, like I said, I'm sure you're capable of staying out of trouble for one night. So, please, for the love of God, don't make me have to come get you," I remind him as I pull the car around to the front of his building.

"I won't." He looks at me. "How steadfast are you on this whole *me not kissing you* thing? Because I gotta be honest. I really want to fucking kiss you right now."

My eyes widen. "No. We are not kissing again, Liam," I say, though I'm silently crying on the inside, subconsciously begging him to just do it. Because I know if he did, I'd throw caution to the wind and go along with it again.

He doesn't kiss me though; instead, he opens the door and steps onto the sidewalk. "Pity, I really like kissing you, Aliyah Monroe. I've never really liked kissing anyone before. You're really good at it."

"Or you're just really horny because you haven't gotten laid since you arrived."

"I've jerked off plenty, don't you worry. To thoughts of you, in case you were wondering." He winks.

"I wasn't. Goodbye, Liam."

"See you tomorrow, princess." With that, he closes the door. And I wait, watching as he disappears through the front entrance of his building.

Once he's out of view, I sigh and lean back against the headrest. How on earth am I going to survive the season?

It was a blissfully peaceful afternoon, alone, without distractions. I've managed to get all of my housework done, laundry included. I should be exhausted from everything I've accomplished in the course of a few hours. The problem is... I'm not. I can't sleep, which is why I'm scrolling through social media at one in the morning.

I know I'm going to regret this tomorrow, this whole not putting my phone down and just trying to sleep. But every time I've tried, I see him. I remember the feel of his arms around me. I remember his lips, his tongue swirling against mine. And then I want to give in and touch myself. I want to pull my vibrator out of my top drawer and think of his body pressed up against me as I make myself come.

I'm refraining from doing that. Some part of me thinks that if I give in to my need, I'm also giving in to the attraction between us, and then it won't be long before I want the real thing and throw myself at the man.

*Liam King liked your photo.*

The notification flashes at the top of my screen. Why on earth is he awake, and why is he stalking my page?

I open my messages and fire off a text to him.

ME:

> Stop stalking my page. And you should be sleeping. It's late.

LIAM KING:

> Not stalking, just getting spank bank material, babe. Which I wouldn't have to do if you were here.

I don't even know how to respond to that. I think

half the shit he says is more for shock value than anything else. Either that or he really is just brutally honest. Before I can come up with a reply, another message appears.

LIAM KING:

Why are you awake? What's wrong?

ME:

Nothing is wrong. I just can't sleep.

LIAM KING:

Did you have another nightmare? How often do you have them?

ME:

No, and not very often anymore.

LIAM KING:

Anymore? So you used to have them a lot?

ME:

When I was a kid, yes.

LIAM KING:

What are they about?

I don't know what makes me type the words. Maybe it's exhaustion, or maybe it's the fact that the man, despite all his faults, is really easy to talk to. Or maybe it's simply that I want to tell someone, anyone, to get it out of my own head. It's not spoken about in my family. *She* isn't spoken about. Whenever I ask about her, my father gets a pained look on his face, and my brothers... they just get angry. So I learned to not ask anymore. I don't like upsetting them like that, especially when I know it's my fault that she left.

ME:

My mother.

LIAM KING:

I see. Well, my mother slept with the coach of the Montreal Rangers. He bragged about her before the SC game.

My eyes bug out of my head. That's why he beat the shit out of his former coach. Why didn't he tell anyone? It's not an excuse, but it's a hell of a lot better than what all the headlines are saying. That he snapped and had a mental break, couldn't handle the pressure, or that he was just another spoiled athlete with an anger problem.

ME:

My mother tried to kill me when I was eight.

Shit! Delete, delete, delete! I hit *unsend* on the

message, hoping it vanished before he could see it. I can't tell him that. I can't tell anyone that.

ME:

> Why didn't you explain what he did?

LIAM KING:

> Because that would hurt her too, and as pissed off as I am about what she did, I don't want to destroy my mother like that.

I let out the breath I didn't know I was holding. He didn't see the message. Thank god.

LIAM KING:

> Go to sleep, Aliyah. Try not to dream of me too much. The real thing is far better anyway.

I smile. I don't doubt that one bit.

# Chapter Twenty

Liam

My arms are resting on my thighs as I listen to the coach's opening talk. This is the first game of the preseason, my first game with the Knights. Over the last few weeks, I've managed to build a rapport with my new teammates. We work well together. The guys on my line have accepted me, and even though we don't know each other personally yet, we know each other's game. We're strong during the practices. Tonight will tell just how strong, though.

I can hear the fans chanting for their team. My team. It's an addictive feeling, being in a packed out stadium, the crowd's excitement palpable. I fucking love it. Live for it.

"Okay, let's start the season strong, boys. Go out there and win!" one of the coaches says.

We all push to our feet and line up behind Peter Franks, the team's starting goalie, as we make our way down the tunnel and skate out onto the ice. We begin with a few warm-ups, taking turns shooting a couple of pucks into the net. Then the announcers call out the starting lineup. When they get to my name, I look up at the crowd. I'm so used to the entire stadium cheering for me, but that's not happening right now. They're cheering, but it's not all that loud and it certainly isn't for me. I guess that PR work I've been doing with Aliyah hasn't paid off quite yet.

Not that I've minded hanging around her one bit. I'd like to say my charm is winning her over, but it's not. I've tried—really fucking tried—to get her into my bed. She's headstrong about us maintaining a professional relationship. It's a pity. I happen to think we'd be fucking explosive together. I haven't kissed her again, been trying real hard to respect her boundaries and all. She also hasn't slept in my apartment since. I glance up into the stands, looking for her and coming up short. I was hoping she'd be here...

Then, right when I'm about to look down again, I spot her. Next to the Sin Bin, with her little group of friends. I've never wanted to be put in that box before, but here I am, praying like hell for a penalty. This woman is bringing out a lot of firsts for me. She smiles and waves. I lift my gloved hand to return the gesture, only to find myself pushed into the boards.

This time, when I glance up, I see Gray glaring back at me. "Don't look at her like that," he warns.

"At who? Like what?"

"Aliyah, my fucking sister. Don't look at her like that. I might be your teammate, but don't think for one second that I won't break your fucking kneecaps if you touch her," he says.

I'd like to think he's just another overbearing, protective big brother—the kind that talks shit but will never actually follow through with any of it. Unfortunately, for me, he's not. Grayson Monroe wouldn't think twice about ruining my career by making sure I'd never walk again... that's if he leaves me breathing at all.

"Dude, I waved. Relax," I tell him.

"Just making sure. Now, come on, we've got a game to win." He pats the top of my helmet and skates off in the opposite direction.

As soon as the coach announces that I'm part of the starting lineup, it sinks in that I'm also competing for the first puck drop of the season. No pressure at all. This is something I've done a million times before. I can do this. I *will* do this.

I take position, my stick ready and waiting for the ref to give us the green light. I look my opponent in the eye, Jason Welch, captain of the Ice Bears. And a real fucking asshole. This isn't the first time I've played against him. It's just the first time in this uniform.

"I hear they gave you a sitter. I've seen the pictures. Hot piece of ass," he says. "Mind giving me her number? She can watch over me anytime, and I can show her how a real man fucks the babysitter."

I don't even have time to react before Gray, who was right behind me, shoves me aside. He throws his stick down, then his gloves come off. I don't think the Bears' fuckwit captain knows what hit him when Gray's left hook connects with the guy's face and knocks 'em backwards. The refs are quick to step in, dragging Gray back towards the penalty box. I watch as Welch pushes to his feet, gets into position, and lines up his stick, ready for the drop with a smile on his face. That fucker just took out one of our best players at the jump. And he knows it. I wish I could blame Gray for coming in so hot, but I can't. I was two seconds away from throwing gloves myself. I'll do one better, though. I'll win this drop, we'll score, and then we'll win this game. We're not going to start the season out with a loss.

Fuck that.

As soon as the puck hits the ice, I'm on it, slapping it back to where Jameson collects it before hitting it up the boards. My legs pump as I keep my eye on the prize, my focus honed in on that little black circle. I manage to get to the puck at the same time Welch does. Slamming my body against his, I push the fucker up against the boards. I want to do so much more, but I know with Gray off the ice for the next five, the team can't be down another player.

I get the puck and slap it over to where Jameson is waiting. He takes it down the ice, rushes the net, swings his stick up, and brings it down again. The puck flies right over the goalie's blocker side and hits the back of the net. The horns sound, and the crowd goes nuts. The team jumps on Jameson, congratulating him for his goal. A goal within the first two minutes of the game.

*This is how you play fucking hockey, boys and girls.*

At the end of the first period, we're up by three. I hit the locker room and plop myself down next to Gray. He looks over at me. "I want him taken out," he says. "Fucking asshole thinks he can disrespect my sister like that." He shakes his head. I can see he's still vibrating with rage.

"What do you want me to do?" I ask, prepared to do whatever it takes. I've been playing hard against Welch the whole first period, banging him up *legally* as much as I can get away with. I'm not afraid to throw gloves. I'm only holding back because, according to Aliyah, I have an image to fix. But that fucker is getting on my last nerve.

"You? Nothing, just have my back because they're going to come at me," he says.

"Don't do anything that'll get you suspended," I caution him.

"I won't. But they're not going to like what I have planned either. Just have my back out there," he repeats.

"Always." I nod and we bump fists.

"All right, listen here. We're up but they're hungry. Keep 'em out of the zone and score. It's that simple," the coach says, and then stares right at Gray. "Monroe, keep it fucking clean out there."

"Coach, the fucker said he wanted to fuck my sister," Gray grinds out between clenched teeth, and the entire locker room goes silent.

"He's a fucking dead man," Jameson says.

"Fuck him up. You can afford a fine, but not a suspension. Keep that in mind," this comes from the owner, our owner, Jacob Monroe himself. I haven't had a whole lot of interaction with the guy, but he's always watching. I can feel it.

The team hollers and everyone jumps up, ready to head back down the tunnel. The moment we touch the ice, Gray and Jameson nod at each other like they're talking a language I'm not privy to. Which isn't far from the truth. These guys know each other inside and out, have been playing together for years. I'm the newbie. It doesn't take me long to figure out what they were planning, though. I win the puck drop against Welch, shooting it back to Gray, who takes off down the ice before passing it back to me.

I pivot with the puck, dodging Welch and maneuvering around him. He comes up beside me, attempting a quick steal. I look up and see that Jameson is right in front of me. I manage to pass it to him. Welch plows forward, and as he does, Jameson ducks, causing Welch to fly over my teammate's back. That's when all hell breaks loose as Gray is coming up hard and fast. He tumbles on top of Welch, and his left blade connects with Welch's face. Blood pools around the Bear's star center, who's sprawled out flat on the ice, unconscious.

The refs, players, everyone crowds around him. Everyone except Gray and Jameson, who look on from a distance. I skate over to them. "You good?" I ask.

"Yep, can't say the same about that fucker, though," Gray mutters under his breath, and I don't know what to say. It looked like a coincidence, an accident. Sure as fuck wasn't the first time I've seen a player take a skate to the face, probably won't be the last time either, but there's something about the way Jameson and Gray share a look that tells me there's more to it than that.

Of course I keep my thoughts to myself as each team heads to their respective benches while Welch is strapped onto a gurney and carried off the ice. The cleaners come out to clear away the blood left behind. I look across the rink to where Aliyah is seated, except she's not there anymore. Her friends are gone too. Maybe they stepped out to the concession area or something.

At the end of the game, as the whole stadium is celebrating the Knights' first preseason victory, I glance over to the penalty box again and realize Aliyah never came back.

*Who the hell leaves a hockey game halfway through?* But then my mind shifts to darker thoughts. *What if something happened to her?*

I head into the locker room. I'm supposed to stay for post-game interviews. But I couldn't care less about the press right now. I dig through my locker for my phone and send Aliyah a message.

ME:

You okay?

The *read* notice appears on the screen but she doesn't message me back.

# Chapter Twenty-One

I had to leave before the game was over. I couldn't handle the sight of all that blood on the ice. My dad's words were taunting me in my head: *If you let any of my players touch you, that ice will be painted red with their blood, and it'll be your job to come up with a creative way to*

*explain how a whole team of NHL players went missing.*

It was Liam's blood I imagined covering that ice, not the player's from the opposing team—the guy who obviously did something to piss off my brother. Instead, I pictured Liam's body sprawled out on the rink, a pool of blood surrounding him because I did let him touch me. And I did let him kiss me. Twice.

I've been able to hold strong ever since, though. I'm not going to give into my urges, no matter how crazy this need to have him is getting. Sometimes I feel like I'm burning up from the inside out. But I don't have a choice; he's not for me.

He's been doing good too. He attends every PR opportunity I've set up for him without complaint. I haven't had to go out in the middle of the night again to find him and make sure he doesn't end up splashed all over the front page of the tabloids. Which I'm thankful for, because I really do love my sleep.

I'm now at home, in bed, with Casper on my lap. I've read Liam's message a hundred times over but I'm not sure how to respond. The fact that I had the image of him being the one bleeding on the ice and how much that terrified me is well... *terrifying me.*

What does that mean?

I can't unpack the feelings I'm having for him. I thought that it was crazy chemistry mixed with strong sexual attraction, but when I envision him being hurt, I physically ache. That's more than just wanting to bang the guy. Maybe if I do take him up on that offer to jump on his dick, it'll help get this infatuation out of my system, and we can go on pretending it never happened. Just like we've been pretending those kisses never happened.

As I'm staring at his message, my phone lights up with his name flashing across the screen. *Shit, why is he calling me?* I look over at the time. It's nine p.m. on a Friday after a game. Most of the guys will be out celebrating their win.

"Hello," I answer the call.

"Aliyah, where are you?"

"Home. Why?" I ask. I can hear club music in the background.

"You're supposed to prevent me from making stupid mistakes, right?"

"I am."

"Then you need to come and help me out."

"What are you doing? Where are you?"

"I'm at that bar ICE with the team. There are puck bunnies everywhere, and I mean *everywhere*," he stresses the last word.

"So, why is that my problem? You're a big boy, Liam. *Leave.*"

"Because I'm fucking horny as all hell, Aliyah. I haven't had sex since I stepped foot in this city, because a certain babysitter won't succumb to my charms."

I smile. If only he knew how hard it actually is for me to fight it. "You're just not that charming, King," I tell him.

"Fuck off. I'm more charming than the prince himself," he says.

"If you say so."

"I do say so. Look, babe, I need you to come here and be the type of fun police you're so good at being. I can't just leave. The guys won't let me live it down, and I *really* don't want to fuck a puck bunny."

"So, then, don't. Tell them *no*. It's your body, Liam. You're in control of who touches you and who doesn't. Did no one ever give you the *it's okay to say no* talk?" I ask him.

"Cute... Please, Aliyah, I need your help here. I can say no, trust me. I might be horny but my cock isn't hard for these women. I don't want them. I want you but that's a whole other problem. If I don't show interest, the team is going to question me. *Your brother* is going to question me. Which I don't really give a fuck, but I'd prefer to die after I've been to heaven at least once, and not a moment sooner."

"Heaven? How much have you had to drink?"

"Nothing. Not a drop. Heaven is where I'm going to be when you finally let me sink my cock into that sweet little cunt of yours."

"Oh my god! Goodbye, Liam."

"Don't hang up. People have phones out and they're taking pictures. Aliyah, if you don't come and help me, I'm going to make sure I get caught in what looks like a very compromising position—the kind of position that will ruin all the hard work we've been doing to clean up my image," he threatens.

"You wouldn't," I tell him.

"Wouldn't I?"

"Damn it. I'm in bed already, Liam."

"I'll make it up to you. Thanks, princess, see you soon," he says. "Oh, and, Aliyah, put some clothes on before you leave your apartment this time." He disconnects the call, and I drop my phone next to me on the bed, contemplating if I should just leave him there to fend for himself.

Really, what did the guy do before he moved here and had me to constantly watch his ass?

He got himself into shit—that's what he did. Damn it. If I don't get up and go, and he does follow through on his threat, I'll be letting my dad down. Not to mention, the lecture I'd get about doing my job.

I throw the blankets off and glance down. Casper looks up at me very unimpressed. "Sorry, buddy, I gotta go. Keep the bed warm for me. I won't be long." *Hopefully*. I sigh, scratching the top of his head as he snuggles back into the comforter.

I get up and walk into my closet. Liam said to make sure I put clothes on. With a smile spread across my face, I dig through my closet until I find the perfect "puck bunny chic" outfit. I gather every-thing up, take it all into the bathroom, and run my fingers through my hair. I don't bother to brush it, wanting that *just rolled out of bed* look more than I ever have before.

Stripping out of my pjs, I slip into the short, blue, leather miniskirt. I then pull a little white crop top over my head, forgoing a bra. I look in the mirror to see the full effect. My breasts are popping out of the shirt, my stomach is on full display, and when I turn, I can just make out the curve of my ass at the hem of the skirt.

I walk back into my closet and find the pair of sparkly blue Jimmy Choos I picked up last year. I haven't had a reason to wear these yet, but they're a perfect finishing touch. I pull a black coat off the hanger and wrap it around myself before picking up my keys, phone, and purse and heading to the elevator.

It's not until I pull up at the bar that I second-guess this little act of defiance. But I'm committed now. I'm all in. I don't even know what I was thinking would happen by wearing this.

Will it piss him off? *Hopefully*.

Turn him on? *Again, hopefully*.

Not that I plan on acting on either of our desires, but if he's going to drag me out of bed to come and get him, then I want to make sure he's suffering too. A case of blue balls will do the trick. That's if what he says about being desperate to fuck me is even true.

I've had boyfriends before, not any my family knew about of course, but none of them have ever spoken to me the way Liam does. So openly and crude. It's getting to the point that I expect it from him. Truth be told, I'm surprised he hasn't slipped up when other people have been around and said something sexual to me. He's careful, though, only ever talks like that when we're alone. I don't hate it either if I'm being honest. I like how expressive he is when it comes to something he wants, although sometimes I can't tell if he's joking or not.

Why would someone like Liam King want me?
He could have any woman he wants. I'm sure all he'd
have to do is look at them and they'd drop their
panties. But he seems dead set on bedding me. I keep
telling him it's the fact that I'm saying no. He just
wants the unobtainable, that forbidden fruit he's not
supposed to touch. It's the only thing that makes
sense.

Before I enter the bar, I take off my coat and
hand it to the security guy standing out front. His
eyes bug out of his head. "Ms. Monroe." He nods
to me.

"Jim, I'm not going to be long, but can you please
hold on to this for me, for just a sec? I know it's not
your job and all, but, well, please?" I ask him.

"Sure thing, Ms. Monroe." He nods again and
wraps my coat over his arm.

"It's Aliyah, Jim. You know that." I smile up
at him.

Jim has worked at this bar for as long as I can
remember. He's always looked out for my brothers
whenever they've gotten themselves into trouble
here.

I push through the front doors. I don't need to
look hard to know where the team is. They always
occupy the back of the bar. But it's the noise and the

crowd of people congregating in that particular area that let me know exactly where I'll find the guys. I don't go up to them straight away. Instead, I head over to the bar and order a soda and lime. As much as I'd love to have the vodka added into the mix, I'm driving, so I don't. Once the glass is in my hand, I bring the straw to my lips and turn around. I make it two steps before I'm met with the shocked and confused gaze of Luke Jameson, one of the players on the team who also happens to be one of my brother's best friends.

"Aliyah, what the fuck?" he asks, his eyes wide, and then he quickly glances over his shoulder. "Come on, man, I'm sore as fuck from that game and now you're gonna make me have to fight more," he whines when his gaze meets mine again.

"How am I going to make you fight more?" I ask, my eyebrows drawn down.

"Because when Gray sees you in here." He points to the floor. "Looking like that." He points to me. "He's gonna go apeshit and start cutting the eyeballs out of every guy in the bar. Fuck, he'll probably even come for mine," he says.

"You're being way overdramatic, Luke. I'm just here to pick up King. Where is he? And I swear to God, if he's gotten into any kind of shit that will come back on me, I will hold you all responsible for bringing him out here."

"He's part of the team. He's gotta celebrate," Luke says. "Besides, the guy needs to loosen up a bit. He's wound so tight over something that he won't talk about."

"He's just settling in. Give him a chance to adjust. You all aren't the easiest group to like." I smile.

"Aw, Aliyah, here I was, thinking we were friends."

"You're on Team Gray, which means I tolerate you because you love my brother. But you and me? Not friends, Luke." I laugh.

"Wait here. I'll go get King and let him know you're here," Luke says and turns around.

Do I wait? *Not a chance in hell.* I follow behind him, up to the back of the bar where everyone is sitting. It doesn't take long for the players to notice me. All of them go silent and look at my brother.

Well, all of them except Liam. "What the fuck are you wearing?" he asks loud enough for everyone to hear.

"You like it? It's part of my new *puck bunny chic* wardrobe." I do a little twirl so he gets the whole effect.

Liam swallows. He opens his mouth, about to say something, but Gray beats him to it. "I'm going to slice all of your fucking eyeballs in half if you don't stop gawking at my sister," he growls. "Lia, where the fuck are your clothes? What are you doing?" He jumps up from the booth and walks over to me.

Liam, who also gets up, stands right next to Gray but in front of me, effectively blocking the view of everyone else at the table.

"I'm here to pick his sorry ass up. He can't be out partying, Gray. You know that."

"He's fine. He's not even drinking, and the man deserves to let loose and celebrate his first Knights' win."

"I don't care if he scored a hat trick, Gray. He's leaving." I fold my arms over my chest, and Liam's eyes go right to my cleavage before he groans and lifts his gaze.

"He's staying," Gray insists.

"Really? Should I call Dad, get him down here, and let him decide where he wants his player?" I ask.

"Go for it. I'd love to see his face with you looking like that. What do you think he'd say, Lia? What do you think he'd *do*?" Gray challenges me.

"Argh, you are impossible. Come on, King, I'm dropping you home and you're staying there."

"Can I at least bring a friend?" Liam asks me with a grin.

I look at him, open-mouthed, *shocked*. He did not just ask me that, did he?

"No," I snap, turning on my heel before I push my way through the crowd to the front door. By the time I reach Jim and retrieve my coat, Liam is hot on my heels. He silently follows me to my car and climbs into the passenger seat. I throw my coat in the back and turn on the ignition.

I don't know why I'm fuming but I am. *A friend?* Can he bring *a friend* home?

"You know I wasn't serious, right? I said that for your brother's benefit, princess."

"You don't need to explain yourself to me. I don't care."

"You sure? 'Cause I gotta tell ya you seem a little pissed off. Which is fine with me. Angry sex is fucking hot," he says.

"I wouldn't know. I don't have sex with people I don't like."

"You can be angry with people you like, Aliyah."

"Shut up," I hiss as my fingers grip the steering wheel tighter. Why does he get under my skin so badly?

# Chapter Twenty-Two

Even when she's angry, she's fucking stunning. I don't get it. I never do this. I never bother engaging with women when they get all emotional or angry. Trust me, I've pissed plenty of them off. Usually, I just walk away. Forget them and think nothing of it... *or them.*

But with Aliyah, it's different. I want her to yell at me. I want her to react to my stupidity. I want her to curse me out, because she's fucking adorable when she does. It's weird. I know. I just haven't found a single thing about this girl that I don't like.

Apart from her choice of outfit tonight. I can't believe she walked into the bar looking like that. Like *this*. I look over at her. So much fucking skin on display. Her skirt doesn't even cover her pussy when she's sitting in the car. I have a clear view of her white lace panties that are so sheer they may as well be see-through.

Fuck, I'm going to die. Her brothers are going to kill me.

*But it'll be worth it.* I grin at the thought.

"Stop looking at me like that," she says.

"Babe, you didn't wear *that* for me not to look," I tell her.

"I told you I was in bed. I never said I was alone, Liam," she says.

What the actual fuck...? I see red. Blood red. And it's not my blood. No, it'll belong to whomever the fuck she's talking about right now.

"Who?" I ask, attempting to keep the homicidal tendencies out of my tone.

Aliyah looks at me briefly before she returns her

eyes to the road. "It's none of your business," she says.

"You're wrong. It's my business because you're mine, Aliyah. If you don't wanna accept that we're destined for each other yet, that's okay. I'm patient. But don't think for one second that I'm going to share you with anyone else, while I wait for you to work up the courage to actually take something you want in life," I tell her.

Aliyah slams a foot down on the brakes. I peer up into the rearview mirror, thanking the hockey gods that they're no cars behind us.

"Get out!" she says.

"What?"

"Get out of my fucking car, now, Liam," she screams.

"No," I tell her.

"You can't say *no*. Get out!" she screams louder this time.

I still don't get out, though. Instead, I lean over the center console, wrap a hand around the back of her neck, and pull her lips onto mine. My fingers dig into her hair as my mouth devours hers. Claiming her, showing her exactly who the fuck she belongs to. And it isn't whatever fucker she left behind to come get me tonight.

I've been patient. I've waited, but now I'm done. I know she wants this just as much as I do. What I don't know is what's holding her back. I've tried to figure it out, trust me. I'm done waiting for her to get out of her head. Now I'm going to drag her out of it, one orgasm at a time.

"Pull the car over, Aliyah," I tell her, putting just enough distance between us that she knows I'm serious. She swallows, and her hands tremble as they return to the wheel. Then she does as she's told, maneuvering the car to the side of the road and putting it in park. "Turn it off," I say.

Aliyah looks across to me. "We... we can't, Liam," she says, her voice shaky.

"Aliyah, turn the car off," I repeat.

She sighs, closes her eyes, and hits the button that switches the ignition off. I unbuckle my seat belt before I reach over and undo hers. Then I pick her up and lift her over the center console, depositing her onto my lap. Cupping her face in both hands, I bring my lips to hers again, more gentle this time. She's still hesitant. I can feel her holding back. My thumb rubs up and down her jawline. And then I move my hands down to her waist, tugging her core into the hardness of my cock. Aliyah lets out a moan and I smile into the kiss.

Pulling back slightly, I look at her. "Tell me again how you don't want this."

"I never said I didn't want it. I said *we can't*. And *we shouldn't*. This isn't going to end well."

"We *can* and we most certainly fucking *should*," I tell her before my lips meet hers for a second time. Regretfully, I have to pull away again. "But not here." I open the door of the car, lift her into my arms, step out, and then turn around and set her on the passenger seat. "I'm driving. You're in no condition to be behind the wheel." I close the door and jog around to the front of her car. As soon as I start the ignition, I glance back over to Aliyah. She looks like she's in shock. I reach over and thread my fingers with hers. "You doin' okay over there, princess?" I ask her.

"Uh-huh. What...? What just happened?" She's staring straight ahead at nothing.

"We just sealed the deal. You're mine now," I tell her.

"I can't be yours, Liam."

"Hate to break it to ya, princess, but you already are, so you *can* be."

"No, you don't understand. He'll kill you," she says.

"Who?"

"My father, one of my brothers—take your pick."

"Babe, I'm not afraid of your family. Let them come at me." I tell her what she needs to hear, because it's obvious she's scared. Truth is... so am I. I'd be mad not to be terrified of that family. But I've never let something like a little fear stop me before.

"You say that now. But I'm not worth the risk," she says.

"You, Aliyah Monroe, are worth every bit of risk there is. Why would you even say that?"

"Because it's true," she whispers. By this point, she's turned her head to stare out the passenger window. But I can tell she's stuck in her head and not really looking at anything in particular. I need to do something about this girl's self-esteem. How can someone so fucking confident in life be so insecure when it comes to *this*? To being desirable? Wanted?

I drive to my apartment and park in the underground garage. We both sit in silence, neither one of us making a move to leave. Eventually, I do get out, walk around to her side of the car, and open the door. Her hands are still shaky when she places one in mine. I pull her out of the car, but don't let go of that hand, even after she's standing. I don't like that she's so unsure about this. I had planned to bring her back here, take her to my bed, and show her just how fucking perfect we can be together. I want to worship the fuck out of that body of hers. I want to do things that will ensure she never has doubts about us again.

I don't want to do any of it while she's so uncertain, though. She needs to want it enough to not care what anyone else thinks. She needs to get to where I'm at.

"You can have the spare room," I tell her when we enter the apartment.

Aliyah's head whips to the side, her gaze boring into me. "What?" she asks, confused.

"You don't want this, Aliyah, and that's okay. I'll just have to wait until you do," I tell her.

"I... I want this. I want you. What I don't want is for you to get hurt because of me."

"I'm not gonna get hurt, babe."

"You will," she says so assuredly.

I don't respond. If that's the only thing holding her back, fear, then I can overcome that for her. Hopefully.

I lead Aliyah into my bedroom and close the door behind me. I walk to the bed, stopping next to it. Then I wrap a hand around her throat and tilt her face upwards, bringing my lips within an inch of hers. "Tell me you want this. Tell me you want me to make you come harder than you ever have before."

"I want this." Her words are a whisper, but I hear them loud and clear. They're the green light I've been waiting for.

I slam my lips onto hers and my tongue delves into her mouth as I push her back down onto the bed, before covering her body with mine. My hands roam up and down her curves. Fuck, she's got a body worth fighting for. The kind men have started wars over.

I groan as I grind my cock between her open thighs. My palm slides up her torso, under her pathetic excuse for a shirt, and cups her breast. My fingers tweak her nipple, twisting, pulling. Her body arches up off the bed and into me. Her hands are going crazy, ripping at my shirt and yanking it upwards. I push up on my knees and bring my shirt over my head.

Her eyes are hungry, greedy, as they run along the length of my body. Then her eyebrows draw down. "Did you get hurt?" she asks, gently running her fingertips over the new bruise forming on my ribs.

"No, I'm fine. I'm a hockey player, babe. It comes

with the territory," I tell her.

She nods her head but continues to look at the bruise. Grabbing her chin in one hand, I force her to look at my face instead. "I'm fine," I tell her again before dropping my arm, fisting the material of her shirt, and tearing it right down the middle. I don't need her wearing that again anyway. Aliyah's breasts fall out of the fabric—full, firm breasts that overspill the palms of my hands. "Fuck, I've wanted to do this since the day I met you."

Leaning down, I take one of her breasts in my mouth, sucking, licking, biting on the skin there while I massage and tweak the other one with my free hand. Aliyah is squirming under me, letting out quiet little moans. It's not enough. I want her fucking screaming so loud the whole building hears her, knows I'm the one giving her pleasure.

I kiss my way over to her other breast and lavish it with the same attention. Not for long though. Because my mouth has somewhere else it'd like to be. I continue to kiss a trail along her flat stomach, twirling my tongue inside her belly button, making her both squirm and laugh. Which brings a smile to my face.

Then I sit up and grab the top of her panties. Sliding the lacy material down her legs, I bring them to my face and inhale her scent. It's fucking amazing. Aliyah watches on, silently, as I spread her legs wide open for me.

"I'm keeping these," I tell her, throwing her underwear over my shoulder.

As much as I want to take my time and ravish her body, I can't. I feel like a starved man who hasn't seen water in days. I bury my face into her mound, and my tongue swipes right up the middle of her wet slit before circling around her hard little bud. I groan as her taste explodes on my tongue.

"Fucking delicious. I knew you'd taste as sweet as you looked," I say, then quickly dip my tongue into her hole, licking up as much of her as I can get. My fingers dig into the flesh of her thighs as I hold her legs down and in place, keeping her pussy spread wide.

I move my tongue back up to her clit, flattening it out. Aliyah's hips lift off the bed as she grinds into my face harder. Her hands grasp my head, holding me down.

*Like I was ever planning on leaving this slice of heaven...*

It only takes another minute before I feel her legs tremble and freeze up. Her body jerks as she calls out my fucking name, her juices coating my tongue. The sounds of Aliyah coming apart for me, under me... Fuck, I've never heard anything more fucking amazing, and I can't wait to hear it again.

# Chapter Twenty-Three

Aliyah

I must be dreaming. I fell asleep in my bed, back in my own apartment, and I'm likely to wake up soon. Because this... this orgasm that just tore through me cannot be real. It felt real, but way too intense and insane to be anything other than a fantasy.

I mean, I've experienced orgasms before. Never anything on this level, though. And that was just his tongue. Jeez, what the hell would his cock do to me if that's the kind of pleasure he can give with his mouth? His very talented mouth.

My body feels like it's floating, little aftershocks of pleasure rocking through me. I open my eyes to find Liam staring down at me, his own full of lust and need. And so blue. Much bluer than I remember. It's a lot to have that look directed at me.

"You doin' okay there, princess?" he asks with a knowing, cocky-as-hell grin on his face.

I nod. "Ah, uh-huh, I'm just waiting to wake up," I admit.

"Wake up?" He tilts his head to the side.

"Yeah, this is a dream, right?"

"You're a fucking dream. Your body is a fucking dream. But this, you and me, it's as real as it's ever been."

I blink up at him. How does this man just come up with these lines? Does he say this shit to every woman who ends up in his bed?

Liam's fingertips skirt up and down my inner thighs, featherlight. He wants my attention, and he has it. Whatever I was thinking leaves my head when he stops just at the apex of my thighs, right next to my core, and then slides lower. My legs involuntarily fall to each side of my body, spread wide. I'm already desperate for his touch again. I want those fingers on me, in me.

More than that, though, I want his cock. And I'm afraid if I don't let this happen right now, I'm going to come to my senses and run out the door. With that thought in mind, I sit up and push Liam down. His back hits the mattress and his arms reach out to grab me around the waist and pull me on top of him. It's exactly where I wanted to be anyway. I shed the remains of my destroyed top from my arms. And then reach behind me and unzip the back of my skirt. Rising to my feet on the bed, I let the skirt drop before kicking it to the side.

"I'm burning that," Liam says, gesturing to the floor.

"That skirt cost me three grand. You're not burning it," I tell him.

"I'll give you four grand if you let me burn it," he says.

"That's insane."

"It is what it is."

I plop back down, straddling his lap while my hands take their time exploring his torso. I have this desperate need to lick the grooves of his abs. So that's what I do. I lean forward and run my tongue around the smooth skin. My fingers find the button on his pants, popping it open before sliding the zipper down. My hand reaches underneath the band of his briefs and finds his cock, hard and weeping precum. Then I lower my head, and my tongue darts out and slides right across the slit at the tip. His taste invades my mouth and it's not enough. I want more. Taking as much of his cock as I possibly can, I hollow out my cheeks and slowly suck as I slide back up again.

Liam's hands fist my hair. "Fuck, babe. Shit." He tugs tighter, until I have no choice but to open my mouth. "If you keep doing that, I'm going to come in that fucking mouth of yours. And as much as I want to do that—God knows I fucking do—I want your cunt more." He grabs me under my arms and drags me up his body. "You want that too, right?" he asks as one of his hands travels down until his fingers are sliding through the wetness of my pussy. He inserts one inside me, and my head falls back on a moan. "You want me to fuck this pussy, don't you, Aliyah?"

His use of my real name, instead of that ridiculous pet name, has my core clenching around his fingers. I nod my head.

*I want that. I want all of that.*

"I need the words, Aliyah. You want me to fuck

you until there's no doubt that you're mine, then say so, babe."

I glare down at him. He's really going to make me say it, isn't he?

"Fuck me, Liam. Now. Before I come to my senses and walk out that door," I tell him the truth, what part of me has been thinking of doing this entire time. Because it knows I should.

He gives me that devilish smirk of his and then reaches into the bedside table drawer, pulling out a string of condoms. He tears one off and then throws the rest onto the bed. "We'll be using all of those before the night's out," he says, so goddamn cocky.

"You're awfully sure of yourself, there, sport," I say.

"I've been waiting weeks for this. You've had my cock constantly rock-hard—my balls have never been bluer, Aliyah. We've got a lot of time to make up for," he fires back.

I roll my eyes. I'll go with it for tonight. But I don't expect it to turn into anything more. I'll go home before he wakes up, make sure there isn't that awkward morning-after discussion to deal with.

"How about less talking and more doing?" I suggest, plucking the condom out of his hand.

I lift up onto my knees, and Liam shoves his

pants down his legs, kicking them off as I roll the condom onto his length. My mouth waters at the sight of him. I really did want to explore his cock with my mouth longer than I did. Holding it in one hand while lining it up with the other, I slowly, so fucking slowly, slide myself down onto him. He's stretching me so damn much there's a slight sting of pain with the intrusion.

"Fuck, you're tight," he curses under his breath, his fingers digging into my hips, almost like he's trying to control himself.

"If you're a two-pump chump, tell me now, so I can at least pretend to have a good time," I say.

Liam's eyes widen at my words. And before I can react, he rolls us over so he's back on top. He manages to do this while keeping his cock buried to the hilt inside me. "That sounds like another challenge, princess. You really think I can't fuck you all night long? Now I have something to prove."

"Prove it then," I taunt him. Liam draws back, his cock slides out until just the tip is left inside me, and then he slams home again. "Ah, shit." I close my eyes. I don't know what part of my insides he just hit with his cock. But hell did it feel good.

He lifts my right leg, holding my knee over his elbow while my other leg wraps around his back.

Then Liam glides in and out of me. Slowly. "The Knights scored five goals tonight, which means I'm going to make sure you score yourself five orgasms. One down, four to go," he says.

"That's not possible," I tell him. No way am I going to come five times in one night.

"I can't wait to prove you wrong." Liam leans over me, his lips connecting with mine. My right knee touches my shoulder and I'm officially bent like a pretzel, my lower body spread wide open for him.

He pushes his tongue into my mouth as he increases his pace, thrusting in and out of me. At this angle, there isn't an inch of him I can't feel. He's hitting every pleasure point I have inside me. One minute, I can feel the upward climb of my climax. And then, all of a sudden, that son of a bitch is soaring through the clouds, taking my sanity with her.

"That's two," I hear Liam say before he pulls out of me. He picks me up and turns me over so I'm flat on my stomach. I'm useless. My legs—shit, my whole body is nothing but Jello right now. Liam doesn't seem to care as he lifts my hips off the bed and thrusts his cock into me from behind. He palms the flesh of my ass. "Fuck, I love this ass," he says.

I have no words. I can hear the sounds coming

out of my mouth as he fucks me. He wasn't wrong. He is damn good at this whole sex thing, and as I feel myself trembling with that familiar feeling in the pit of my stomach, I'm having second doubts about the whole *not being able to come five times* in one night.

We haven't even been at it for half an hour, and I'm coming up to my third. This has never happened to me before, not even with my vibrator. Liam's hand wraps around my hair and he pulls my head upwards. His lips connect with my neck. "This is better than any of the fantasies I've ever had about fucking you, Aliyah Monroe," he growls in my ear. "I want you to come for me again, princess. Come all over my cock. Coat it in those delicious fucking juices of yours."

"Oh god!" I'm a mess, my hips pushing back onto him, meeting his thrusts. "I need…"

"What do you need?" he asks me.

"I don't know," I cry out.

"I know what you need. I've got everything you need buried deep inside your cunt right now. Fucking come for me," he grunts, increasing his pace, hitting home each time. Then I feel one of his hands curl underneath me, his fingers press into my clit, and like he's just tapped that huge red detonation button, I come, hard and fast. My body slumps forward, spent. I'm sprawled out on the bed. Liam withdraws his cock and lays his body next to mine. His hand runs up and down my back. "That's three. Two to go," he whispers, like it's some sort of secret between us.

I sigh into the bedsheets. I don't think I can do this two more times. Like I said, I'm spent. And then he rolls me over to my side, his body flush against my back. Liam lifts my leg, placing it on top of his, and I feel him slide into me. Gently. His hand cups my breasts, alternating between massaging and tweaking my nipple. He continues to slide in and out of me with slow, languid movements. Almost like he's trying to savor the connection between us.

"Do you feel it?" he asks.

"Feel what?"

"How fucking good we are together. It's like your body was designed for my cock."

"Mmhmm," I mumble, pushing my ass against him, trying to get him to speed things up a bit. This whole slow-movements and tender-touches bullshit is too intimate, and it's going to trick my head into thinking this is more than what it is.

Liam grips my hip to hold me still. "Let me take my time with you, Aliyah," he says, his mouth pressed to the shell of my ear. "I'm not ready to be done with you yet."

*Not yet, but soon. Two more to go, right?*

That's when my walls start to creep back up. I need to protect myself. I close my eyes, clench my core to squeeze his cock, and moan. I make my legs quiver, mimicking the aftershocks of another orgasm. When I'm done, Liam pulls out and rolls me over so I'm flat on my back. He positions himself between my legs and stares down at me, his eyebrows drawn together.

"What's wrong?" he asks me.

"Nothing. Why?"

"Bullshit. You just tried to fake an orgasm. What the fuck is wrong?" he repeats.

"I didn't fake anything."

He lifts a single eyebrow.. "Yes, you did. I'm not some chump who can't tell the difference between a woman *coming* and a woman *faking it*."

I don't even know what to say to that. How the hell could he tell? I've faked plenty of orgasms before, and guys never seem to know the difference.

"Aliyah, you need to tell me what's wrong. Are you hurt? Did I hurt you?" he asks, pulling back so that he can check over every inch of my body. I have no idea what he's looking for, or what he thinks he'll find.

"No, I just... I don't know. That was intimate. We're supposed to be fucking, Liam. That's what this is, not whatever it was you were trying to do."

Without saying a word, he gets off the bed and walks into the bathroom before slamming the door behind him. I look up at his ceiling with a sigh.

Great, now he's pissed off. What the hell did I say that could have possibly pissed him off? I mean, this *is* just fucking. Isn't it?

# Chapter Twenty-Four

I walk out of the bathroom after I've had time to put my emotions in check and cool off. Too fucking intimate, my ass.

*It's just fucking.* That's what she said.

I should be embracing that, glad she only wants to fuck me and nothing more. But for the first time in my life, I want the *more*. I don't know when that switch happened. It sure as hell started out with me just wanting to fuck her. The woman's fucking hot. I mean, who wouldn't want to fuck her? And, then, somehow, it shifted to me wanting *her*. Not just her body, but her.

When I find the bed empty, my blood goes cold. "Aliyah?" I call out, leaving the bedroom and heading down the hall. I wasn't in the bathroom that long, so where the fuck did she go? "Aliyah?" I call out again, only to be met with silence. She fucking left.

I storm back into my bedroom and throw on a pair of sweats and a shirt. I pick up my keys—thankfully I left my car in the garage before going to the bar tonight. She can run all she wants, but I'll chase. For one, I need to make sure she actually gets home all right. And two, I really need to find out what the fuck happened. Why would she fake an orgasm after having three really fucking good, really fucking *real* ones?

I jump into my car, drive over to her apartment, and park out on the street. I know I shouldn't enter the code to her building, the one I might have memorized after the first time I saw her type it in. Knowing I shouldn't doesn't stop me from doing it, though. I slide into the elevator and enter the same code. It'll take me right up to her apartment. As soon as I step foot inside her foyer, I know she's here. I can hear the shower running. I head to her bedroom, sit on her bed, and wait. Her male roommate—AKA Casper, your friendly neighborhood cat—comes and plops down on my lap.

Twenty minutes later, the water in the shower turns off. And not long after that, Aliyah opens the door, a cloud of steam billows out, and her steps falter when she sees me propped up on her headboard, my hands tucked behind my neck and my ankles crossed, waiting for her. Her hair is piled up on top of her head in a messy bun. She's wrapped in a white towel and, fuck me, I want to lick those little water droplets that run down her collarbone.

"Wh... what are you doing here?" she asks me.

"Why'd you run?" I counter.

"I asked you a question first," she says, walking into her closet.

"You ran. I chased," I tell her with a shrug.

"Why?"

"Nope, my turn. Why'd you run out on me?" I repeat.

Aliyah steps out of the closet with a Vancouver Knights sweater on. It only takes me a second to realize that it's mine. The one I made her wear a few weeks ago. I don't think she noticed she grabbed it.

"One of us had to think reasonably, Liam. That shouldn't have happened," she says.

"That's not what you were saying while you were screaming my name. Give me one good fucking reason why *we* shouldn't happen?"

"Because you're you, and I'm me," she says simply.

"That's the exact reason *we* should happen."

"My father will kill you. I know you think I'm overreacting, but I'm not. My family, they're not like other families, Liam."

"I'm aware. I'm not worried about them."

"You should be."

"You want me to go and ask your father's permission to date you? I will, and I won't leave his office until I get it," I tell her.

"No, do not do that." She gasps and her eyes widen.

I slide off the bed and walk towards her, stopping once we're nearly toe-to-toe. Cupping her cheek, I lift her eyes to meet mine. "There's another reason, a reason you're not telling me. Something in that pretty little head of yours is holding you back. I can't help you defeat those demons if you don't tell me what they are."

"I can't," she says.

"I already told you I'm a patient man, Aliyah Monroe. I'll wait until you can tell me," I say. "Come on, I'm tired, and we've got another early morning skate tomorrow." I take her hand and lead her over to her bed. Pulling the blankets back, I pick her up and lay her down before climbing in beside her. Then I cover us both with the blanket and wrap an arm around her waist.

"What are you doing?" she asks.

"We're going to sleep, Aliyah. We can talk about what happened later."

"You can't sleep here, Liam." She rolls over to face me.

"I'm not leaving," I tell her.

"What if..." She stops short.

"What if *what*?" I urge her to continue.

"What if I have a nightmare again and wake you up? You should just go home."

I frown. Does she really think that? If she has a nightmare, I *want* her to wake me up. I want to comfort her, hold her and let her know that nothing is going to hurt her while she's in my arms. So I tug her closer and tell her as much. "If you have a nightmare, I'll be right here. I don't care if you wake me up. I don't care if you hog the bed, steal all the blankets. Fuck, I don't even care if you snore like a goddamn freight train. I'm not going anywhere, Aliyah."

"Why?" she asks.

"What do you mean *why*?"

"Why me?"

"Because I haven't been able to stop thinking about you since the day I walked into my apartment and found you standing there waiting for me. When that fucking asshole Welch talked shit about you out on that ice, I wanted to throw down my gloves. I've never wanted to throw gloves over a woman before. I've never cared enough to let anything anyone says bother me," I tell her. "Well, apart from my mother."

"So I'm like your mother?" she says, and I nearly choke on air.

"Fuck no. I don't want to devour my mother." I shudder at the thought. "Gross, Aliyah."

"Wait... you said Welch talked shit about me on the ice. What'd he say?"

"He said he wanted your number so he could show you how a real man fucks the babysitter."

Aliyah's eyes widen. "That's why Gray hit him."

She nods as if she's answering her own question. "And then the skate to the face..."

"Yeah, I'm still trying to figure out how the lucky son of a bitch managed to make it look like an accident," I admit.

"He's good." Aliyah shrugs. "You know, if he did that to someone who just talked shit, what do you think he's going to do when he finds out you actually have fucked the babysitter?"

"I didn't fuck the babysitter. I fucked my future girlfriend." I smirk.

"Future girlfriend?"

"Yeah, I figure you're not ready to label this." I gesture between us. "But one day you will be. So, future girlfriend it is."

"It honestly scares me to think about how your mind works. It's like you have your own Liam King logic going on in there."

"Go to sleep." I kiss her forehead.

"If I wake you up, I'm sorry and ignore anything you might hear me say."

I laugh. "Deal."

"Oh. My. God!" a high-pitched female voice squeals before the sound of a door slamming shut has me jumping out of bed.

Aliyah sits up and groans. "Phoebe, what are you doing here?"

"What am *I* doing here? What is..." Phoebe points to me. "...he doing here?" she whispers.

"Why are you whispering?" Aliyah asks her.

"Because your brother's in your living room. I told him to let me wake you up because you like to sleep naked and he didn't need to see that," she says. Phoebe reaches behind her and locks the door, right before the handle starts rattling.

"Pheebs, what's going on in there? Open the door," a male voice yells out from the other side.

"Just a sec. Your sister is naked. Jesus, Jonah, let her get dressed," Phoebe yells back.

"Aliyah?" the voice calls.

"I'll be right out, Jonah."

"What's he doing here? He's supposed to be at school," Aliyah hisses to Phoebe. Me? I'm just standing here, looking between the two of them, still trying to figure out what the fuck is going on. "You have to get rid of him," Aliyah urges, her tone panicked as she jumps out of bed. "He can't find Liam here, Phoebe." Then she takes me by the hand

and drags me into her closet. "Stay here until I come and get you—*don't make a sound*," she stresses the last few words.

"What? Aliyah, I'm not hiding in your fucking closet," I say and attempt to brush past her.

"Yes, you are. Please, just let me get rid of him."

The pleading look on her face, the desperation in her eyes, is what has me giving in and sitting my ass down on the carpeted floor of her wardrobe. I mean, if you've gotta be stuck in any closet, hers ain't a bad one to choose. It's fucking nice in here. Aliyah has a fondness for designer labels. Everything is so orderly, color-coded, and on display like a museum exhibition. The back wall is floor-to-ceiling shoes. I grin as soon as the idea pops into my head.

*I'm going to fuck her in every pair of heels she owns.*

I can't hear shit, and I feel like I've been sitting in here for ages when the door finally opens. Except it's not Aliyah who greets me on the other side. It's her friend Phoebe. "Aliyah went to breakfast with her brother. You need to leave before they come back," she says with an icy clip to her voice.

"She left?" I ask.

"Yep, so hurry up."

"Okay." I walk back into the bedroom and pick

up my phone and keys from the bedside table where I left them last night.

"Oh, and, Liam," Phoebe says as I'm turning to head out the door. I pivot back to face her. "Aliyah isn't the kind of girl you fuck around with. She's the kind of girl you keep. If you hurt her, it won't be her brothers you'll have to worry about. It'll be me. And I have no qualms about burying your body in one of my family's oil wells."

"You're right. She is the kind of girl you keep, and I plan to do just that," I say as I step into the elevator. Then I pull out my phone and send Aliyah a message.

ME:

Call me when you're free.

ALIYAH:

You need to get your ass to the rink before you're late.

Fuck, she's right. I jog over to my car, jump behind the wheel, and break just about every road rule on my way to the stadium. I make it into the locker room as everyone else is changing.

"What happened to you?" Gray asks.

"You don't want to know," I tell him, and a little guilt that I spent the night with his sister seeps in. I shut that shit down quick, though. I don't owe the man anything. I saw Aliyah first, met her first, liked her first. Bro code doesn't apply in this case. At least that's what I'm telling myself.

Again, I thank all that is holy that I don't have sisters to worry about—my mother's already more than I can handle.

# Chapter Twenty-Five

I'm sitting at breakfast with my brother Jonah. But I can't stop thinking about Liam, about all the things that were done and said last night.

I pick up my coffee and eye my brother over the rim of my cup. "So, are you going to tell me why you're not at school?"

"Can't I just want to visit my little sister?" he says, then quickly tries to change the subject. "How's the job going?"

"Nope, nice try but not gonna happen. Jonah, why are you here?" I press him.

"A friend needed my help, so I came to help them. Thought I'd stop in to see you as well." He looks at me, his eyes scrutinizing my every feature. "You look different. Good. Are you good?"

Out of all my brothers, Jonah is the one who worries about me the most. Don't get me wrong, they all worry. They all try to wrap me in cotton wool. But Jonah, he sees beneath my masks. He sees the torment that goes through my head.

"The nightmare's back," I tell him.

Jonah's room was right next to mine when we were growing up. He heard every single one of my nightmares. Then again, I think the whole house did because I'd wake up to all of my brothers, my dad, and some of my dad's soldiers standing in my bedroom. Sometimes, when I was too exhausted from battling with my own mind, I'd sleep in Jonah's room with him. He'd stay awake and talk to me about random things until I finally drifted off. I never had the nightmares when I was with him. Come to think of it, I didn't have any last night when Liam held me either.

"When did they start?" Jonah asks me.

"A few weeks ago."

"How often?"

"A few times a week."

"The same one?" he continues his line of questioning.

"It's always the same one," I remind him.

"Aliyah, you're safe. No one is going to do anything like that to you again. She can't touch you. Ever. Again." He says *she* and not *Mom*.

I know that I shouldn't be so scared. I get that she hasn't returned in all these years, but what if she does? What if, one day, she's just waiting at my door? Or in some dark corner? I know it's stupid. But no one ever said that fear had to be logical.

"I know," I lie, then decide to take a page out of his book and move this conversation along. "Tell me about this friend you had to help. Is it a girl?"

"Yes—and, no, I'm not telling you who it is."

"Why not? Do I know her?"

His face goes stoney, solid like a block of ice. It does that when he doesn't want to give away any details. Which tells me I *do* know her.

"Who is it? That look you have tells me it's someone I know."

"What's been happening here? How are all your friends?" Jonah says instead of answering.

"Same, same. Nothing new."

"Are you dating anyone?" he asks, and I do a double take.

"What?"

"Are you dating anyone?" he repeats.

"Why? So you can go and make them disappear?"

"Something like that." He smiles.

"I'd never tell any of you unless it was really serious and I was in love. Just keep in mind that if I ever do bring a guy home..." Jonah's groan interrupts me. I wait for him to finish before stressing my point. "*If I ever do bring a guy home*, I love him. And if anything were to happen to him, I'd never forgive any of you."

"You know we just want to protect you. We're looking out for you, Lia. You had a shitty start to life, one that wasn't your fault. One that we should have stopped long before it got to where it did. We should have known what was happening. You don't understand the guilt we all live with for not knowing," he tells me.

"What are you talking about?" Honestly, I'm confused.

"No one knew what she was doing. You never said anything. And Dad... he blames himself, and he won't ever stop blaming himself for allowing someone—*anyone*—to hurt you like that."

"It wasn't his fault. It was mine," I say.

Jonah shakes his head. "None of it was ever your fault. I know you think it has something to do with you, but I promise you it didn't. She was sick in the head, Lia. She was always the problem. Not you."

"She didn't do those things to you or Gray or Vinny. It was me, Jonah. It's okay. You don't have to try to sugarcoat it for me," I tell him.

"No, she didn't, but I wish she had. I'd trade places with you in a heartbeat, just so you wouldn't have gone through it."

I believe he would too. As much as I complain about my brothers' overbearing ways, I know it comes from a good place. "Why didn't she love me?" I've never asked this question before, but maybe if I can figure out what it is about me that's so unlovable, I can finally fix it.

Maybe then I'll be worthy of the attention Liam gives me.

"She was jealous of you. That's all it was. She

wanted to be the center of Dad's world. And then you came along and he was besotted, Lia. You've always been Dad's favorite—shit, I think he loves you more than he even loves that fucking hockey team of his."

I smile. "I don't think he loves anything more than his team."

"You're wrong. You are the one thing he cares about more than anything else in this world."

"He cares about all of us," I'm quick to correct.

"He does, but you more so. I'm okay with that, because I get it. You're my favorite too." Jonah grins. "And I don't want to ever hear you say you're not loveable, because that's not true either."

"Maybe," I say, but it's hard to believe him. "We should go. I have to get to work."

The moment I step foot inside The Castle, I'm met by Gray. "Dad wants to see you," he says.

"Why?"

"No idea. Come on." He holds his arm out for

me to step in front of him. "What'd you get up to last night after you left the bar?"

Shit, please tell me he doesn't know. You can't tell that someone had the best sex of their life a few hours prior just by looking at them, can you?

"I dropped Liam home and then went back to my apartment, where I was rudely woken up by Jonah this morning. Any idea why he's in town?" I ask, a single brow arched in question.

"Nope. I didn't know he was," Gray says, taking his phone out of his pocket, probably to text Jonah to find out why he's not at school.

A few minutes later, I walk into my father's office. "Shut the door," he says.

Gray closes the door behind us, so I go and sit down on one of the chairs in front of Dad's desk. My brother then fills the chair next to me. "You summoned me," I say to Dad.

"How are things going with King?" he asks me, and I feel all the blood drain from my cheeks. I need to work on my poker face if I'm going to continue this thing with Liam behind everyone's back.

"It's going well, so far. I think all the positive PR is working. His jersey sales numbers are up by twenty percent, and that was before last night's win," I tell my father.

"Good." He spreads out a range of images of Liam at various events. "We need to start sending out some of our other guys on these things. It can't become the Liam King show. This is a team. It needs to look like a team effort," Dad says.

Gray picks up a newspaper clipping from a few weeks ago when Liam went and taught the youth league. It's a photo of him handing the puck he signed to that little girl. "Where was this taken?" Gray asks me.

"Ah, just some local youth camp," I say.

"Which one?" He hasn't taken his eyes off the picture. *Weird.*

"One of the ones we sponsor, down the road a bit."

"Get rid of their coach. I want to coach those kids myself," Gray says.

Both my father and I look at him like he's lost his mind. "What? You can't do that," I tell him.

"I can and I will," Gray says, folding the clipping in half before shoving it into his pocket.

"You're on the road too much. The season is just starting and you're going to be away a lot. Those kids need a coach all season, Gray. Not whenever you happen to be in town and not on the ice yourself."

"Okay, then get me an appearance. I'll help out

whenever I'm free." My brother pushes to his feet and heads to the door. "I got shit to do. Catch you both later," he says and walks out.

"That was odd." I look to my dad.

"Yeah," he agrees, but then goes back to talking about Liam. "The first away game is next weekend. You need to travel with the team."

"What? Why? You never said anything about traveling," I complain.

"Because you're the only thing keeping that boy out of trouble. Whatever you're doing, it's working. Keep doing it," Dad tells me. I'm almost certain he wouldn't be saying that if he knew exactly what I was doing with his player last night.

"Okay. Whatever you need me to do."

"We're hosting the Knights' dinner at our house in three weeks. Make sure you're there too."

Argh, I hate those black-tie dinners he hosts. "Can I bring my friends?" I ask.

"Charlie? Sure."

"All of them, Dad."

"Fine, but you'll be working, Aliyah. I don't want King making a fool of himself."

"I actually think he's okay, Dad. I don't think he's going to do anything stupid. He wants this to work just as much as you do," I say.

"Maybe, but he fucked up."

"Do you know why he fought his old coach?" I ask.

"No, do you?" Dad fires back at me.

I consider telling him the truth. Maybe if he knew, he'd think differently of Liam. But I quickly decide against it. If I tell him, I'll be betraying Liam's trust, and that's something I don't want to do. Instead, I shake my head, stand from my chair, and walk around my father's desk. I lean down and kiss his forehead. "Love you, Daddy," I say.

"You too, Lia." He nods, his sign that this conversation is over for now. I'm just about at his door when he stops me again. "What was Jonah doing at your apartment this morning?"

"How'd you know he was there?" I ask.

"I know everyone who comes and goes from your apartment, Aliyah. Do you honestly think I'm not continuously watching over you?" he says and, again, I feel the color drain from my face. He knows. He has to know.

"I don't know why he was there. He mentioned something about being in town to help a friend." I shrug.

"Which friend?"

"He didn't say." I walk out before Dad can ask

me about any other guests visiting my place. That's not how my father works, though. He wasn't really asking me about Jonah. It's clear he knows everything my siblings and I do. No, he was *telling me* he knows Liam was at my apartment last night without ever having to say the words.

Shit. How do I arrange for someone to go into witness protection?

# Chapter Twenty-Six

It's the team's first away game. Aliyah is sitting at the front of the plane, next to her brother and father. I want nothing more than to drag her back here and sit her next to me. I want to talk to her. I want to touch her. She's scared that her dad knows about us, while the fact that she's slowly admitting that there is an *us* is a win in my book.

Over the last week, she's spent every night at my place, in my bed. We've been fucking like rabbits and it's not enough for me. I need her all the damn time. I know she's still holding back. She's not convinced that we're a lasting thing. Or at least she doesn't want to believe it.

I also know she's been hurt by someone. I'm not sure who, because whenever I ask her about it, she either shuts down and refuses to talk or she distracts me by putting my cock into her mouth. She hasn't had any more nightmares, though. I've even tried to stay awake to listen to her talk in her sleep, like she says she does. But nothing. She sleeps peacefully all night, in my arms. I fucking hate that she's insisting on keeping us secret, but then again, sneaking around is fucking fun. Especially when I pulled her into the cleaning closet at the stadium yesterday.

I smile at the memory.

When she stands up and walks to the back of the plane, towards the galley, I follow her. I glance behind me and see that everyone is going about their business, either sleeping or buried in their devices. I step up behind her, my arm stretching around her waist.

"I miss you," I tell her, and Aliyah shoves an elbow into my ribs. I don't move though. "Is that all you got?" I chuckle.

"Do you have a death wish? Is that what this is? The thrill of living a little dangerously?" she hisses.

"No, I have a *you* wish. I want you, Aliyah. I need you," I say, nibbling on the side of her neck.

"Oh my god, stop." She steps to the side. "We can't do this here."

"But you want to," I tell her.

"That's not the point. I want you to stay alive more."

"Will you come to my room tonight?" I ask her.

"Will you be alone?" she counters.

"What kind of question is that?" I'm taken aback, physically stumble at the accusation.

"I don't know. It's an away game. You're in a town where you can take a puck bunny back to your hotel room and never have to see her again when you leave in the morning."

She can't be fucking serious. I shake my head. "That's fucked up. The fact that you can stand here and even think that is *fucked up*. Tell me, Aliyah, do you want me to go out and fuck some random chick?"

"I don't care what you do." She shrugs one shoulder.

"Bullshit. You're a fucking terrible liar," I say. This is another one of her attempts at pushing me away. It's not the first and it won't be the last. "Why do you keep trying to sabotage us?"

"I'm just trying to stay within the realms of reality. And the reality is you're eventually going to find something shiny and new, and forget I exist. It's okay. I get it. It's how it works."

"Whoever the fuck hurt you did a real number on your self-esteem, Aliyah Monroe."

"Shut up," she hisses, picks up the bottle of water she came for, and barges past me to the front of the plane.

Her father looks at her, and then looks back. His eyes connect with mine. Then he's coming towards me. Fuck, this is not what I wanted to deal with today. "King." He nods, opening the fridge. "You need something?"

"No, sir," I say and wait.

He takes out a packet of chocolates. "These are her favorite. Whenever she's in a bad mood, I feed her these, and it's like whatever pissed her off never happened," he says, and then walks off.

Well, that was fucking cryptic and weird as hell.

But in my mind, I'm mentally taking note of the brand and flavor. I plan to get a truckload of that shit delivered to my apartment. Because, let's be honest, I fucking piss her off more often than not.

There's a light tap at the door. I open it to find Aliyah standing on the other side. I grab her arm and pull her into my room, shutting and locking the door behind us. I don't wait before slamming my lips down on hers. I pick her up and shove her back against the wall. Her legs wrap around my waist. We should probably talk about whatever pissed her off earlier. But right now? This moment when we're both starved for each other, nothing else in the world matters. All I want is her. I want everything she's willing to give me.

I drag my lips away from hers. "I don't know what you're doing to me. I don't know what it is about you, but I can't get enough. I'm not sure I ever will."

"You will," she says, and there's a sadness in her eyes.

I shake my head. I'll work on unpacking that shit later. Right now, I need to be inside her. "I hope you got some rest on the plane, because we're not sleeping much tonight, babe." I walk over to the bed. "Get that off," I tell her, nodding at her dress.

She smirks. "You're bossy. You know that?" she says as she lifts the hem and pulls the fabric over her head. She's left in a matching black lace panty and bra set.

"Fuck me. Were you wearing that on the plane?" I ask her.

"Well, yeah." She shrugs.

"Tell your father he should buy a jet with a bedroom."

"Sure, I'll make sure to add on... *so that I can fuck my boyfriend in the back while the rest of the team is on board the flight too*. I'm certain he'll be more than willing to accommodate me," she says. The smile on my face is fucking huge. "What are you smiling about?"

"You just called me your boyfriend." My grin widens.

"You're a strange one. I said *my boyfriend*. That could be anyone, doesn't have to be you," she says.

"It's me." I nod confidently. She can talk all she likes, but I know whose bed she's in every night.

"Your ego is beyond measure."

"It's well deserved. Have you met me?" I lift my shirt over my head and throw it to the side, before I undo my pants and let them fall to the floor. "I mean, you've seen and felt what I can do with this," I say, fisting my cock before dragging my palm up and down its length.

"It's okay," she says.

"Just okay? That sounds like a challenge. I'll just have to keep on fucking you until you admit I'm the best you've ever had."

"You don't know who else I've slept with."

"Nor do I ever want to know." I screw up my face. "As far as I'm concerned, it doesn't matter anyway. Your cunt is now molded to the shape of my dick. I've imprinted myself inside you, Aliyah Monroe. This pussy is mine. Only mine," I tell her, cupping a hand over the top of her lace panties.

"Mmm, pretty sure I still own the deed to this body," she counters.

"Nope, that deed was signed, sealed, and delivered the first night you let me in," I tell her. "I'm like a vampire from one of those shows you watch. You only have to invite me in once."

"I know you think you're cute and all, but can you hurry this along?"

I slide her panties down her legs, spread those thighs wide open, and stare down at her glistening lips. My mouth goes dry. "Fuck, you're beautiful." I sigh.

"Me or my pussy?"

"Both, but I was talking to *her*. Give me a minute. She and I have some business to attend to," I say as I crouch down and lower my face to her mound. "I'm fucking obsessed with you. It's like you've put a damn spell over me I just can't shake. And your taste, best fucking thing I've ever had in my mouth," I talk directly to her cunt.

"Really? I find that hard to believe," Aliyah says.

I look up. "I wasn't talking to you. I was talking to her. Stop interrupting, princess."

She laughs and lies back on the mattress. "Well, don't let me keep you from your riveting conversation," she grumbles with a sarcastic wave of a hand.

I refocus my attention on her pussy, dragging my tongue up from the bottom to the top. My lips close around her clit, sucking it into my mouth. I groan as I bury my face against her. There's something about her scent, her taste, that just has me ensnared in its trap. Although I'm not exactly looking for a way out either. Aliyah's hips buck off the bed. She reaches up and pulls a pillow over her face as she screams into it.

She's so responsive to my touch all the time. She fucking comes so easily. I love it. I continue licking and sucking and nibbling on her until her hands pull my head away.

"Get a condom. Now," she demands.

"Now who's being bossy?" I ask her.

"Shut up and wrap that thing already. Please, Liam, I need you inside me."

"Well, fuck, babe, when you beg so pretty like that…" I rip the foil packet open with my teeth and roll the condom down my length. I line up my cock with her entrance and—

"Liam King, I know you're in there," a voice calls out from behind the door.

Aliyah's eyes widen, and I freeze. "What the fuck is she doing here?" I hiss to myself.

"Who is she?" Aliyah asks. "Actually, it doesn't matter. You don't owe me anything. Give me a second to fix myself and I'll get out of your way."

"What the fuck? Aliyah, no. *She's* my fucking mother. And you're not going anywhere. She is."

# Chapter Twenty-Seven

*Aliyah*

His mom. *His mother* is knocking on the door and I'm naked. Well, technically, I still have my bra on. I reach up and push Liam off me. He lands on his ass on the floor.

"Ow, what the fuck?" he hisses.

"Oh, please, like that hurt. You're a fucking

hockey player. You get hit harder than that on a good day," I hiss back at him as I reach for my discarded dress. I pull it over my head. "Where are my panties?" I look around, then over to where Liam is tugging his pants up his legs.

He spots my underwear on the floor and shoves them into his pocket. "I'll keep 'em for ya." He winks.

"I am not meeting your mother with no panties on."

"She's not staying," he says, pulling his shirt over his head. My eyes flick around the room again. There's a desk in the corner with a chair. I drag a second chair over and grab the little hotel notepad and pen. Liam stops and looks at me. "What are you doing?" he asks, tilting his head to the side.

"We're working. That's why I'm in here. We're going over the upcoming events you're scheduled to attend."

There's another loud bang on the door. "I can hear you in there, Liam. Open the fucking door," his mother yells out.

Liam swings the door open. His mother pushes past him and then stops when she sees me. I swallow the lump in my throat. "Hi, I'm Aliyah, Liam's PR rep for the team," I say, standing to greet her.

"You can leave," she says, dismissing me with a wave of her hand.

"No, *you* can leave," Liam tells her, and I look between the two of them.

"We can finish this later, Liam," I say, picking up the notebook and pen and holding them to my chest.

"No, we can't. We're not done here, Aliyah," he says between gritted teeth.

"Oh, please, drop the act, son. Get rid of your little groupie. We need to talk." His mother huffs, crossing her arms over her chest while pretending I don't exist.

"What did you just call her?" That vein at the top of Liam's head, the one that sticks out whenever he's annoyed, it's pulsing now.

"I said *get rid of the groupie*. We need to talk," she repeats.

"First, she's not a fucking groupie. Second, I have nothing to talk to you about." Liam holds the door to his room wide open. I walk towards it, almost make my way through too, but he stops me. "Don't leave," he says. He's pleading with me, begging me to stay. I can see it in his eyes. So I hang back. "Mom, you need to go."

"You haven't answered my calls or messages. Matty said you won't tell him what your problem is."

"My problem? You want to know what *my* fucking problem is? You. You're the fucking problem. Now, get the fuck out of my room and out of my life," Liam yells.

I hear some doors open and close. Great, the whole team is on this level. But it's not the whole team that comes to the door. It's Gray and Luke.

"What the fuck is going on?" Gray asks.

"His mother turned up and won't leave," I tell my brother.

"Liam, this isn't like you. What's going on? What happened?" his mother asks. "Is it her? Did you let some bitch sink their claws into you? Is that what this is?"

"What the fuck did you just say?" *This* comes from Gray as he pushes his way past me and into the room.

"Gray, stop. Leave it. This isn't our business." I pull on his arm.

"Anyone who talks shit about you, Lia, makes it my fucking business," he growls.

"Oh, great, you picked a good one there, son. She's probably fucking the whole team behind your back," his mother says, and my mouth hangs open in shock.

"Excuse me? You don't even know me. I work for

the team. I'm not sleeping with the players. You want your son to talk to you? Maybe you should have thought about that before you fucked his goddamn coach. What kind of mother does that? He's not ready to talk to you. You need to give him space. Then, maybe one day, you'll be lucky enough to earn his forgiveness. But, honestly, now that I've had the pleasure of meeting you myself, I wouldn't hold your breath. Liam is a good guy, which is an anomaly, considering he was raised by someone like you," I say, pointing back to Liam. I'm furious right now. How dare she come in here and cause problems for him. "You need to leave before I have security drag you out."

Liam steps up next to me. I didn't realize I'd moved and am now facing off with his mother. "Aliyah, shit. It's okay," he whispers so only I can hear him.

"No, it's not okay, Liam. You've worked fucking hard to overcome the image you only had because of something *she* did. I won't let her come in here and talk shit. I won't let her come back into your life just to mess it up."

"Okay, I think it's time you leave," my father's voice comes from behind me.

Gray and Luke close in on Liam's mother.

"Come on, we'll walk you out," Gray says to her in that tone that stresses it's not a suggestion but an order.

"Liam, you need to talk to me. We can fix this. I didn't mean to. It just happened," she says.

"You don't just accidentally fall onto my coach's dick, Mom," Liam tells her.

"That's why you beat the shit out of him?" my father asks, as Gray and Luke escort Liam's mother down the hall. The door shuts behind them, and then I'm left in the room with the two people I'd like to keep as far apart as possible. My father and the guy who, only minutes ago, was giving me a mind-blowing orgasm. "Is there a reason my daughter is in your hotel room, Mr. King?" Dad prompts, and I pray for the floor to swallow me whole.

Please, for the love of God, now would be a good time for an earthquake or some other form of natural disaster.

"We were working, going over the schedule for the next few weeks, Daddy," I say.

My father looks at me, and then at Liam. "Is that true?"

My eyes bore into Liam's profile. *Please just lie. Just go along with it.* That's the message I'm trying to get across, but I can tell by the look on his face that he's about to do the exact opposite.

"No, sir," Liam says.

"Then what exactly is my daughter doing in your room?" my dad repeats.

"We're dating, been dating for a few weeks now," Liam says.

I step in front of him, like I'm enough to protect him from whatever my father has in mind. "Daddy, I can explain…" I say.

"You can explain? How, Aliyah, with more lies?"

I flinch at my father's words. He hates being lied to, more than anything else in this world. And I just flat-out lied to his face.

"It's not her fault, sir. I asked her to keep things quiet between us. I wanted to make sure what we have is solid before we let the opinions of others affect our relationship."

"I appreciate that you're trying to cover for her right now, but there's no need. She's my daughter. She'll always be my daughter. You're the one who's disposable to me."

"Dad, no. He's not disposable. Not to me."

My father looks in my direction, and then above my head. "I'll be in my room. Aliyah, I expect to see you within the hour." Then he walks out. Just walks out the door. Without another word.

"Shit, what the fuck, Liam? Why would you tell him that?" I hiss the moment my dad is out of earshot.

"Because he's your father and I wasn't going to lie to him," he says simply. "I'm also getting tired of hiding this. I want you, Aliyah. I want the whole fucking world to know that you're mine."

"Oh, yeah, and when you end up at the bottom of an ocean wearing a pair of cement shoes, whose will I be then, Liam?" I yell. I'm frantic, my brain whirling, trying to come up with a way to fix this.

"That's not going to happen." Liam wraps an arm around me and pulls me into his chest.

I let myself sink into his touch. "I knew this had an expiration date. I *know* that. But I wasn't ready for it to end yet," I admit.

"Nothing is ending, princess. We're only just beginning. Our story doesn't have an end."

"Every story has an end, Liam," I say.

"Not ours." His lips press to the top of my head. "I like you way too much to let you go."

"I have to talk to my father, see if I can offer up my firstborn or something as leverage," I joke.

"You're not giving away our child," Liam says, sounding almost serious.

"Don't worry, I'm never having kids."

"What? Why?"

"Because some people aren't mother material. I don't have mothering genes." I shake my head and push out of his hold.

"Well, that's the bull-shittiest bullshit I've ever heard in my life," Liam says.

"Just... maybe lock your door. And if Gray comes looking for you, hide," I tell him as I walk out into the hallway.

It isn't long before I'm holding my breath while I knock on the door to my father's suite. "It's open," he calls out. I walk in and find him sitting by the window, nursing a glass of whiskey. "Come sit. Want a drink?" he asks me.

"No," I say, lowering myself down on the chair opposite him.

"How long has this thing between you and King been going on?"

*Right, straight to the point, I guess.*

"A few weeks," I tell him. "But you don't have to worry. It's not going to last."

"Why? Has he hurt you?"

"No, it's not going to last because it's me. I'm not

269

meant for what he wants. Liam wants a full-on, committed relationship with labels and all. He just doesn't know yet..."

"Doesn't know what?" my father asks, staring at me like he's trying to see past my physical person and into my soul.

"He doesn't know that I'm not lovable. He likes me, sure. But to have a long-term relationship, you need love, and that's not going to happen because it can't." I shrug.

"What the fuck? Why on God's earth would you think you're not lovable?" my father growls, and then downs his entire glass of whiskey.

We don't do this. We don't have heart-to-heart talks. I do that with Jonah, not anyone else. "Because that's what she said."

"Who?"

"My mother," I say and watch as my father's face hardens.

"Aliyah, your mother was a raging psychopath. You have no idea how much it haunts me to have to admit to myself that she did what she did to you, in my house, under my nose, and I was too blind to see it." He shakes his head.

"It wasn't your fault. I tried, Daddy. I tried really

hard to be good. But I kept messing up, and it's my fault that she left," I tell him.

"None of what happened is your fault, and she didn't leave, Aliyah. *I* got rid of her. No one will ever lay a hand on my daughter—on any of my children— and live to talk about it."

I blink. *Did he just admit to killing her?*

"But she was your wife," I gasp.

"She was insane is what she was. We had an arranged marriage. I never loved her, Aliyah. But you, I fucking loved you the minute you were born, more than I've ever loved anything in my life—don't tell your brothers that," he says, and I swear I see the makings of a grin before he locks it away. "She couldn't handle it. I knew she was jealous of you, but I didn't know the extent of it. I never would have let that happen to you had I known..."

"I always thought that you resented me because I made her leave," I admit for the first time.

"No. Never. I could never resent you. You're my daughter, Aliyah," he says.

"I'm sorry."

"Does he make you happy? I've noticed you've been different. Is it because of him?"

"He does," I say. "What are you going to do?"

"Nothing. I'm gonna do nothing. If King makes

you happy, then I'm happy. But the minute he causes a single tear to fall from your eyes, I'll make *his* bleed," my dad threatens.

"Really? You're not gonna make him disappear?"

"Not unless he gives me a reason," my dad says.

"Can you make sure the boys leave him alone too?" I know it's a stretch but I have to ask.

"*That*, I can't promise." Dad laughs.

"Great," I mumble under my breath.

"Aliyah, you are the most loveable person I've ever met. The fact you've been thinking you weren't all these years breaks my fucking heart."

"When I first started seeing Liam, the nightmares came back. *She* came back. I guess old wounds were just cut wide open."

"Do you need to go back to therapy? I can have someone do house calls."

"No, I just need time," I say, hoping it's the truth.

"You know that boy's already in love with you, don't you?" my dad tells me.

"No, he's not."

"He is. You'll see."

"How do you know?" I'm curious if it's really that obvious to everyone who isn't me.

"Because he knows I hold his whole career in my hands, and he still admitted to being with you. He was prepared to endure whatever fallout would come, because he wants to be with you regardless."

I stare at my dad. I have no idea if that's true. I can't imagine Liam being in love with me.

Lust? *Sure.* Borderline obsessed with my vagina? *Absolutely.* But love? *I don't know about that one.*

"You lied to me to keep him safe. That means you care about him too, because you've never lied to me before *that one* came along." Dad juts his chin towards the door, in the direction of Liam's room.

"You're right. I haven't." Because I never had something worth lying about, I guess.

# Chapter Twenty-Eight

I'm pacing up and down the room. I want to go and knock on her father's door and demand he give her back to me. Which is absurd. She's not a fucking possession, but she *is* mine. I don't give a fuck who tries to tell me otherwise.

I pick up my phone and send her a message.

ME:

Please tell me you're okay.

I throw the phone down on the bed when there's a knock at the door. Opening it, I find Aliyah standing on the other side. I take my time running my eyes up and down her body.

"Get in here." I grab her hand and pull her into the room, before shutting the door behind her. I wrap my arms around her waist and tuck her up against my chest. She's so much shorter than I am. Her head rests right under my chin. "Are you okay?" I ask while holding her tight.

"I'm okay. I had a good talk with my dad," she says.

"How likely am I to end up as fish food?"

"Not as likely as I would have thought," she tells me. "I don't get it. My whole life, he's warned me not to date. Even before you arrived, I made some off-handed comment about letting the whole team do what they wanted with me, and he threatened to paint the rink red with their blood."

"Wait... You said what now?" I pull back to look down at her.

"Relax. I was trying to make a point, stress that

they couldn't control what I did. Trust me, I'm usually a three-date minimum kind of girl."

"Three dates? It took me a gazillion."

"Ah, we've never officially even been on one," she says.

"I'll fix that. When we get home, I'm taking you out. Maybe I'll hire an air-writer to scrawl a message across the sky, so that all of Vancouver knows we're official."

"Do not do that. You still have my brothers to deal with. They're not going to be as understanding as my dad appears to be. Which I still find bizarre."

"What'd you talk about?"

Aliyah steps back to look at me. "My mother, mostly. I had no idea my parents had an arranged marriage."

"Some arranged marriages end up the happiest," I tell her.

Aliyah shakes her head. "For as long as I can remember, I've blamed myself for what happened between them. My father lost his wife, and it was all because of me. It was my fault."

"Why would it be your fault?" Shit, this is a topic I haven't been able to figure out how to approach. Ever since she sent and immediately *unsent* that message, I've been wanting to ask her.

"My mother tried to kill me. More than once," she says, looking down. "She would say that it was my fault, that I wasn't a lovable child." Aliyah touches the scar on her wrist. "This was her last attempt. That's what my nightmares are about, her slicing into my arm. It was the worst pain I've ever felt in my life, and there are some nights where I can still feel it. Like it's really happening."

I blink, pulling her in and holding her a little tighter. "I think you just might be the most loveable person I know, Aliyah Monroe," I tell her.

Do I love her? *I'm pretty certain I do.* Does it scare the fuck out of me? *Absolutely.* I'm just not sure I'm ready to tell her yet.

"That's exactly what my father said." She smiles up at me.

"Well, he's a smart man," I tell her, then add, "He did acquire the best player in the NHL after all."

Aliyah laughs. "He did. But if you tell Gray I said that, I'll deny it."

"Your secrets will always be safe with me, princess."

"Thank you."

"Can we go to bed now? I have four hours before I have to be up again." I lead her over to the bed.

"I should go back to my room," she says.

"Why?"

"So you can sleep."

"If you leave, I won't sleep a wink. Get in." I hold the blankets back, waiting for her to climb under them.

Aliyah pulls her dress over her head, reaches behind her back, and removes her bra. My eyes greedily take in the view she's giving me. As soon as she's in bed, I hop in next to her and cover us with the blankets. We're both silent as I pull her into me, resting her head on my shoulder as my hand runs up and down her back.

"Liam."

"Yeah."

"Don't ever risk your career for me again. I don't want to live with that kind of guilt," she says.

"Okay," I agree. What I don't tell her is that if it's a choice between her and hockey, I think I might just choose her. The fact she'd never ask me to choose, that just makes me love her all the more.

I love hockey. Live and breathe it. But Aliyah...? Whenever I'm with her, I feel like I've just scored the shootout goal in a Stanley Cup game. It's a high I've only ever felt on the ice, something I've been chasing my whole life. Now, I have it right here in my arms and I don't plan to ever let it go.

"Do you think we're a little insane? This is crazy fast. I don't even know what your favorite color is," she says.

"Brown, the color of your eyes. That's my favorite color," I tell her, and feel her body relax and her breathing even out. That's when I close my eyes and let sleep take over.

ME:

Are you going to watch the game?

ALIYAH:

Yes, my friends own a box. I'll be sitting up there with them.

ME:

Friends? What friends?

ALIYAH:

Just family friends. No one important.

Coach yells something in my direction, and I throw my phone into the locker before following the guys out through the tunnel. We're playing our first away game against the New York Bobcats. They're a good team, but we're better.

I skate out onto the ice for warm-ups and my eyes immediately search the box windows. I find Aliyah standing close to the glass, watching the rink. Then I spot the four guys surrounding her.

"Gray," I call out. He skates over, shaving the ice up before stopping in front of me. "Who is that with your sister?" I ask him.

Gray follows my line of sight, his glare landing on Aliyah right as one of the assholes wraps his arm around her shoulder. I see fucking red, and an insane amount of jealousy overwhelms me. I don't know what to do. I want to walk up there and rip the fucker's arm off his fucking body.

"The Valentino brothers, friends of the family," Gray says and then looks back at me. "Why?"

"No reason."

"They're not the sort of people you want to fuck with, King. Trust me on that," he says, and turns around to slap one of the pucks into the net.

I might not be able to go up there and rip that guy's arm off my girl right this second, but I can take my frustration, anger, whatever the fuck it is I'm feeling out on the ice. My stick rises up and I swing, hitting the puck as hard as I can. It doesn't go anywhere near the net. Instead, I send it flying right into the plexiglass. It bounces off and comes straight back at me. I lift my gloved hand and catch it before dropping the puck back to the ground and hitting it as hard as I can again.

"You good, King?" Jameson asks.

"Never been fucking better," I grind out while swinging at another puck on the ice.

"King, get over here now," one of the coaches, the one who still hates me, yells out from the bench.

I skate in his direction, really hoping he doesn't say anything to piss me the fuck off. Tonight is not the night. When I get over to the side, I find Mr. Monroe standing next to the coach with his hands in his pockets. "Coach. Sir." I nod to Aliyah's dad.

"King, what the fuck crawled up your ass?" the coach asks.

"Nothing, Coach," I say, avoiding looking behind me to where Aliyah is up in that box with her so-called *friends*.

"Give us a minute," Mr. Monroe says to my coach while gesturing for me to stay. Coach looks between us before he grumbles something and walks away. Mr. Monroe waits for him to be out of earshot, then turns back to me. "I respect that you didn't lie to me. But don't confuse that respect with approval. You want to date my daughter? Prove that you're worthy of it. Fuck up once, and I'll be waiting. Because if you hurt her, I won't just hurt you, King. I'll fucking destroy you."

"Yes, sir."

"That anger, that jealousy you're feeling right now. Deal with it on the ice and leave it there. A little word of advice? Aliyah is stubborn and strong willed. She doesn't take well to being told what to do."

"I'm aware," I say.

"Good. Now, do me a favor and win tonight. Those Valentinos are way too fucking cocky and put five hundred grand on the Bobcats to win."

My eyes bug out of my head. Who the fuck bets five hundred grand on a hockey game?

"I'll win because that's what you pay me to do, sir, and no other reason," I say. But what I'm really thinking is that *I'll do anything to make those assholes lose their money.*

# Chapter Twenty-Nine

I'm sitting next to Romeo Valentino, getting ready to watch the game. His family owns the box with probably the best view of the ice. My dad and his dad have been associates for as long as I can remember. They do business together. Romeo and I have always had a good friendship, although it's his wife who I adore the most. I just won't ever admit that to him.

"I really wish you would have brought Livvy tonight. How did I end up the only girl in here with you lot?" I ask him.

"Pfft, do you know how many women would kill to trade spots with you and be at the center of this Valentino sandwich?" This comes from Romeo's older brother, Matteo.

"Please do tell, Tao?" Matteo's wife Savvy enters the room, looking less than pleased by his comment.

"It's a hypothetical, babe. I'd never let it happen. But you can't deny the truth. I mean, look at me." He waves a hand down his body.

Savvy rolls her eyes at her husband's antics, and I just laugh and return my attention to the game. I'm used to their bullshit.

"Wanna make it interesting?" Luca, Romeo's twin, asks me.

"Make what interesting?" I say.

"The game? A shot for every time your brother gets knocked on his ass." He holds up a bottle of gin.

"Pass. And, really, have you not seen Gray play? He does the knocking," I scoff.

"You know you're rooting for the losing team anyway. The Bobcats are going to win," Luca says.

"In your dreams maybe." I chuckle, staring down at the ice as the players take position. Something's up with Liam. I watched him during warm-ups and he seemed off. Not just off. But *pissed* off. Then I watched again as Coach Malcom and my father had a talk with him. I want to go down there and find out what's wrong, but I know I can't.

"Does Grayson know?" Theo, the oldest of the four, steps up next to where I'm standing by the glass.

"Know what?"

"That you're with that fuckwit King?" he grunts.

"First of all, he's not a fuckwit. And second, no, he doesn't know, and we're going to keep it that way, aren't we, Theo?"

"Sure, it's none of my business. Not until he hurts you. Because you know damn well if that happens, I'll be the one holding him down while Gray skins him alive."

"You guys really need therapy, you know that?" I say.

"Finally! I've been telling them that my whole life," Savvy chimes in.

"Okay, shut it. The puck's about to drop," Matteo says.

We watch in silence as the puck drops and Liam

wins it over the Bobcats player. He passes it to Gray, who rushes down the ice. Liam and Luke are quick to take off after him. Liam shoulder-checks one of the Bobcats, knocking him into the boards as Gray passes him the puck. They're in the zone. He takes a swing and the puck hits the post and rebounds off the net.

Luke is right there to capture the puck and take it around the back, looking for an opening. Liam manages to push past the Bobcats player trying to block him. He's being more aggressive than usual. He takes the puck and then passes it to Gray, who slaps it towards the net. The Bobcats goalie catches it and effectively blocks the shot.

Liam loses the next puck drop, which I'm assuming he's not taking too well, considering he's just knocked the other guy on his ass. The Bobcats player gets up and throws his gloves off. Liam, though? He just stands there with a smile on his face. How do I know this? Because his smug-ass expression is plastered on the jumbotron.

"What the fuck is that dude's problem?" Romeo asks.

"No idea, Lia. It's your team. You got any clue?" Theo muses.

"Nope. Fresh out," I say. I don't look at them, my

attention solely focused on what's happening on the ice.

*Don't do it,* I silently plead, begging Liam not to do what I think he's about to do.

Those pleas go unanswered. As soon as the Bobcats player swings, Liam's gloves are off too. It's like he's been possessed. He's unstoppable. Coaches, refs, other players all try to get between the two of them. Liam won't relent though. He throws punch after punch after punch to the guy's head, before he gets him to the ground and then he's on top of him.

Gray and Luke step in and drag Liam back. When he's on his feet again and being pushed away from the player he just laid out on the ice, he looks up into the boxes. Directly at me. His eyes are wild, and the noise of the crowd is drowned out as I get lost in that intense blue color. He doesn't drop his gaze, not even when he's shoved into the penalty box. He just keeps staring up at me. Then the cameras follow his line of sight, and the next thing I know, my face is up on that damn screen.

"Guess lover boy ain't too happy about something." Theo shrugs.

"Shut it." I shove an elbow back, hitting his right arm.

"Ouch, who taught you how to hit like that, Lia?" he grunts.

"I have three brothers," I remind him.

"Speaking of, looks like *that* one might have just caught up on current affairs." Theo nods down to the rink, where Gray is looking from me, to Liam, and then back to me again.

"Great."

"This should make things interesting." Matteo chuckles.

I don't answer. I do, however, spend the rest of the game glued to the glass, watching as the Knights continue to play dirty. They win, though. And not just win but kick ass. Seven to two. The final buzzer just went off, announcing the end of the game.

I hold my breath as Gray skates over to Liam. They exchange a few words, and then before I know it, Gray gut-checks Liam, right where I know there's no protective padding. I run from the box, fully intending to rush out on that ice to stop my brother from killing my boyfriend. By the time I make it to the tunnel, the guys are walking down together with my father right behind them.

I march up to my brother and push at his chest. "You asshole," I scream. Gray grabs hold of my wrist, preventing me from hitting him again. "Let me go," I seethe.

"Let her fucking go right now," Liam growls—yes, growls. He steps in front of me, forcing my brother to drop my wrist.

"You seriously want to go again, asshole?" Gray says.

"If you touch her like that, I'll fucking kill you. I don't care who the fuck you think you are," Liam says, not backing down one bit.

"Enough. Grayson, locker room now," Dad tells him.

"Pops, you can't seriously be okay with this. The fucker's not even close to being good enough for her." Gray throws an arm in Liam's direction.

"You're right. He's not. The fact is no one is. But she's happy, and that's what matters, son. Now step aside before I let your sister rip off your balls."

"This is bullshit," Gray mumbles under his breath before aiming his glare at Liam. "Watch your back, King, 'cause I sure as shit won't be watching it no more." Then he shoves past him, continuing down the tunnel towards the locker room.

"Good game," my dad says, turns on his heel, and follows my brother.

Liam spins around on me, his face hard, his teeth grinding together. Great, now he's pissed off at me.

"What the hell is your problem?" I ask him, folding my arms over my chest.

"Nothing. Go back to the box with your *friends*," he says, putting extra emphasis on the last word.

"You know what? Fuck you, Liam King. I will go back to my friends. At least they're not immature asshats with a stadium-size chip on their shoulders," I yell at him.

"Do whatever you want. You and I both know you'll be knocking on my door later, begging my cock to fill that sweet little cunt of yours," he says so low that I barely hear the words. I do hear them though.

"You're dreaming if you think that's ever going to happen again." I laugh. "Argh, I knew I should have stayed away from you and that disease-riddled cock of yours."

"Diseased? Really, Aliyah? Might want to drop by the clinic then, considering you've been riding it nonstop for the last three weeks." Liam smirks. "You know there's a closet just down the hall there. We could go inside and angry-fuck the shit out of each other. It'd be hot." His voice does that thing where it drops an octave.

"You're serious." My eyes widen.

"As a heart attack. You're fucking hot when you're mad."

I must be insane, because no less than a second ago, I wanted to kill him myself. And now, I just want to take the bastard up on his offer.

*What the hell is wrong with me?*

# Chapter Thirty

Looking at Aliyah right now, it's hard to even remember what we're fighting about. I don't give her time to decide. Taking hold of her hand, I drag her into the closet. I saw an equipment manager coming out of here earlier and immediately tucked the idea of fucking Aliyah against a pile of hockey equipment into the back of my mind. Spinning her around, I press the front of her body up against the door. I always find her tiny, but with the extra height my skates are adding, she's even fucking smaller than usual.

My hand wraps around her front, inching underneath her jersey. "I fucking hate that you're wearing another man's name on your back," I tell her.

"It's my brother's name, Liam, not another man's."

"It should be mine. You should be wearing my name, only my name." I cup her breasts and tweak her nipples through the lace of her bra.

"Maybe if you weren't such an ass, I would wear your name," she says. I chuckle as my mouth meets her neck. Aliyah tilts her head to the side, giving me full access to her skin. "Why did you fight that guy?"

"I was pissed off, and he was there," I tell her.

"Why are you so pissed?" She pushes her ass back into me. I'm still in full uniform. Ever wear a cup with a raging boner? Yeah, it's not fun.

I step back and undo my pants, letting them drop to the ground before removing my cup and my lucky underwear. "I was irrationally jealous. I've never been jealous before, Aliyah. I don't fucking like it."

"You were jealous? Of what?" She turns her head to glance at me from over her shoulder.

"My girlfriend was sitting in a box with another man's arm around her," I grit out while fisting my cock.

"Your girlfriend, huh? Do I know her? How would she feel about you being in here with me right now?" She smirks.

"Cute." I step forward again, press up against her, and reach around her waist, looking for the zipper and button on her jeans. Then I slide the fabric down her legs. She kicks off her shoes and steps out of her pants and underwear. Spinning her around, I cup her ass and she jumps up, wrapping her legs around me. "My girlfriend thinks she's a comedian."

"Better than being a babysitter to a hockey player who can't seem to stay out of trouble," she counters. My lips slam down on hers, hungry for her taste. She moves her hips, pushing her wet pussy up and down my cock.

"Fuck, I don't have a condom," I curse under my breath.

"I don't care. I'm on the pill."

"What about all those diseases you keep claiming

I have?" I raise an eyebrow at her as my bare cock slides into her opening.

"Fuck! Ah, I don't know what you're talking about. I've never said any such thing," she hisses.

I prop her up against the wall so I have the leverage to fuck her the way I like. Pulling back, I thrust forward, hard, over and over again. Aliyah screams out as her legs tighten and her pussy convulses around my cock.

"Fuck, I love hearing you scream like that," I tell her, before covering her mouth with my own and swallowing the rest of her sounds.

As soon as she comes down from her orgasm, I pull out and my cock squirts all over the outside of her pussy. I run my fingertips through my cum, massaging it into her skin. "Tell me again how you're not my girlfriend?" I ask her.

"Shut up. Nobody likes a know-it-all, Liam."

I laugh. I can't help it. Whatever we were arguing about or fighting over is long forgotten as we both put our clothes back on.

"How hurt are you? Gray got you good," Aliyah says, looking at the bruise covering the left side of my temple.

"I'm fine, and what he got was lucky," I grumble.

"Sure he did." Aliyah smiles. "I don't like that you're fighting because of me."

"I've never had a better reason to fight," I tell her.

I don't know how I let Aliyah talk me into coming here. Actually I do. She said she was going with or without me, and I wanted to be with her. That's how I ended up at a club, sitting in a booth with a bunch of people I don't know, and her brother who isn't shy about hiding his true feelings for me. Luke at least seems to be playing Switzerland and is refusing to get between us, while Aliyah is sitting next to me, chatting away with one of the wives who came with the four guys from the box. They've all introduced themselves—all also sent me glares like they're waiting to cut my fucking head off.

I'm not stupid. I know who these guys are. After Gray mentioned how they're not people to mess with, I Googled them. I knew I'd heard the name Valentino before. Once I figured out why, it didn't surprise me that Aliyah's family is friends with them.

"I'm going to dance," she announces. I go to

stand, looking to follow her out of the booth, when she pushes me back down. "I'll be with Livvy. You don't have to come."

"But what if I wanna dance with you?" I pout.

"You can. Later. When we're naked," she whispers in my ear before walking away laughing. Fuck me, now I'm stuck sitting here, with her grumbling brother, while I've got a fucking hard-on and images of her dancing naked in my head.

"You know she'll get bored of you, right?" Gray says.

I look over at him. "That's not possible. Unlike some of us, I'm not fucking boring." I smirk.

"Well, damn, he's got you there, Gray," one of the Valentino brothers hollers out. I don't remember who's who. I don't really care to learn their names either.

"Fuck off, Matteo," Gray says and drags his phone out of his pocket. He taps on the screen before turning the device over to me.

"Who is this?" he asks, pointing at his phone.

There's a picture of that little girl and her mom pulled up on his screen. "A kid from that youth league appearance your sister made me do," I tell him.

"What's her name?"

I look at him, and my brows draw down. She was a sweet kid, a tough-as-shit little girl who's going to run circles around all the boys her age. "Why? What do you want with her? She's just a fucking kid, Grayson," I snap.

"What's her name?" he asks again.

"I don't know. Graycee or something like that." I shrug.

"Graycee... and is that her mother? The woman behind her?"

"Yeah."

Grayson curses under his breath, then stands, pockets his phone, and walks away without another word.

"Well, fuck me. Talk about being knocked for six by a blast from the past." Matteo lets out a low whistle. Everyone at the table turns to him. No one asks but the question is there, thick in the air. "That was Kathryn Kilgor. Come on, you didn't recognize her?"

"Who the fuck is Kathryn Kilgor?" the Valentino twins ask at the same time.

"You two are too young to remember, but back in college, Gray was obsessed with the girl, barely let her out of his sight. When she disappeared, I assumed he offed her because it was like she never existed. He flipped a switch and, poof, it was like *Kathryn who?*"

"I remember her," Theo says.

Luke and I share a look before we both get up and walk in the direction Gray stormed off towards. I might not know the guy that well yet, but we are friends—well, if you look past his obvious hatred for me right now, that is.

"Hold up. Let me get Aliyah," I tell Luke.

"You get that Monroe. I'll go find the other one and make sure he doesn't do something stupid."

I nod and we part ways. It only takes me a second to find Aliyah on the dance floor. It's not hard. She's the fucking hottest chick here. She's like a beacon. Everyone with a dick is watching her sway those hips. I walk up behind her, wrapping an arm around the front of her body, across her shoulders, and I pull her into me.

"We need to go. Something is off with your brother," I tell her.

Aliyah spins around in my arms and looks up at me. "He just found out his teammate is screwing his little sister. I think he's going to need time, Liam," she says, locking her hands around the back of my neck.

Her body doesn't stop moving. My palms slide

down, stopping at the curve of her ass. "No, it's something else. He was asking about the girl from that little league stunt we did. The kid and her mother."

"Huh, I thought I recognized the mother from somewhere but I couldn't remember where," she says.

"Someone mentioned the name Kathryn," I tell her, and her eyes widen with recognition.

"Oh, shit. This isn't good. Come on, we gotta go. Why didn't you say we had to go?" she asks.

"Pretty sure that's what I started with."

"Yeah, but I thought that was just your way of trying to get me into your bed."

"There's never a second that I'm not thinking of ways to get you back into my bed, princess." I thread my fingers with hers, waiting for her to say goodbye to her friend, and then I lead her out of the club.

# Chapter Thirty-One

I was young but I remember Gray bringing Kathryn home for the holidays one year. It's the only time he's ever brought a girl over to meet the family, and the only time we ever saw her. Then, like many uncomfortable topics in my household, she was never spoken of again.

I don't know what is going on with Gray, or why he's asking about her and her daughter now—although there's also this feeling in the pit of my stomach that tells me I do know. I just really hope for everyone's sake, especially Kathryn's, that what I'm thinking isn't true. The timeline makes sense, but I really don't think Gray would handle that kind of betrayal from anyone.

When we get back to the hotel, I head straight to my brother's suite. "Let me talk to him. I'll meet you in your room when I'm done," I tell Liam.

"Are you sure?" He looks to the door.

"Liam, he's my brother. He's not going to do anything to me," I say.

"Okay, yeah. Call me if you need anything." He leans down and briefly kisses me.

I pull back, wait for Liam to walk away, and knock on my brother's door. "Gray, open up," I yell out. He might not open up to many people when he's in a mood, but I know my brother, and he's never *not* going to open his door for me.

Sure enough, a few seconds later, the door swings open and Gray sticks his head out, looking up and down the hallways. "Did the neanderthal actually let you out of his grasp?" he asks me.

"Shut up, and don't call him that. He's your

friend," I remind my brother, walking past his bulky frame to get into his room.

"No, he's not. A friend wouldn't bang my sister behind my back."

"Would you rather he do it in front of you? Actually, don't answer that. That came out wrong." I shake my head. "It doesn't matter. I'm not here to talk about Liam."

"Are you okay? What's wrong?"

I walk farther into the room and notice that all Gray's shit is out and he's packing up. We don't leave for another day. The team all voted to spend their day off in New York before we fly back to Vancouver. "Why are you packing already?"

"I booked my own flight. I gotta go home early."

"Does this need to get home early have anything to do with Kathryn?" I ask him.

Gray stiffens, but quickly recovers. "Who?"

"Don't play dumb. You know who. Kathryn, the girl you brought home that one time when you were in college. The same woman in that picture that you took from Dad's office. The one with the little girl Liam signed a puck for."

"This really doesn't concern you, Lia."

"You know... you, Vinny, and Jonah always overreact and think you need to protect me. I get it now.

I've never had a reason to want to protect any of you before, because I didn't think anyone was capable of hurting you. But she did. She's hurt you and, honestly, I want to go and rip her hair out of her head for even daring."

"Lia, I'm telling you it's nothing. I want you to drop it," Gray says.

"Do you think she's yours? The little girl? I couldn't put my finger on it, but there was something about her..." I say.

"No, I don't think she's mine," he says. "Lia, listen to me. You want me to stay out of your... whatever it is you have going on with King? Then stay out of this. It doesn't concern you."

"It's a *relationship*. You can say the word, Gray. It won't kill you."

"No, but you might." He smiles.

"Maybe." I sit down on one of the sofas. "Are you really okay?"

"Yes, I appreciate your concern, Lia. I do. But you're my little sister. I'm the protector here, not you."

"I can protect you too, you know."

"I don't doubt it, and if ever I need a bodyguard, you'll be the first person I call." He smirks.

I smile, knowing he's full of shit, but I'll take it. "What are you going to do?"

"I'm going to go coach youth league."

"Liam said that Matteo told everyone he thought you killed Kathryn and that's why she disappeared."

Gray laughs. "Matteo is a fucking idiot." He shakes his head. "She left because she didn't like the kind of life our family leads."

"You're a hockey player," I remind him. We fall into silence, as Gray continues to pack his bag, before I finally break it again. "Can you do something for me?"

"Anything," he says.

"Can you please not hit my boyfriend?"

"Anything but that, Lia." His smirk turns into a full-on grin.

"Please, Gray, I really like him and he makes me feel like I matter," I say.

Gray's eyebrows pull down in the center. "Aliyah, you have mattered since the day you were born," he tells me.

"Not to everyone." I shake my head.

"To everyone who counts."

"Either way, I want to keep him. Don't scare him off, please."

"If he was going to run, he would have done it

already. Unfortunately, the fucker doesn't scare that easily—either that or he's just too fucking stupid," Gray scoffs.

"He's not. Stubborn as hell, but not stupid."

"You really like him, huh?"

I nod my head.

"Boyfriend?" He says the word like it's painful.

"Yes, but don't tell him I called him that. I'm holding out on the whole commitment thing a bit longer. He wanted to put a label on us from the start, and I think he's out of his mind. But right now, things are good. Well, apart from my brother hitting him with a damn hockey stick."

"You're happy?"

"Extremely." I smile.

"Don't worry, Dad already told us all we aren't allowed to cause any real damage to the fucker."

"Well, Daddy did pay a lot of money for him to play on the team."

"No, it's because he said you deserve to be happy and he's right. You do deserve happiness, Lia. Just wish it was with someone who wasn't on my fucking team."

"Okay, well, good talk, bro." I stand from the sofa. "Please try to keep a level head. Whatever you're going to do, make sure it's something you can live with afterwards."

Gray nods his head silently. I can see the turmoil in his eyes. It's breaking my heart, and right now I hate this Kathryn woman for putting that look on my brother's face.

I lean up and kiss his cheek. "You are not just your family, Gray. You are Grayson fucking Monroe, one of the NHL's best players. You're going to end up in the hall of fame. You're kind and loyal, and I couldn't ask for a better brother. Don't let anyone make you feel like you're not worth it," I tell him.

"Right back at ya, sis," he says.

I smile and leave him to his packing. As I'm walking up the hall to Liam's room, I pull out my phone and send Vinny a text.

ME:

> Gray is coming back early. Make sure he doesn't do anything life-alteringly stupid.

VINNY:

> It's Gray. He's always doing something life-alteringly stupid.

ME:

> This is true. But he's bent up about Kathryn resurfacing. With a kid.

The ringtone on my phone blasts through the otherwise quiet hallway. "Hey."

"Is it his kid?" Vinny asks me.

"He says no. But I'm not convinced."

"Where is he now? And where the fuck did she turn up?"

"He's in his hotel room packing, and apparently Kathryn's the mother of a girl from the youth league that Liam and I visited a few weeks back. Gray saw her in the newspaper clipping." When I turn the corner, I find Liam standing in the hallway, waiting for me. Our eyes meet. "Vinny, I gotta go. Just keep an eye on him."

"Wait. Hold up. What's this shit Dad's saying about you having a boyfriend?" Vinny asks.

I roll my eyes. "Bye, Vinny. Talk later." I hang up and a message pops up right away.

VINNY:

This conversation isn't over, Lia.

I put my phone back in my purse and approach Liam. "Did you lose your room key?"

"No, I was waiting for you," he says.

"Out in the hall? Why?"

"No idea." He shrugs.

"Well, do you think we can go in there now?" I point to the door behind him.

Liam smirks. "Or I could fuck you up against that wall over there and add exhibitionism to our list."

"Our list?"

"Our sex list."

"We don't have a sex list." I laugh.

"Oh, but we do. It's up here." He taps a finger against his head. "Every single time, place, position, number of orgasms. It's the list."

"You're insane. And, no, we are not adding exhibitionism to that list."

"Yet. One day, you'll let me." He turns and opens the door.

"Never. That's not happening, Liam King."

"You said that about letting me fuck you, and you let that happen a lot now. So you should know that *never* does not mean never. It just means until you change your mind."

# Chapter Thirty-Two

ALIYAH:

Score big on the ice and you might just score when you get off the ice too.

I'm in the locker room, getting a filthy look from the coach, probably because I'm not supposed to be on my phone during these team pep talks. I couldn't care less, though. I'm not ignoring my girlfriend.

ME:

> I score every night you're in my bed. Which is every night. You really should just move in already.

Over the last two months, our relationship has been great. There have been fights, disagreements, and lots of make-up sex afterwards. But the majority of the time, we're so fucking good it's unbelievable. I don't know how I felt the littlest bit of joy before Aliyah was around. I don't think I ever did.

"King, whenever you're ready, we're waiting for you," Coach yells out.

"Sorry, Coach." I throw my phone into the locker behind me. Tonight, we're at home, playing against the Dallas Dolphins. They're a shit team and winning isn't even a question in this case. I don't know what the coach is all up in arms about.

"All right, hit the tunnel. And remember, if you lose tonight, you'll all be the laughingstock of the league," Coach calls after us.

"Try not to fuck up, King," Gray says as he walks in front of me.

"I don't lose," I tell him.

"What was up with that game against Philly two nights ago?" he fires back.

He's referring to the game we lost by one point. "That was you being a fucking asshole and spending half the game in the penalty box," I say.

I don't know what's going on with him. I know Aliyah is worried about her brother, but he's keeping whatever the fuck his issue is close to his chest. Choosing to take it out on the opposing players. And me, on the ice. I know he's purposely letting me get hit more often than I should be. He doesn't even try to stop them half the time. Not that I care. I can handle being shoved into the boards a few times a night.

"So what you're saying is you can't win without me. Got it." Gray shrugs.

I don't respond. Instead, I skate out onto the rink. The crowd is loud tonight, and as I look up into the stands, I see more people wearing my number. More Knights fans have started embracing me, claiming me as one of their own. But they're not who I'm looking for. I glance over to the penalty box and find her. Aliyah, sitting right next to it, with her friends. I skate over to that side of the ice, skidding to a stop just before the boards.

"Show off." Aliyah laughs.

"Stand up and turn around," I tell her.

"No," she yells back. She's wearing a Knights jersey but there's no number on the front of it, so I can't be sure if it's mine or not.

"Aliyah, don't make me jump over this wall," I warn.

She sighs and pushes to her feet. When she finally turns around, albeit reluctantly, I see my name scrawled across her back.

"Nice shirt." I wink at her before pivoting on a skate and heading in the opposite direction to where everyone is warming up.

Two minutes left on the clock during the third period and we're up by five. There's no doubt who's taking this game, not that there ever really was. The ref drops the puck and I win, slapping it over to where Gray is supposed to be, except he's not there. No, his gloves and stick are in clear view but not him.

Because he's on top of some poor fucker who must have looked at him the wrong way.

Four Dallas players then start in on Gray. Yeah, fuck that. By the time I reach them, Luke already has one of them pulled off Gray and is throwing fists with the fucker. I join the chaos. I might not be best buddies with the guy, but he's still my fucking team-mate. And I'm not going to sit around and let anyone beat on one of my teammates.

One on one, that's fine. But four on one?
Fuck no.

I get hit on the head with something solid. When I look up, I realize it was a stick. Some dirty fucker just hit me over the head with a stick. I see red. Fisting his shirt, I pull my right arm back and land him square in the jaw. His head tips to the side and blood splatters out of his mouth. By the time the refs are able to lock it down, we have four players in the Sin Bin and Dallas has three. How the fuck one of their players got off, I have no idea.

I look to where Aliyah should be, right next to me as I sit in this damn box. She's not here. She's gone. "She doesn't like blood. Has a thing about seeing blood on the ice," Gray says. "That's why she leaves whenever a fight breaks out or shit like that."

"She loves hockey though," I say.

"She does, just not the fighting part of it. She's petrified of skates—well, the blades anyway."

"Understandable." I nod. I get why she doesn't like blood or sharp objects. Her own mother sliced her wrist open when she was just a little kid.

"What do you mean by that?" Gray asks me.

"Just with what she's been through, I get why she doesn't like blades or blood."

"She told you?" He tilts his head to the side, like he's trying to figure something out. I nod my head. "Shit. She doesn't talk about that. With anyone," he says more to himself.

I feel a sense of pride that she feels comfortable enough with me, safe enough with me to talk about that time of her life.

I'm out of the stadium as quickly as I can be when the game finishes. I left before the interviews were over. They can send me a fine for skipping out early. I don't give a fuck. I need to make sure my girl is okay. She sent me a message saying she had a headache so she went home early and that she'd see me tomorrow. Sometimes I wonder if she knows who she's dating. As if I'd ever not turn up to see her...

I let myself into her apartment and look up at the camera that sits above her door. I know her father monitors who comes and goes. Aliyah hates it, but I like it. You can never be too safe, right?

"Babe, you here?" I call out. The apartment is dark, silent, so I make my way into her bedroom and find her curled up on the bed.

She opens her eyes when she hears me enter. "Liam, I thought we were meeting up tomorrow," she says.

I toe off my shoes and pull my shirt over my head. Leaving my sweats on, I climb into the bed, place her head on my chest, and wrap my arms around her. "Why didn't you tell me that the blood bothers you?" I ask her.

"Because it's stupid. We don't need to make a big deal about it," she says.

"It's not a big deal, but I want to know. I want all of it, Aliyah. The good, bad, ugly—not that it's possible for you to have an ugly anything."

"Nice save." She laughs.

"I thought so." I shrug a shoulder.

"I don't like blood, and I don't like blades. But mostly I don't like seeing you get hurt. I know it's your job and you love it, but I feel every hit, every body-check. Not physically obviously. But when you hurt, I hurt," she says.

"So I guess that means you kinda like me, then, huh?"

She slaps a hand against my chest. "Well, you're so insistent that you're my boyfriend and all, I figure I should learn to like you. Some would call it *Stockholm*."

"Do you remember the first day we met?" I ask her.

"How could I forget? You came running out of the shower naked."

"You enjoyed the show."

"You killed a spider with a hockey stick while you were naked. It was hilarious."

"I was shit scared of that damned spider. I killed it for you, because when I looked at you and saw the fear in your eyes, I wanted to erase it. It forced me to face my own fears."

"I know. Your hands were shaking."

"Spiders are fucked-up creatures. I don't like 'em." I run my hand up and down her arm. "The point is, whatever your fears are, I want to conquer them with you."

"Or... I can just go on about my life ignoring and avoiding them?" she says.

"There is that too," I say. "Did you have fun with your friends tonight?" I ask, changing the subject.

"They want to have dinner."

"Okay."

"With you," she clarifies.

"Okay, and you don't want to?"

"I don't want them to grill you, which I know they will."

I laugh. "Babe, I survived your father and all three of your brothers. I think I can handle your friends. Arrange the dinner."

"I will, but don't say I didn't warn you," she huffs.

# Chapter Thirty-Three

Liam pulls into the lot at the Castle. I've been so busy texting back and forth with the girls—mostly threatening them with bodily harm if they embarrass me tonight at the dinner we've planned for them to officially meet Liam—I didn't notice where he was headed.

"Why are you here?" I ask him.

"Come on," he says, shutting off the engine and getting out of the car.

"Liam, the stadium's not even open. No one's here," I say, unfastening my seat belt and following him anyway.

Liam holds up a set of keys. "Just so happens I have the keys to *the castle*, princess."

"How'd you get those?"

"Aliyah, I'm King. The King. Why wouldn't I have keys?" he deadpans.

I can't help but laugh at his corniness. "I'm set to inherit this *castle* and I don't even have keys," I remind him.

"Maybe I'm just on better terms with the owner than you are."

"Doubtful." I smile.

Liam takes my hand in his and leads me over to the door. He unlocks it, gets to the wall, and freezes. "Shit, no one told me the code for this thing," he says.

"But aren't you supposed to be the *King of the Castle*?"

"Not funny. Call your dad and ask him for the code before his army comes in, guns blazing, thinking we're breaking into the joint."

"Move over." I enter the alarm code into the wall panel, and the high-pitched beeping stops.

"You knew that was gonna happen and you didn't warn me," he says.

"I like watching you squirm." I laugh. "Also, my dad's *army* would only shoot you, not me." I shrug.

"Well, that's comforting to know." He entwines his fingers with mine. "Come on."

When he leads me out to the ice, I realize that all the lights are already on. "What are we doing here?" I ask him.

"Skating."

"You spent three hours on this same ice already today. Do you really need to skate more?"

"Yes, and I'm not skating alone, Aliyah, because you're skating with me," he says.

I back up, letting go of his hand. "No, I'm not," I say, shaking my head at him.

"Yes, you are. We're facing fears together, remember?"

"No, what I remember was agreeing to ignore and avoid them at all costs." No way am I getting on that ice in a pair of skates. Nope, not happening. I've gone my whole life without being able to skate. I think I can go the rest of my life just fine without it too.

"Aliyah, you own a stadium. You own a hockey team. You can't be scared of skating."

"Correction, *my dad* owns this place and the team. Not me. I'm good. I'll just sit here and watch you skate," I say, planting my butt on one of the chairs.

Liam kneels down in front of me and takes hold of my hands. "Aliyah, do you really think I'd ever let anything happen to you? I need you to trust me. I'll catch you if it looks like you're going to fall. I won't let you fall," he says.

"It's not falling I'm afraid of," I tell him.

"The blades are on your feet. They're not going to cut you."

"I've seen plenty of people get cut from the blades." I lift a questioning brow.

"In hockey, yeah, but we're skating, not playing hockey. And it's just the two of us here. No one else, babe. Please, just let me show you."

"Show me what?"

"How fun it is to glide along that ice." He smiles at me.

It's that smile that wins me over. "Promise you won't let me fall?"

"Promise."

"What if *you* fall?" I ask.

Liam gives me that cocky look of his, the one that says: *Do you even know who I am?* "Babe, I think I can manage to stay upright on a pair of skates."

"I've seen you fall," I remind him.

"Again, in hockey, not just skating around the rink. We'll go slow."

"Okay. But if I do this, you have to take me to Cal's Diner afterwards for burgers."

"Deal." He smiles again and drops the bag he had slung up on his shoulder. He opens it and pulls out a brand-new set of white skates and a pair of socks.

I slip off the boots I was wearing and take the proffered socks from him. I keep the ones I already had on and place the new ones over the top. A little extra warmth won't hurt in this cold-ass stadium. I then squeeze my feet into the skates.

"How did you know what size to get me?" I ask him when I discover they fit perfectly.

"You're my girlfriend. I know your shoe size," he says, as if it's really that easy.

"I don't think that's in the boyfriend/girlfriend handbook," I tell him.

"There's a handbook?" He looks up at me with genuine shock on his face. "How do I get a copy?

That would have been useful a few months back..." he says the last part more to himself.

"Why? Need some pointers?"

Liam shakes his head. "I think you talk more smack than any hockey player I've ever faced off against." He laughs.

"It's a gift."

Liam finishes lacing up his skates and stands, holding his hands out for me. Sucking in a big breath of air, I accept his help and climb to my feet. My legs wobble a little but not too much.

"Do not let me go," I tell him. Liam shrugs, wraps his arms around my waist, and lifts my feet right up off the floor. I lock my hands behind his neck and hold on for dear life. "What are you doing? Stop! Put me down!" I yell as he starts walking. He steps out onto the ice and glides us into the center of the rink, right on top of the Knights' emblem.

"Okay," he says, lowering my feet to the ground or, in this case, the ice. He doesn't let go of me though.

I struggle to hold myself upright. I have no idea how these guys make this look easy. It's *not* freaking easy. My feet are sliding around like a baby deer learning to walk, and if it weren't for Liam holding me upright, I would be flat on my face.

"Stop. You need to relax. Stop moving your feet," he tells me.

"How? I'm standing on ice, Liam. *Ice.* They won't stay still!" I scream at him.

"Okay, if you want to move, let's move," he says, and then proceeds to skate backwards while dragging me along for the ride.

"Okay, okay, I'll stop!" I yell out. I'm absolutely petrified right now. I can't believe this is happening. How am I in the middle of an ice rink?

Liam stops, and I try to keep my feet still and my body upright. My fingers are digging into his arms so hard I wouldn't be surprised if I'm drawing blood. "That's it. You're getting it. Just relax and know that I have you. I'm not going to let you fall, Aliyah, not ever."

What I don't tell him is he's too late. I've already fallen, so freaking hard. I've fallen for *him.* I'm not ready to tell him that though. A huge part of me still thinks he's going to see me for who I am, realize that I'm not worthy of him. Also, he's full of shit right now, because I don't have this. Not even close.

"I want you to push outwards with your feet. Move with me," he says.

"I can't."

"You can. Stop looking down and look at me.

Look at my face, princess. Dance with me," he says with that magical grin of his.

"Oh, so now you're a figure skater too?" I joke. I shouldn't have said it. I realize that now. Because Liam bends down, picks me up under my thighs so my legs wrap around his waist, and then he's off, skating down the ice and spinning. "Oh my god!" I yell out. "Okay, I get it! You can skate. Stop."

He doesn't stop, but he does slow up a bit. He also doesn't put me down. "You know what? I think this is better anyway. I prefer having you in my arms. Whenever we go skating together, I'll just carry you," he says.

"Whenever? This is a one-off, isn't it?"

"Aliyah, you own an ice rink."

"Again, I don't own shit. My dad does."

"Same thing. We're going to have many skating dates in our future," he says.

"This is a date?" I screw up my face. "Can't you just take me out to the movies or something normal?"

"Skating is normal," he says, allowing my body to slide down his until I'm back on my feet.

This time, when I stand, Liam lowers his mouth to mine. His arms hold tight around my waist as he pushes his tongue past my lips. I let myself get lost in his kiss—well, let's be honest. I don't think I have any other option but to get lost in his kiss. It happens every time he kisses me. I thought this feeling would wear off over time, but I've kissed this guy every day for the last few months, and this feeling is still just as strong as it was the first time.

Liam pulls away. "You're doing it, babe. You're skating," he tells me.

I look down at my feet, which are slowly moving along the ice in sync with his. "Oh my god, I'm skating!" I say excitedly, and then my feet decide to wobble and give out from under me. I don't fall though. Because, just like he promised, Liam holds firm, keeping my body upright.

"You're so fucking cute," he says, kissing me on my nose and then again on my lips.

# Chapter Thirty-Four

I should have taken Aliyah's warning about her friends more seriously. Fuck me, I'd rather go a round with all of her crazy-as-fuck brothers than be drilled by these girls. The minute I sat down, the questions started coming. Aliyah has been giving her friends death glares, which they all ignore.

"So what are your plans with Aliyah long-term? Can we expect wedding bells anytime soon?" her friend Charlie asks.

"Don't answer that," Aliyah says to me, and then turns to her friend. "Charlie, seriously, enough."

"What? I just want to know what his intentions are and all," the girl says with a smile. "Do you have four friends, Liam?" Amanda asks me.

I furrow my brows. "Why?" I'm not sure where she's going with this question.

"Well, if you're gonna marry our girl here, we're all in the bridal party, which means you need to match the number. Four of us, four of them," she says.

I have no idea what the fuck she's talking about. "We're eloping," I tell her, because if planning a wedding involves all of Aliyah's friends, then fuck that. I'll just whisk her off somewhere quiet instead.

"No, we're not. And we are not getting married," Aliyah says.

"Yet," I clarify.

"*Aw*, look! He so wants to put a ring on it," Aliyah's friend Nicole says.

"Oh my god! Stop, all of you. Leave the guy alone," Aliyah hisses at them.

"It's okay. I can handle it," I tell her.

"You shouldn't have to. They're being ridiculous. I swear they are not usually this insane," Aliyah says to me.

"Don't listen to her. They are always fucking insane," a deep voice calls out from the other side of the table. I whip my head around to find four men dressed in well-fitted suits.

"Why are you here?" Aliyah and Charlie ask at the same time.

"We gotta go. Breach on the home front," one of them says. Charlie immediately stands and picks up her bag.

"Wait... What do you mean? What's going on?" Aliyah asks.

"You too. Let's go," the guy says to her. Aliyah rummages through her bag.

"What's wrong?" I ask her.

"My phone, I need my phone," she says, finally finding it. She presses some buttons and puts the phone to her ear. "Gray, what's happening?" I don't hear what her brother says on the other line, but Aliyah's eyes widen as she looks up at me. "Yes, he's with me." A few seconds later, she cuts the call and stands. "We have to go to my father's house," Aliyah tells me. The panic is gone from her voice and a more robotic version of Aliyah takes over. A version I've never seen before.

I stand from my chair, because she's not going anywhere without me and honestly she's freaking me the fuck out right now, then hold out a hand. "Come on, I'll take you."

The four men step in front of us. "Liam, these are Charlie's brothers. Ignore them," Aliyah says.

"We have four cars that will follow you—two from the front and two from the back. Do not try to lose 'em," one of the brothers says before they all turn and walk away with Charlie sandwiched between them.

Once we're in the car, I take hold of Aliyah's hand. If I don't, I'm worried she'll chew her whole nail off. "What's going on?" I ask her.

"I'm sorry. I shouldn't have let you get involved with me. But you are, and now I have to drag you along with this mess," she says.

"Whatever's happening, it's going to be fine. And you could drag me through the pits of hell and I'd still be one hundred percent in it with you," I tell her.

"A few warehouses were blown up tonight. It's a direct attack on my family and Charlie's, and until they narrow down the threat and eliminate it, we're going to be kept under lock and key," she says.

I look over at her. "How often does this happen to you?"

"A few times over the years. It's usually resolved really quickly though," she says. "On the bright side, Gray was the one who insisted I bring you. He said that because everyone knows we're dating, you'd be a target too." She smiles.

"You're happy I'm a target in some *Godfather-*style mafia war?" I ask her.

"No, and my family isn't mafia. I'm happy that my brother likes you enough to make sure you come home with me, to make sure you're protected."

"Your family *is* the fucking mafia, Aliyah, and your brother likes you enough, not me."

"Maybe, but we don't use the word mafia."

"What do you use then?" I ask her. The topic of what her family does isn't something we've ever discussed.

"Business." She shrugs.

"Business." I laugh, because how can I not? This situation is absurd. We're not living in an episode of the *Sopranos*. I follow the GPS directions to the address Aliyah punched in. I haven't been to her father's house before—can't say this is the kind of situation I wanted to be invited to, but it is what it is.

"I'm really sorry," she apologizes again.

"You don't have anything to be sorry for."

"You could get hurt because of me," she says.

"Babe, I'm a hockey player. Getting banged up is in the job description." I smirk.

"It's not the same thing." She sighs.

"I know. But you can't help who your family is, just like I can't." I still haven't spoken to my mother. Honestly, the way she treated Aliyah back in New York pisses me off more than the fact she slept with my fucking coach.

Matty has been calling nonstop, trying to be the peacemaker. He wants us all to be together for Christmas. I've told him he's more than welcome to spend the holidays at my place, but no way am I going home. Aliyah is a lot closer to her family anyway. It makes more sense for us to stay here. Not that we've discussed holiday plans yet. I'm just assuming at this point. I mean, everyone knows where this woman goes, I go.

I pull up to a huge gate. There are three men blocking the entrance. When they see us, they move aside and the gate opens. My jaw drops as I drive up to the house. "This is where you grew up?" I ask.

"Yep. Trust me, a house may look big and pretty, but more often than not, what goes on inside it isn't what it seems."

Turning the car off, I look over at her. "Does being here bother you?"

"Sometimes. I mean, I have good memories here too. But sometimes the bad ones take over and bring me right back to that place. Like if I walk past a closet that she used to lock me in or something like that."

"She locked you in fucking closets?" I growl.

"She did."

"How the fuck did nobody know this was happening to you?"

"She only did it when my father wasn't home. Which was a lot. He was home more after she left though," Aliyah says. We both know her mother didn't leave voluntarily, but if that's how she wants to process things, then that's what we're sticking with. "Come on." Aliyah opens her door and steps out of the car. I follow suit, coming around the other side to grab her hand.

"What are the chances your father will let me into your bedroom? Maybe we can create our own memories here, the X-rated kind," I suggest.

"Uh, sure, if you're prepared to get shot." Aliyah laughs.

"For you, always."

"Don't ever get shot for me, Liam King. I mean it."

"How about we both try not to get shot, babe?" I tell her.

"Deal."

I keep hold of her hand and follow her into her family home. It's huge. This house isn't just a mansion; it's a mansion on steroids. This is one-percenter stuff right here. I wonder what Aliyah would think if I ever did take her back to my hometown. The difference in how we grew up has never been so glaringly obvious until right now.

Her family is right. I am not good enough for her. I don't think I ever will be, but fuck if I'm ever letting her go. This girl has my heart tied to hers. She doesn't know that yet. I haven't figured out how or when to say those three words to tell her exactly how I feel.

# Chapter Thirty-Five

I'm filled with trepidation at just the idea of bringing Liam here. I don't visit this house often, usually only for family get-togethers. I see my dad at The Castle almost every day so I don't feel the need to visit him at home. I moved out the day I left for college and have never spent the night since. The house haunts me. I've never told my father this of course. I don't want to burden him. There was also the whole *no boyfriend* thing my father and brothers were so hung up on forever. It was easier to just not live with any of them if I wanted to have any kind of sex life.

Although, now that I'm having sex with Liam, I don't think what I was doing before can be put in the same category. I don't know if it's the chemistry, or if it's just the man himself, but sex with Liam is mind-blowing. The kind of orgasms you read about or see in movies. The kind that I always assumed were fictional. Guess what? They're not. If you're not having those out-of-body experience orgasms that send pleasure through every fiber of your being, then you're not with the right partner.

Just thinking about it has me wanting to drag Liam up to my old bedroom and let him give me some of those X-rated memories he offered.

"I know what you're thinking." He leans in and whispers into my ear.

"No, you don't." I laugh.

"You're thinking you want to take me up to your bedroom. You're thinking about my cock filling that wet cunt of yours, and you're thinking about the orgasm you know you'd have if you did."

My breath hitches. "How…" I look over at him, and with the cockiest smirk I've ever seen, Liam winks at me. Just winks.

"Lia, you good?" My brother Vinny's voice breaks me out of my Liam King trance.

"Uh, yeah, what's going on?" I ask him.

"What's he doin' here? This is family business and he ain't family," Vinny says, jutting his chin in Liam's direction.

You'd think my brothers would be over the whole *Aliyah has a boyfriend* thing by now. It's been months! But, no. Especially not Vinny. Gray is coming around a lot quicker than I expected, and Jonah sends me messages every day to ask if Liam's treating me well. He's waiting for me to reply with a *no* so he can make his move.

"You know I can just take him to Vegas and marry him. Then you'd have to acknowledge him as family. If that's what it takes, I will," I threaten Vinny.

"Aliyah, you run off and get married without me and I'll make you the world's fastest widow," my dad says, his voice echoing down the halls.

I hold Liam's hand tighter, scared he might just try to run now that he's amongst the crazy that is my family. Liam gives my hand a reassuring squeeze.

"Sir, I'll make sure to save you a seat at the front of the chapel," Liam fires back.

*Holy shit, he did not just say that.*

"King, you are not marrying my daughter in fucking Vegas," Dad grunts.

"Okay, no to Vegas. How about Vancouver?" Liam tries again.

I look at him with wide eyes. I don't even have words. He has to be kidding, right? He is always making jokes. That's all this is.

"Vancouver, we can make work," Dad agrees.

"Ah, hang on a hot minute. I'm right here," I tell them.

"Your point?" Dad asks.

"First, if I want a Vegas wedding, I'm having a Vegas wedding. And, second, we're not getting married. No one has even asked me," I say.

"Yet." Liam smirks.

"Well, either way, if I'm not there, then neither is he. You're my only daughter, Aliyah. I've been dreading the day I'd have to walk you down the aisle since the moment you were born," Dad says.

"Then why would you want to be there?"

"Because *you're my only daughter*," he repeats, "and it's my job as a father to make sure you get everything you've ever wanted. If that includes him, then I'll make sure that happens."

I mean, the sentiment's there, but then I have to wonder what my father would do if I wanted Liam and Liam didn't want me back.

"For fuck's sake, Dad, are we really entertaining this shit? Lia, you're not getting married. Period," Vinny grunts and then stomps off.

"Daddy, what's happening? Why are we here?" I ask him.

Dad looks at Liam and then to me. "Precaution, that's all."

"For how long?"

"Hopefully not long. I'm on my way out. I'm leaving Vinny here with you. Try not to piss him off any more than he is," Dad says.

"Hold up. If you're leaving Vinny here, who's going with you?"

"I have people, Aliyah. And Grayson and Jonah are already waiting in the car."

"Okay." I nod my head. I hate this part of our lives. I know whatever my father and brothers do, it's not safe. I let go of Liam's hand and throw my arms around my dad. "If you don't come back, I'm going to run off to Vegas and marry him," I whisper in his ear.

"I'll be back." Dad pats my shoulder and then

steps away. Before he gets to the front door, he calls out, "No boys in your room, Aliyah. He can have a guest room, on the opposite side of the house."

I smile. I wasn't really going to take Liam up to my old bedroom, but now that I've been told I can't... Well, let's just say I've never really liked being told what I can and can't do. So...

"Come on, we're going to my room and you're delivering on those X-rated memories you promised me." I pull Liam's hand towards the staircase to the right of the foyer.

"Ah, princess, not that I'm complaining or anything, but are you sure that's a good idea? You did just hear what your father said, right?" Liam asks me.

"Are you serious? You're choosing this moment, right now, to listen to my father? You've already broken his number one rule—*don't touch his daughter*," I remind him.

"Well, yeah, but that wasn't in his house. This is a lot more disrespectful, and I happen to like your father," Liam says.

"Liam King, if you don't take me up to my room and fuck me right now, I'm going to go up there on my own, dig out one of my old vibrators, and do it myself. Without you."

Liam groans. "Lead the way, babe," he says.

I know my boyfriend and the thought of me pleasuring myself without him drives him freaking crazy. He wants to be the only thing to give me pleasure. It's one of his odd quirks—one I don't mind him having.

# Chapter Thirty-Six

Aliyah opens a door and pulls me in. Her hands land on my chest as she pushes me up against the wall. I know I had reservations about doing this here, in her father's house, but every single one flies out the damn window when she drops to her knees in front of me. Her hands frantically pull at my belt. When she gets it undone, she goes straight for the button and the fly. Then her hands are reaching into my boxers and she's taking hold of my cock.

I look down at her as her tongue darts out, and she licks her lips. "Hungry?" I ask her.

"Starved," she says and then lowers her mouth.

"Fuck." My hands reach down and scoop up her hair, holding it back from her face. I like watching her as she sucks me off. It's a sight to behold. Fucking gorgeous. "You suck so fucking good, princess."

Aliyah looks up at me, smiling around my dick briefly, before she goes back to the task at hand. She takes me as far down her throat as she can manage, gagging a little before sliding back up my length. One of her hands wraps around the base of my shaft, while the other reaches under and cups my balls. I yank my pants down farther, giving her better access.

A moan leaves my mouth, and my head falls back, hitting the wall she shoved me up against. I can feel that telltale tingle at the base of my spine, and my balls tighten. "Shit, babe, I'm going to come," I warn her.

Aliyah doesn't let up. No, she fucking increases

her pace, her head bobbing up and down on my cock, her hand cupping and massaging my balls. She presses a finger into that magic spot between my balls and my asshole. My knees buckle and my thighs shake as my body seizes up. I hold her head still and my hips jerk as my cock empties inside her mouth. When she's drained me of everything I have, I pull back and watch her swallow, which is so fucking hot. I drop to my knees and my thumb swipes up the little bit of cum that's spilled out of her mouth.

"Suck it off," I tell her. And like the perfect fucking goddess she is, Aliyah sucks my finger into her mouth, twirling her tongue around the tip, cleaning any remnants of me. "I fucking love your mouth."

Aliyah releases my thumb with a pop. "Just my mouth?" she teases.

"No, I also love your cunt, your ass. I fucking adore your tits," I say, about to admit that it's not just her body I love, when a loud crack sounds out through the house.

"Shit, get up. Get dressed." Aliyah panics.

I've just gotten my belt done up when her bedroom door slams open. I jump in front of her, not knowing what the hell is going on.

"I'm sorry, Lia. You have to go in," Vinny says.

I glance over my shoulder at Aliyah. She looks petrified. "What the fuck is going on?" I ask.

"There's a panic room, in the back of her closet. Get her in there. Now," her brother tells me in an eerily calm voice. There are more sounds going off throughout the house, which I now recognize as gunshots.

I turn to Aliyah. "Babe, come on." I take hold of her hands.

Aliyah shakes her head. "I can't."

"You have to. Come on, Lia. I need to go and help the guys before we all get slaughtered here. Go in there. Use the phone to call Dad," Vinny says and then looks to me. "Get her in there. The code to open the door is Gray's jersey number."

Before I can respond, he disappears down the hall. It's not until I watch his retreating back that I notice the two pistols in his hands. When the sounds of shots being fired, glass breaking, and men slinging insults at each other increase, I turn around and pick Aliyah up. I need to get her in that room. I throw her over a shoulder, run towards the back of her closet, and find the little keypad on the wall. I type in her brother's number, twenty-two, and the wall opens up.

Then I enter the room, the wall clicks back in place, and I set Aliyah down on her feet. "No, get me out of here. Let me out. I need to get out." Aliyah bangs on the door. She's screaming, tears pouring down her face.

I wrap my arms around her. "It's okay. I've got you. Aliyah, calm down. It's going to be okay," I tell her, hoping like fuck that it is *in fact* going to be okay.

"It's not. I need to get out. Don't let her shut me in here again," Aliyah sobs. She starts grabbing at her chest. She's fucking hyperventilating. I have no idea what's happening. I feel fucking helpless right now.

"Aliyah, you need to calm down. Breathe slowly. In and out. Come on, babe." I pick her up again and sit down on the floor with her in my lap. I hold her face in my palms. "Please, just listen to me. Listen to my voice. Breathe in." She stares at me with watery, fear-stricken eyes and it fucking breaks my heart. But she does listen and takes a huge breath. "That's it. Good. Now out slowly. Again, breathe in." We repeat this process until her body starts to relax and her breathing evens out. Her fingers are gripping my forearms, her nails digging into my skin, but I don't care. "You're okay. I'm here with you. You are not alone, Aliyah. We're here, just you and me," I tell her.

"I'm sorry," she says.

"It's okay," I reply, my eyes flicking around the room. It's small. There's a little sofa in one corner, a bar fridge against the wall, and above it hangs an old-school telephone. Then I remember what Vinny said. "Should we call your dad? Your brother said to call him."

Aliyah nods her head but she doesn't move. Her grip on me has loosened slightly but she's still holding on tight.

"What is it about this room that made you panic?" I ask, while stroking my hand through her hair.

"She used to lock me in here. My mother," she says so quietly, almost like speaking the words will somehow make the woman appear. "Sometimes, when my dad was gone for the night, she wouldn't let me out till the morning."

Holy fucking shit, I wish I could bring this woman back just to strangle her myself. "I'm sorry."

"It's okay. I'm sorry I freaked out."

"Don't be. Come on, let's call your father." I want to get out of this room and disappear with Aliyah. I want to take her away from her fucked-up family so she's never put in danger again. But the reality of the situation is that she'll always be Jacob

Monroe's daughter, and somehow I think she's probably safer under his watchful eye than off on the run.

Aliyah picks up the phone. "Daddy, they're here," she says and then listens to whatever he has to tell her. She nods her head but doesn't reply. Then she holds the phone out to me. "He wants to talk to you," she says.

"Hello."

"King, do not leave that room until either I or one of my sons opens the door for you. No one can get in there. You two are safe as long as you stay put."

"How long?" I ask.

"How is she?"

"Not good," I tell him.

I hear him exhale and curse a few times. "I'm on my way. It won't be long. Just distract her," he says.

Something tells me the way I usually distract his daughter isn't what he has in mind right now. "I've got her. Just get us the fuck out of here," I say, before hanging up and placing the phone back on its receptacle on the wall. I look over to Aliyah and smirk, letting my eyes roam up and down her body. "Your dad told me to distract you."

"I don't think he meant what you're thinking," she says.

"What am I thinking?"

349

"That you want to devour me?"

"I always want to devour you, Aliyah," I tell her. Because it's the truth. No matter how much I have this woman, I don't think I'll ever get enough of her.

# Chapter Thirty-Seven

Liam's eyes are full of lust. You wouldn't think I just emptied the man not even half an hour ago. I wonder if he takes supplements or some shit. It's not normal how often he can perform. Not that I'm complaining. I'll take Energizer Liam any day over a two-pump chump.

Although now, being trapped in this room, the last thing I want to do is fool around. What I want is to get the hell out of here. I'm trying really hard not to panic again. I'm so embarrassed by how freaked out I got.

I look to the door, feeling that same panic creeping up my neck again. "Liam?" I ask.

"Yeah."

"Talk to me. Tell me something about you that I don't already know."

"Okay, but you have to promise not to laugh," he says, his expression suddenly serious.

"Promise," I say.

"Come, sit down." Liam sits crossed-legged on the floor. I plop down in front of him. "Okay, what I'm going to tell you can never leave this room, like ever."

"Okay." I nod my head, curious as to what he's going to say.

"When I was in the fifth grade, there was this girl, Chelsea Stevens." He smiles. "She was *the* girl at school. Every boy wanted to be her boyfriend, and I was no exception."

I try to picture Liam as a little kid. I can only imagine the kind of trouble he would have gotten into.

"Anyway, she did figure skating. And I was already playing hockey at this point, so I thought how hard could it be to dance around on the ice? I was already a great skater," he says.

"I'm sure you were." I laugh.

"The best the youth league had ever seen," he deadpans. "I signed up for her figure skating class and made sure I was assigned to be her partner."

"So you danced with her? And it made her fall hopelessly in love with you?" I ask him.

"Not exactly." He looks away briefly before his eyes settle back on me. "Nobody told me I'd have to do the splits, spin around a million times a minute, and shit like that. And I used to be a bit cocky, thought my shit didn't stink."

"Used to be?" I interrupt him.

"Yes. Used to be," he says with a scowl that I do my best not to laugh at. "Anyway, I went out on the ice and tried to copy the same moves the teacher had instructed me to do."

"What happened?"

"I spun and spun so damn much that when I went to land on a split, I tore a muscle in my groin."

"Ouch."

"Exactly. I had to be carried off the ice. I couldn't

get up. The whole class was laughing at me, including Chelsea Stevens," he tells me.

"Aw, I'm sorry you didn't get the girl."

Liam shakes his head. "I couldn't play hockey for weeks afterwards."

"Whatever happened to Miss Chelsea Stevens?" I ask him.

"Oh, I got her in the end. I taught her how to give a blowjob in ninth grade." He smiles proudly.

I blink at him. "Seriously? That's your embarrassing story?"

"It *was* embarrassing. I broke my groin trying to figure skate just to impress some chick."

"I had a crush on this boy in tenth grade. I was obsessed with him. I even doodled my first name with his last name in my schoolbooks," I say.

"I hate him already," Liam grumbles.

"Vinny and Jonah found out. Gray was away at college. But the other two invited him over, showed him every weapon in Dad's private arsenal. Then they proceeded to explain, in vivid detail, how they'd use each and every one on him if they ever caught him around me."

"I think I'm liking your brothers a little more each day." Liam smirks.

I slap his chest. "It was mortifying. He didn't

know I liked him. That boy didn't even know who I was, and my brothers scared the crap out of him."

"Babe, it's impossible for any guy to not notice you. You're the hottest fucking chick I've ever seen."

"Thanks?" I question.

"You know, your brothers could tell me how they'd dismember me as graphically as they'd like, but nothing will ever scare me away from you."

"I feel like I'm doing a well enough job of scaring you away myself," I admit.

"Why would you think that?"

"Because I just had a full-blown panic attack, Liam. We're hiding out because my family is involved in the not-so-legal side of business, and we have God knows who shooting up our house."

"You are not your family. Are they a little dodgy? Sure. But that's not going to scare me away."

"What if they don't win this time?"

"What do you mean?" he asks.

"What if my dad doesn't come and open the door? What if they get to him first?"

"Have you met your father? There is no way he's not coming to open that door for you, babe. And your brothers? Do you really think they're going to leave you locked in a room with me? They don't like you anywhere near me." He laughs.

"You're right," I say.

"Of course I am. Come here." Liam holds his hands out.

I climb into his lap, turning my body around so my back rests against his chest as he leans against the wall. His arms wrap around me, and right here is where I feel safe. I rest my head on his shoulder and close my eyes.

"Aliyah, babe, wake up," Liam's voice whispers in my ear, his fingers brushing along my cheek.

I open my eyes, blinking away the unconsciousness. I'm met by my father's worried face looking down at me. "Took you long enough," I say as I push myself up and off Liam's lap.

*How long have I been asleep? Shit, his legs must be numb.*

"Sorry, took a little longer to clean up than I thought. Come on, let's eat." My father turns around and disappears through my childhood bedroom closet.

I look back down at Liam. "Are you okay? You should have woken me up," I tell him.

"It's okay. You only drooled a little bit," he says, rising to his feet.

"I don't drool!" I yell at him.

"My wet shirt would say otherwise." Liam laughs. I look at his shirt and, sure enough, there's a damp spot on his shoulder.

*Oh my god, kill me now.*

"Don't worry, babe, I happen to be a fan of your bodily fluids." He winks.

"Let's never mention this again. Come on, if we don't go down to the dining room, Dad will send one of the boys up here to get us." I reach for Liam's hand and lead him out of my bedroom.

"So, we just go and have dinner and pretend that today didn't happen?" Liam asks me.

"That's usually how it goes." I shrug.

"That's fucked up, Aliyah," he says.

"I know. I'm sorry. You don't have to stay. I get it if you want to leave."

"Are you staying?" he asks.

"Yes." I answer.

"Where you go, I go," Liam tells me.

# Chapter Thirty-Eight

I glance around the house as I follow Aliyah through the hallways. Nothing looks out of place. From the sounds of it, I was expecting to see everything smashed and shot up. But other than a few bullet holes I've seen in the walls, there isn't a single piece of broken glass. We were in that room for hours. So long I lost track of time. I do know that it's now morning. So it's been at least half a day.

This is next-level messed up. The fact I had to spend the night in a panic room with my girlfriend, because her family is into criminal activities, should have me running. But it doesn't. I can't think of anything that would have me leaving this girl behind.

When we enter the dining room, her father is seated at the head of the table, all three of her brothers filling the spots on one side. Aliyah pulls me around, opposite them, and sits in the chair closest to her father. I pull out the seat next to hers.

"Are we really doing this, Pops?" Vinny asks.

"Yes," Jacob says. "You two have a game tonight. Are you going to be good for that? I've made excuses for you both for missing morning skate," he says, looking from me to Grayson.

"I'm good." I nod.

"You good, Gray?" Jonah elbows Grayson in the side.

"Gray, what's wrong?" Aliyah asks her brother when he groans at the contact.

"Nothing, just got a graze," Gray answers her.

"You got shot?" Aliyah gasps, stands from her

chair, and rushes around to the other side of the table. "Show me. Why isn't the doctor here?"

"It's fine, Lia. The fucker only scratched me. I've had worse injuries from playing hockey," Gray says, swatting her hands aside.

"Still, you shouldn't play tonight, if you're already hurt," Aliyah says, then turns to her father. "Dad, tell him he can't play."

"Lia, if I don't play, who's going to make sure your little boyfriend here doesn't get smashed up out on the ice?" Gray laughs.

"How I've managed to stay alive before I joined the Knights is unfathomable," I deadpan.

"We're playing Montreal. You really think they're not going to come at you with everything they've got?" he asks me.

"We've played them three times already. I've survived." I shrug. We've also won all three times we've gone up against my old team. I'm not worried in the slightest about doing it again. They can throw everything they have at me. I'll still be standing in the end.

"Suit yourself. I'll step back tonight and see how you fare." Gray shrugs.

"Don't do that. If he gets hurt, I'm gonna kick your ass, Gray," Aliyah threatens her brother as she moves back to her seat.

"Aliyah, I'll be fine," I tell her.

"If you're not, I'll kick your ass *and* his," she says, pointing from me to Gray.

"The Knights are top choice to win the Cup this year. Let's keep it that way," Jacob says.

"We're going to win the Cup," I tell him.

"If you can refrain from beating up your old coach long enough to score," Vinny sneers.

Before I can respond to his comment, Aliyah picks up a fork and hurls it across the table at her brother. He easily dodges it and the fork hits the tiled floor behind him.

"Vinny, for the love of God, can we not just enjoy one meal as a family?" Jacob grinds out.

"Me? She's the one who threw a fork at me." Vinny points at his sister.

I look around the room. As fucked up as they all are in their own right, it took me sitting here at the dining table with them for me to realize that they are a *family*. They're fiercely loyal to each other and bicker like all hell. I never had this growing up. It was always just me and my brother and sometimes our mother. I need to give Matty a call today and find out what he's doing for the holidays.

"You deserved it," Jacob says to Vinny before

addressing his daughter. "And, Aliyah, sweetheart, practice your aim. His head's big enough that you shouldn't have missed."

I chuckle under my breath, which just gets me another glare from Vinny. Jonah and Gray laugh while Aliyah picks up her knife, inspecting it, then looks over at her brother like she's going to throw that too.

"If you even think about it, I'm going to pull out the old photo albums, especially the one when you were thirteen, had braces, and were ugly as fuck," Vinny says, and Aliyah drops the knife back down to the table.

"It's not possible for you to have ever been ugly," I tell her.

"Oh, I was most definitely ugly," she says with a confirmative nod.

"No, you weren't," her father says.

"Thanks, Daddy." She smiles up at him.

Everything calms down once our plates are piled up with pancakes, bacon, and eggs. We eat in an almost silence with Jacob asking about the team, trying to pull intel from Gray about the comings and goings of the rest of the guys. When Gray refuses to give his father anything but a shake of his head, Jacob turns to me, and I dodge those questions like they're looking to steal my puck in a tied game.

"What good is it having you two on the team if you won't give me any of the gossip?" Jacob asks.

"Well, I win games. Not sure what he's there for." I smirk over at Gray.

"I wear the C."

"Of a team your daddy owns." I laugh. I know damn well Grayson's earned that captain title. But it's still fun to hold it over him that he's stuck under his father's thumb.

"Please tell me we're trading him at the end of the season," Gray mumbles under his breath.

"If you trade him, I'm going too," Aliyah is quick to say, and I grin.

"He's dying a Knight. I'm not having your sister leave town," Jacob tells his son.

"Okay, well, this has been great and all, but we have to go. I have plans." Aliyah stands from her seat and that's my cue to follow her.

"What plans?" Jonah asks. He's been really quiet, just observing everyone like he's taking notes.

"Plans that don't include you, Jonah. And shouldn't you be at school?" she fires back.

"I would be if Vinny didn't fuck up a deal," Jonah complains.

"And on that note, we're leaving." Aliyah bends down, kissing her father on the cheek. "See you tonight, Dad."

"I want you near the players box, preferably in the tunnel, Aliyah. Not over at the penalty box with your friends."

"Why?"

"Because I want you close," Jacob snaps a little quicker than usual.

Not gonna lie. Having Aliyah in the box or near the box isn't a bad idea. I always like to keep her close.

We're halfway through the second period. Montreal is up by one. Gray was right. For some reason, they're out for blood tonight. Why tonight and not any of the other times, I have no idea. But if it's blood they want, it's blood they'll get. It just won't be mine.

I slam my left shoulder into Garrison, their best defenseman. His body smashes into the boards. Gray is right there, fighting for the puck. He eventually gets it out and slaps it over to Jameson, who sends it flying right over the goalie's glove and into the net. The horns sound off and the red lights flash as Jameson does his little dance around the end zone.

Garrison shoves at me. "Asshole," he hisses on his way towards the bench. This was a man I once considered my friend. I was at his wedding, his son's baptism. And all it took was me being traded for him to forget all of that.

"Yeah, I'm the asshole," I scoff.

"Yeah, you are. We had it in the bag. The Cup was ours and you had to go and lose your shit, all because your mother's a dirty whore," he grunts.

"What the fuck did you just say?" I ask at the same time as I drop my stick and shake my gloves off my hands.

I get one punch in before Gray is pulling me back. "He's not worth it. He's trying to get to you, King. Let it go," he says.

"Back off. I'm going to fucking kill him," I yell.

"No, you're not. You're going to do your time in the box and make that look on my sister's fucking face disappear." He shoves me towards the bin.

I turn around and see Aliyah. She's standing next to her father. Her fingers are pressed to her lips and I know she's chewing her nails. She only does that when she's nervous. I mouth an apology. I know she hates the fighting part of hockey. I get it. But it's also part of the game. I take my place in the bin and keep my eyes on her across the rink. She relaxes the moment I enter the box. As soon as the three minutes are up, I'm off and chasing the puck.

The Knights managed to prevent Montreal from scoring during their power play, and not long after I hit the ice again, the buzzer goes off, announcing the end of the second period. So everyone makes their way off the rink and heads into their respective locker rooms. I hang back in the hall with Aliyah.

Picking up her hands, I inspect her nails. "You need to stop chewing these," I tell her.

"I know," she says. "Are you okay?"

"Never been better." I smile. "I have the world's hottest fucking girlfriend."

"That's a matter of opinion." She laughs.

"And it's only my opinion that matters."

"Well, I happen to have the world's hottest boyfriend," she says.

"And here I was, thinking you were attracted to my sparkling personality," I feign offense.

"You have a personality? Where?" she asks me,

making a point to look up and down the tunnel, only to come up empty.

"Funny. Come on, let's get in there," I say while leading her into the locker room. It's not until I walk in and see all the guys in various stages of undress that I want to march her back out. "Aliyah, close your eyes."

"King, get over here," one of the trainers calls me to him.

"Go, before you get fired," Aliyah says, shoving me in his direction.

By the end of the third period, we're tied, so the game goes into overtime. Three on three, Gray, Jameson, and me up against Montreal's top three.

We take five shots at the net, and each one is caught by their goalie. Montreal gets two shots at ours. The timer sounds off and we go into a shootout. Montreal's goalie is good, but ours is better. They got one in the net and we end up with two, Grayson having scored the winning goal.

They teach you about the importance of sportsmanship when you're in the youth league. Guess those lessons didn't quite stick with Montreal, though, seeing as the opposing players—the same ones I once considered family—breeze by me without touching gloves. When Jameson and Gray notice what they're doing, my teammates drop their fists and follow Montreal's shitty example.

# Chapter Thirty-Nine

I roll over on the bed and watch as Liam walks out of the bathroom with nothing but a towel around his waist. I'm not sure how we've been dating for seven months already. Every day I wait for the newness of this relationship to wear off, but it doesn't. If anything, I fall more and more. Of course I haven't told him those words yet. I want to, but with the team having made it through to the playoffs, I didn't want to mess with his headspace.

We have a week off before the Knights play against Nashville in the final game. Which means, once again, I can't tell him now, even though the words are on the tip of my tongue.

"See something you like, babe?" he asks, running a hand down his perfectly sculpted abs.

"That depends. Does it come with a side of ice cream?" I counter.

"It could be arranged."

"Then I like it very much," I say, licking my lips.

Liam steps towards me. He drops his towel on the floor as he kneels up on the bed and fists his cock in his hand. "What do you want more? The ice cream or my cock?"

"Mmm, that's a hard decision," I tell him.

"Princess, make your choice," he says.

"You, my choice is always you." I smile, and my tongue darts out, wetting my lips as my eyes stay glued to his cock. The same cock he's presently rubbing up and down with the palm of his hand.

"Take off your shirt," Liam demands. I don't have to be asked twice. I rip the shirt off and throw it over the side of the bed. Liam straddles my upper body, cupping my breasts in his hands. "Fuck, I love these," he says, massaging the flesh.

"I would never have known." I smile up at him.

"Well, maybe I need to fuck them real good, just so you don't forget how much I fucking love them." He groans as he reaches over to the bedside table and pulls out a bottle of lube.

Squirting the liquid on my chest, he rubs it all over my breasts before he pushes them together and slides his cock between the tight opening. Nobody has ever done this to me before Liam. He loves it. And I'm not opposed. It's hot. Watching his face, seeing the pleasure and the lust in his eyes as he stares down at me, that look he's giving me right now —he might as well be feeding me an aphrodisiac. My core pulses with need, wanting him to move down my body and fill that emptiness with his cock.

"Fuck, so fucking good, babe," he groans.

"Liam, I need you to fuck me," I say.

"You need me to fuck you?"

"Yes, it's a need, not a want," I tell him.

"Well, I'd hate for word to get out that I've not been meeting all your needs. What kind of boyfriend would I be, then?" he asks.

"The ex kind of boyfriend." I laugh.

"Oh, she has threats," he says as he lets go of my

body and moves his farther down mine. "I'd love to see you try to make me your ex, babe. I promise you that it will be a fight you will never win." He picks up my legs, spreading me wide open, as he stares down at my lace-covered pussy. His fingertips run along my pelvis. "I think you should get a tattoo right... *here*."

"A tattoo? Of what?"

"Property of Liam King, with an arrow pointing down to your cunt."

I laugh at the absurd things this man says. It's weird how we can have whole conversations while enjoying each other's bodies like this—again, something I've never experienced before Liam.

"That is never happening," I tell him.

"Do I need to remind you that you once said *this* would never happen?" He waves his finger between the two of us. "Like I said, I always get what I want. It's just a matter of being patient, wearing you down," he says.

"Liam?"

"Yeah, babe."

"Shut up and fuck me already," I tell him.

Liam takes hold of the top of my panties and tears them down my right leg. Moving the lacy material to the side, he slides his fingers through my wet folds. "I fucking love how you're always ready for me," he says.

I wrap my legs around his waist. He lines his cock up with my entrance and thrusts inside in one fluid quick movement. I still for a second. It always takes me at least a second to adjust to his size. Liam stays buried inside me. Leaning down, he captures one of my nipples in his mouth and sucks. My back arches off the bed as lightning bolts of pleasure radiate straight to my core.

"Holy shit." My hands hold his head to my breasts. "Don't stop," I demand. My hips start moving up and down and my pussy clenches around him.

"Fuck, I love your cunt," he curses under his breath, releasing my nipple from his mouth. I purposely squeeze him tighter.

*Thank you, Kegel exercises.*

"So you've said once or twice," I moan as the tip of his dick hits that magic spot deep inside me.

All the chitchat falls away with Liam's increase of pace. He moves his hands to my thighs and lifts my legs, bending them over my laid-out body so my knees are up at my shoulders. At this angle, he gets even deeper. My hands cling onto his forearms as he fucks into me with everything he has—*and let me tell you, ladies, this man has a lot to give.*

I feel my stomach tighten, thousands of nerve endings coming to life. "That's it. Let go for me, princess. Fucking come all over my cock," Liam grits out between clenched teeth. He moves one of his hands between us and presses on my clit, detonating my entire body. Liam's movements stiffen. He jerks into me over and over until both of our orgasms have us panting for breath. Then he falls next to me on the bed. "Shit, we forgot to use a condom. Again.".

"It'll be fine," I huff out, trying to catch my breath.

"I'm not worried. I think you'd make perfect babies," Liam says, and my blood goes cold.

"I can't have kids, Liam," I whisper.

"You can't? Or you won't?" he asks. We've been here before. Had this conversation more than once. He just doesn't seem to get it.

"I can't—well, technically I can. You know that. But I just... I can't. What if I'm like her?" My biggest fear would be having a child and not being able to love it.

"If you don't ever want to have kids, I'm okay with that. But don't let such a monumental decision be made because of her. I didn't know your mother,

Aliyah, but I do know you. And you're sweet, kind, and fucking perfect in every way. You are nothing like the woman who did that to you." He dips his head towards my wrist.

"Maybe. But it could be genetic," I suggest.

"We both have fucked-up mothers—granted yours is far worse than mine. But we are not our mothers, Aliyah."

"Do you think you're going to forgive her?" I ask him.

"I'm paying her bills. Her husband left her. But I'm not ready to talk to her. Not after the way she treated you."

"So, how much should I bet on this Stanley Cup game? I mean, what are the odds of the Knights winning?" I ask, rolling over to face him.

"You did not just ask me that. Odds? Babe, we are going to annihilate them. There is no way that Cup isn't coming home with us."

"I like your confidence," I tell him.

"It's not confidence. It's a simple fact," he says.

# Chapter Forty

*Liam*

W e're just about to go out on the ice. It's the game every hockey player dreams of playing. The Stanley Cup Championship. I've been here a few times. This is my first as a Knight though.

It was a rough start, joining a new team, especially after how I left my old one. But Aliyah has made settling into Vancouver easier. She makes it feel like home. I'm planning on using all of my spare time over the break convincing her to move in with me. She says she'll be interning with her dad, learning the managerial ropes so to speak, because babysitting problem players indefinitely is not her life goal.

Speaking of her father, I've been summoned to his office, which is why I'm walking up there, dressed in my gear sans the skates. Why he wants to see me ten minutes before we're due to go on the ice, I have no idea. Aliyah is down in the box with her friends, waiting for the game to start.

*I wonder if I can make a detour to see her before duty calls.*

I tuck that thought away and knock on Jacob Monroe's door. I wait until I hear his booming voice call out for me to enter. I push inside and find him pacing up and down the length of his office with a glass of whiskey in his hands.

"Shut the door," he says.

I've never seen this man so unraveled. Straight away, my internal alert system goes haywire. "Where's Aliyah?" I ask, ready to run out the door. Something's wrong. I can feel it.

Jacob points to a screen on his wall. "She's in the box. She's safe. For now," he tells me.

*For now? What the fuck?*

"What do you mean for now?" I ask aloud.

Jacob turns to me, setting his glass on the desk, as his eyes lock with mine. "I need you to throw the game. We have to lose," he says.

I blink. I must have heard him wrong. Surely I did not just hear my boss, the owner of the Vancouver Knights, ask me to throw the fucking Stanley Cup game?

"I'm sorry, what?" I attempt to clarify.

"I've been trying to find these fuckers all week. There's not a single trace as to who the fuck is sending this shit." He picks up a manilla folder and drops it down in front of me, his hands shaking.

I open the folder and fall onto the sofa behind me. "What the fuck is this?" I grab the first piece of paper—no, not papers. *Clippings.* Words pasted on a blank sheet, but it's the message they form that has my body going rigid.

***Lose the SC or lose her.***

Underneath the ominous threat is a picture of Aliyah sitting in a coffee shop with her friend Amanda. This was taken yesterday. I remember her leaving the apartment, wearing that exact dress.

"They're threats, all of them. Against Aliyah. If we don't lose... I don't know who's behind this, but I'm not willing to risk my daughter's life for a fucking trophy."

"Does Grayson know?" I ask, skimming through the stack of letters, all saying the same general thing. Throw the game, or something's going to happen to Aliyah. I was just talking to her brother down in the locker room. He looked like he was ready to win. I would have known if something like this was sitting on his shoulders.

"No, he can't know. He will go in half-cocked, trying to find the asshole and putting her at greater risk. You know that as well as I do."

I stare at the paper in my hand. I can either win the Stanley Cup and risk losing my girlfriend, or throw the fucking game and lose my whole career. Because, let's face it, if I get caught throwing the game, I'm done for.

I wouldn't have hockey. The sport I love. But I would have her. She'd be safe.

There really isn't even a fucking choice here. If it comes down to it, I'll always choose her.

Pushing to my feet, I hand Jacob back the folder. I don't even know what to say to him.

"I'm asking you to do this because I know you

love her. I'm just hoping you love her more than you love the game," he says.

"I'll do it. I'll throw the game, but afterwards, I'm marrying her," I tell him. I was planning on asking her anyway. This will just make it easier for her to say yes. I walk out of his office and head straight for Aliyah. There are six men guarding the door. They're not usually here. When they see me, one of them nods and steps aside.

I walk in and Aliyah rushes over to me. "What's wrong? Why are you here?"

I wrap my arms around her, burying my face in her neck. "I just wanted to see you," I tell her.

"You can see me after you win." She laughs.

I lift my head and stare into her eyes. "I love you, Aliyah Monroe, so damn fucking much," I tell her the words I have been so hesitant to say, for fear of scaring her off..

Aliyah gasps. The whole room goes silent at my declaration. "I love you too," she says.

My lips slam down on hers, my tongue delves into her mouth, and all too soon I pull away. "Wait for me up here, after the game. I'll change, then come and get you," I tell her.

Aliyah's brows pull together but she nods her head. "You've got this, Liam King. You are going to go out there and kick ass." She grins, and I feel the ache of guilt in my chest. Not because of the choice I made—I'd make it all over again—but because I hate keeping something from her.

"You're right. I've got this," I tell her, but it has an entirely different meaning when I say it.

"What the fuck is your problem?" Gray shoves me into the boards when the puck goes over the top of the net, hitting the plexiglass behind it.

I look around. I want to tell him, tell him we have to fucking lose. Tell him why. But I don't. Instead, I look up at the box and see her face.

*I've got this,* I remind myself.

I can make sure our team holds off on scoring again and figure out a way to let the other team through our defenses. There're three minutes left on the clock and we're tied. I had us at one down, and then Jameson scored a fucking goal. I guess I never realized losing could be so fucking hard, especially when you're trying to make it look like you're playing to the best of your ability while missing every fucking shot.

I don't have much of a choice as I skid to a stop in front of the puck, swing like I'm intending to pass it back to Jameson, and watch as the puck bounces off the skate of one of Nashville's wingers. He has a clear run down the ice and he fucking takes it. I go after him, at a third of my normal speed, but before I make it to the other end of the rink, Grayson is there and manages to steal the puck and break away.

He flies back down to our end, and I'm right there waiting for his pass. I call out to him. He takes one look at me and makes a move like he's going to pass it my way. Instead, he turns his body and swings, and I watch in horror as the puck soars over the blocker side of the goalie. The sounds, the lights, the noise from the crowd—it all falls away.

There's one minute left on the clock. We've just fucking won the Stanley Cup. *Fuck.*

I rush across to the bench, jumping over it, and run on fucking skates down the tunnel. Everyone is yelling at me, wondering what the fuck I'm doing. But I only have one thing on my mind. *I need to get to her. I have to get to her.* We were supposed to fucking lose. Before I make it up to the box, Aliyah is running down a hallway towards me.

"Liam, what's going on?" she rushes out the moment she reaches me.

"We need to get out of here."

"Tell me what's going on," she repeats.

"I will, as soon as we're out of this fucking stadium," I tell her. Bending down, I tear off my skates as quick as I fucking can, take her hand in mine, and lead her to the side of the building. The team's lot is on the left, gated off with private access only. "Fuck, I don't have my keys," I curse out, hitting the metal door and pushing it open.

"It's okay. I've got mine." Aliyah squeezes my hand. Just as we reach her car, I hear the crunch of gravel behind us. I turn around and jump in front of Aliyah.

"You were supposed to lose," a deep voice calls out, his face obscured by a mask, right before he fires two shots from the pistol in his hand.

Aliyah screams and the guy runs off. Fuck, she got shot. I turn around—my first thought that I have to get her out of here, to a hospital—and my legs go weak. I grab onto her. Her hands land on my chest, as she screams even louder.

"It's okay," I tell her.

"Fuck. Help! Someone help us.!" she yells out to the empty lot.

"Aliyah, are you hurt?" I ask her, a sudden burning sensation ripping through my body.

"Liam, you've just been shot and you're asking me if I'm okay?"

*That* finally has me looking down at myself. I can see blood all over my jersey, feel the warmth spreading through my chest. "You're not hit?" It seems like a stupid question when all evidence points to no. But I need to hear it for myself.

"No, but you are. Shit. Hold on." Aliyah pulls out her phone. I look her up and down, realizing she's okay. That I did something right. Then the ground spins and I fall to my knees.

Aliyah reaches out, trying to catch me, but she never had a chance. I'm more than twice her size. My back hits the ground, I look up into the night sky, and everything goes black.

# Chapter Forty-One

"He's going to be okay, Lia," Gray says, wrapping an arm around my shoulder. "What if he's not? This is my fault. I never should have gotten him involved in our world," I tell my brother.

"Like you could have stopped him. That stupid

son of a bitch loves you. Fuck, he chose you over fucking hockey, Lia. If that's not love, I don't know what is," Gray says with an odd edge to his voice. "I just fucking wish someone would have let me in on what was fucking happening. I could have prevented all of this." That edge... it's guilt. I hear it now.

The door to the hospital opens and Liam's brother rushes in, followed by their mother. "Shit, Aliyah, you okay?" Matty asks me.

I shake my head, step out of Gray's arms, and walk over to Matty. "I'm sorry. I couldn't..." I don't know what to say exactly.

He hugs me close to his chest. "Shh, don't. He's going to be fine, and if he sees you crying when he wakes up, he's going to be pissed at all of us," Matty says with a half smirk.

"I can't..." I shake my head and pull out of his arms. I glance over to his mother, who is leaning over Liam's bed, clutching his hand in hers. She's whispering something to him but I can't make out the words.

She pulls upright again and turns to me with a look of disgust and outrage on her face. "I think you should leave," she says. "This is a family matter."

I gape at her. *Is she for real?* There is no way I'm leaving this hospital room.

"Mom, stop. She's not fucking leaving." Matty is quick to come to my defense.

"But *I* sure as fuck can make sure *you're* escorted out of the building," Gray adds.

"Stop! Everyone needs to stop and shut up!" I scream. Walking over to Liam's bedside, I sit down and bury my head next to his pillow. "Please wake up. I need you to wake up now. You can't leave me here to deal with this shitshow, Liam King. Wake up."

I feel a hand brush my hair back. I don't bother to pick up my head. I don't have the energy. Not until I hear his voice. "Aliyah? You good?" he asks me. He sounds a little hoarse but cocky as ever.

My head snaps up, my eyes meeting his. "Am I good? You were freaking shot, Liam. Am I good? No. I'm not good," I croak, letting the tears fall freely down my face.

Liam reaches up a hand and wipes my cheeks. "Marry me," he says.

"What?" I ask, certain I'm hearing things. Or maybe I'm dreaming...

"Marry me," he repeats.

"I think you're high on pain meds or something, Liam," I whisper.

"I'm not. Just say yes. Please."

I nod my head. "Yes, but only if you ask again when we're not in a hospital and you're not doped up on drugs," I tell him.

"Deal."

"King, you fucking asshole. You should have told me." Grayson stalks forward, cursing under his breath while waving an accusatory finger in Liam's direction.

"I told him not to," my father says, walking into the room. "Liam, the doc says you're going to be fine. Just a couple of through-and-throughs. Lucky for you, the bastard missed anything vital."

"What about hockey?" I ask my dad.

"Well, he's got a few months of recovery ahead of him before he gets back out on the ice again," Dad says. "But—"

Liam stops him short. "What's happening? Did you find him?"

"Vinny did." Dad nods. Nothing else needs to be said, and no more questions are asked about who *he* was or what my family did to *him* or *them*.

Everyone knows—well, almost everyone. Liam's mother and brother remain in the dark, and my father will make sure it stays that way. He explained to the rest of us what happened, why Liam was so frantic after Gray scored that winning goal, why he was trying to throw the game in the first place, and everything he was willing to give up to save me.

"Thank you," my dad says to Liam.

"You don't need to thank me," Liam tells him. "There is nothing I wouldn't do for her."

Dad nods, and Liam's mother scoffs. "Liam, we need to talk about this," she says from where she's still standing on the other side of his bed.

Liam's brows furrow. "Mom? Why are you here?" he asks her.

"Because you're my son and you were shot— thanks to this woman," she says, gesturing a mani-cured nail in my direction.

I try to let go of Liam's hand, but he only holds on tighter. "This woman is about to be my wife. You will not disrespect her. Thank you for coming, but you really shouldn't have," he says.

"Liam, I'll be back. You need anything, bro?" Matty chimes in.

"No, I'm good."

"Come on, Mom, let's go," Matty says, throwing an arm around his mother and steering her towards the door. "He needs time—that's all," he tells her.

I don't know what to do. I don't want to be the type of person who comes between a mother and her son, but I know this feud began long before I was around. Though, now that I think about it, if she hadn't done what she did, I never would have met her son in the first place. In a way, I guess I should thank her for being such a shitty parent.

As soon as Liam's mother and brother are out of earshot, my dad clears his throat. "Grayson, let's go."

"What? Why do I have to go?" Gray argues.

"Because I said so. Come on," Dad says more firmly this time. Then he looks to me. "Aliyah, sweetheart, call me if you need anything."

"Thanks, Daddy." Silence falls over the room when everyone is gone, and it's just me and Liam. The only sounds are the machines beeping in the background. My body slumps and more tears fall down my face.

"Come up here. Lie down with me," Liam says.

I shake my head. "No, I can't. You're hurt."

"I'll be more hurt if you don't humor me, princess," he says. The bed is big enough for the both of us, so I do as he asks. I climb on and curl up next to him, careful not to jostle the frame too much. "I don't like seeing you cry," Liam says.

"And I don't like seeing you hurt. Especially after I gave you strict instructions to never take a bullet for me," I remind him. "I was so scared. I thought you were dead, Liam. Don't you ever do that to me again." I tap the back of my hand against his arm.

"I'll do my best," he says with a grin.

"I'm thinking... a Vegas wedding," I say after a moment's pause. "Just the two of us."

"I thought you said you never wanted me to do this again?" He laughs, gesturing to the bandages around his side. "Your father already warned us what would happen if we ran off and eloped."

"Okay, so maybe not Vegas. How about Scotland? We could go to a castle—a real one—and you could be the king there too."

"I've never been. But, honestly, I don't care where we get hitched as long as you end up as Mrs. Aliyah King," he says, kissing my temple.

And I couldn't agree more. I'd be happy to marry this man in a courthouse. I don't need the whole fairy-tale princess wedding I once envisioned for myself. All I need is him, which is exactly how I know Liam King truly is my *one*.

"I love you." I lean up and lightly brush my lips over his.

"I used to think hockey was the greatest love of my life. I didn't need anything as long as I could play. I was wrong, so fucking wrong. Because you, Aliyah Monroe, are *it* for me. *You* are my greatest love."

**Continue to follow the Vancouver Knights' family with *Know The Score*. (Grayson and Kathryn's story)**

## Vancouver Knights Series

Break Out (Liam and Aliyah)

Know The Score (Grayson and Kathryn)

Light It Up Red (Travis and Lillianna Valentino)

Puck Blocked (Luke and Montana)

# About the Author

About Kylie Kent

Kylie made the leap from kindergarten teacher to romance author, living out her dream to deliver sexy, always and forever romances. She loves a happily ever after story with tons of built-in steam.

She currently resides in Sydney, Australia and when she is not dreaming up the latest romance, she can be found spending time with her three children and her husband of twenty years, her very own real life instant-love.

Kylie loves to hear from her readers; you can reach her at: author.kylie.kent@gmail.com

Let's stay in touch, come and hang out in my readers group on Facebook, and follow me on instagram.

Made in United States
North Haven, CT
10 January 2024

47283375R00220